INCO

John Burrowes is the au   books, including *Jamesie's People* and *Benny: The Life and Times of a Fighting Legend*. His other books include *My World On Wheels*, about an Australian sportsman, which became a bestseller in that country, and *Frontline Report*, about his experiences as a reporter in three wars.

Formerly Assistant Editor on a Scottish daily newspaper, he is currently resident in Oman where he edits the leading newspaper. His family is from the Gorbals and his background gives him the highest qualifications to write about this renowned and colourful area in Glasgow, and a deep personal insight which helps to bring *Incomers* alive.

available in Fontana by the same author

Fiction
Jamesie's People

Non-fiction
Benny: The Life and Times of a Fighting Legend

P.'s
3 3
~~35~~   N3! RV3
4 4
81
142
173
207

H Sutherland
8 Roseburn Dr
Cumnock
Ayrshire KA18 1DH

14th Aug, '89.

JOHN BURROWES

Incomers

FONTANA/Collins

First published in Great Britain
by Mainstream Publishing Company 1987
First published in Fontana Paperbacks 1988

Copyright © John Burrowes 1987

Printed and bound in Great Britain by
William Collins Sons & Co. Ltd, Glasgow

Contents

This book would not have been possible without the help of many of the Incomers themselves, as well as others whose incoming happened in previous generations. Among those who so willingly devoted their time and energy in my research and to whom I am most sincerely grateful were the Khalid family of Glasgow and London, Shahid, Ghulam, Javaid, Messrs Sharif, Ali and Shaheen, the Sher family of Sialkot and the Malik family of Gujrat in the Punjab, Mr Durrani of *The Pakistan Times* and Anim Abd-Allah, in Lahore, Dan Grant and Samia for their understanding of what *Incomers* was about, and Bryan, Betty and George for their special knowledge of the licensed trade.

As in *Jamesie's People*, the book from which *Incomers* is the sequel, most of the places and many of the events in this book are based on historical fact and every effort has been made to adhere to those facts. There are people such as the Incomers, but all of the characters depicted are the author's creation and bear no similarity to people living today.

Prologue

I

Star's mother, Isa, found it difficult to accommodate to Pollokshields, and the sophistication and snobbery of the neighbours in
St Andrew's Drive where she and Star had agreed to come and
live with Star's Uncle Sammy several months ago. She missed
her own people from the Gorbals tenements – their rough
cheerfulness, their straightforward way of talking, their uninhi-
bited laughter. So, like Sammy, she often made the forty-minute
trek to her old home of an evening to meet friends in one of the
pubs and catch up with the latest gossip. If she was out late she'd
arrange to meet Sammy rather than walk home alone.

One evening in the spring of 1949 Sammy and Star were up
waiting for Isa to come home. They sat in Sammy's enormous
front lounge, the room he had told Star was bigger than the
Parlour, Lochwood and Tripe dancehalls put together, laughing
loudly when he recollected the one called the Tripe and described
how it had been so small they had to seat the small band on a
platform over the dancers!

'I'm surprised she hasn't rung by now to say where she is,' said
Sammy. 'It's unlike Isa.' Restless, he hauled himself out of his
deep armchair to turn the radio on for the late news. They
listened to the headlines, before the newscaster's crackly voice
turned to other topics:

'Reports have been coming in from our correspondent in
north-west India about isolated incidents of violence between
different religious groups in Amritsar. In the last week alone
several people have been killed, property looted and burned,
in the Muslim section of the city. Local observers fear the
situation may worsen, although law and order has largely been
restored in the area since the serious rioting that followed the
final withdrawal of British authority from the area over a year
ago. Recent events have, however, led to many remaining

7

Muslim families hurriedly packing their bags and leaving for a new homeland in Pakistan. Many thousands have already made the journey . . . .'

'I'm sure I don't see quite what they're fighting about,' Sammy broke in as he switched the radio off. 'They've got what they wanted, the Indians, haven't they? Independence, I mean.'

'I don't know,' said Star thoughtfully. 'I was talking to a girl at college whose brother came back from India last year when the company he worked for folded. Apparently, making a new Muslim country, Pakistan, has created more problems than it's solved because it's so artificial. Millions of people were left in territories that mean something different now. By the stroke of a pen on a map Hindus and Sikhs who wanted to stay Indians found themselves in a Muslim country. And everyone was frightened because they didn't understand, so the different groups started hating each other.'

'They seem to be sorting it out a bit, though. All these Muslims going off to be with the others in Pakistan.'

'But what a journey with all their children, and having to settle in a strange land and start all over again. And there might not be jobs or homes for them all.'

'I suppose so.' He chuckled. 'At least you and your mum didn't have that problem coming to live in the 'Shields with me, eh? Where can Isa be? She should have been home hours ago.'

When the phone did ring ten minutes later it was the police.

Sammy put the receiver down and when he came back into the lounge his face betrayed bewildered disbelief.

'Star,' he said softly. She rose to meet him and he put his arms round her. 'Star, it was the police. They've found Isa. She'd collapsed in the street. A heart attack, they think. Star, they don't know if she'll last the night.'

II

The Indian soldiers had come to their villages for them in tanks whose big cannon guns showed them that their fear of the unknown was no longer. Their fear was now of the known there

8

in its reality with .303s that had long bayonets fixed and bren carriers with their automatics mounted and loaded. And those tanks with their menacing cannons.

The *maulvis* and the peers and other elders of the villages pleaded with the soldiers. 'We have told our Muslim people,' they said, 'that they must not harm the Hindu or the Sikh men and women. We will stay peacefully here in India.' But they spoke to ears that heard but did not heed.

'You must go now,' said the officers, impatiently thwacking their swaggersticks on their legs in an identical fashion to the way other officers used to do, the ones with the pale and red faces who had now gone away. 'All Muslims must leave within one hour. You can only bring what you can carry. No livestock or other property. Everything must be left. This is an order. Those who disobey will be punished.'

And all that day and night and the next day and the night of that day and the next day and night after that they rounded them up in the little villages and the larger ones. They herded them, just as they did the black, nonchalant water-buffalo, to the camp at Chabal Kalan, south of Amritsar in the far north-west of India. After three weeks at the camp, during which they were rationed to a small bowl of rice or wheat flour every day, there were 100,000 of them gathered. And throughout the zone there were other similar camps. Then the soldiers ordered them to start marching in the direction of the west; in the direction of the land they said was the 'land of the pure' . . . Pakistan.

And so they went forth with their young and their old, with their sons and their daughters but without their flocks and without their herds, just as the children of another land had gone forth. The children of Allah were on their way to their Promised Land.

Weakened by the meagre rations and the numbers of young and old, they could only manage eight miles a day. Because they were young and fit, the three men they called Maqbul, Rasool and Javaid walked more than twice that distance each day as they went up and down the long column, helping the elderly, carrying them back and forth over dried creek beds and rocky outcrops as they headed overland towards the trunk road to the north of Chabal Kalan which came all the way from the heartland of India to the far north-west and down which Genghis Khan himself had come with his hordes. The three men kept the discipline too when the food lorries came, restraining the greedy, and punishing the occasional thief. And together they would sit and talk at night after they had worshipped their Allah with the *isha*, the fifth prayer of the day, said at that time of nightfall when it was no longer possible to distinguish between a white and black thread. They had been strangers prior to the long march but were now the firmest of friends, tied by the bond of hardship.

There was Maqbul, fast-talking, always with a smile and a joke, broad-shouldered from his days on the small family farm, the youngest in a family of two sons and a daughter who were also on the march with their parents. They had named him well, for Maqbul meant 'the popular one'. Their little farm had been near Sultanpur. With their uncles and aunts and cousins and their other Muslim neighbours his family had been rounded up and escorted to the big camp at Chabal Kalan, a heritage of centuries of husbandry terminated with the arrival of a lumbering tank. It had been on the first march from Sultanpur to the big camp that they had been joined by two men who came running across the fields towards their column.

'Thank God we're with our people,' the two men, Rasool and Javaid, had said to the first man they had met and who had come forward to shake their hands . . . Maqbul. 'We've been running for miles,' they said, between great gulps of the water he had fetched for them.

That night they had told their stories.

'I was living in the suburbs of Amritsar,' said Rasool. 'My father was a senior civil servant. One of the most senior men in the Punjab. I went to Aitchison's College and have just finished university.'

Javaid whistled. 'Aitchison's eh . . . the Chiefs' College. You must be rich, Rasool. Very, very rich.'

'Yes, Javaid, we were very rich. *Were*. Anyway, I was home for the summer vacation and the crowds came that night. There were many Muslim families in the district and they knew where to find them. First of all they burned the Mosque and killed the *maulvis*. Then they went round the houses. I didn't know they were in our place till I heard the screams. We had quite a large bungalow and I was in the verandah guarding the back. It was the screams. I'll never forget the screams . . . they were my parents and my sister Nazia. And before I could get to them the house went up in flames. I could see the Sikh police just standing there with their sword sticks and not even attempting to intervene. The flames stopped them from coming to the back of the house and I got away.'

He had fled from his home through the small orchard of evergreen mango trees, leaping the irrigation channel into a neighbour's garden orchard and on into another and when he did stop to look back there was just a pall of heavy black smoke in the sky and the distant shouts of rejoicing . . . the crazed merriment of the horde whose killing had quelled some of their fear of the unknown. Just as he had regained his breath he had turned to run again when a young man leapt out from the cover of a tree. He was holding his hands out to block the way.

'Stop, *yaar* (friend). You're a Muslim like me.'

Without hesitating, Rasool picked up a big stone to defend himself.

'How do I know you're Muslim? You're wearing the *lunghi* of the Hindu. You want to waylay me and trick me to going to your people.'

'I swear to Allah I'm Muslim.'

'You lie. What comes after the first prayer of the day?'

'After the *fajar* there is the *zohar* then *asar*, *maghrib* and *isha*. But I have not been a good Muslim. I don't say my five prayers every day, I have never had enough money to give *zakat* nor have I been on the *haj* pilgrimage.'

'Every Muslim knows the *al-fatiha*. Say it.'

'Of course, *yaar*. In the name of Allah, the Beneficent, the Merciful, praise be to Allah, Lord of the World, the Beneficent, the Merciful, owner of the Day of Judgment, Thee alone we worship, Thee alone we ask for faith, show us the straight path, the path of those whom Thou has favoured, not the path of those who earn Thine anger, nor of those who go astray.'

Rasool put the stone down and held out his hand. '*Yaar*.'

'My name is Javaid. I'm from Lahore. I was in the district staying with a cousin. I have been on the road for two days now, but I only travel at night taking my direction from the stars. Stay

11

with me, *yaar* . . . you're wearing Muslim dress and they'll spot you right away. We will be safe once we meet up with one of the big groups heading for Pakistan.'

Rasool was still in shock and he had wept as he recounted the story of how his family had been killed. 'It was just an hour ago. Look, that smoke high in the sky. That was my family's home. Our whole world was there . . . now it has gone. The crowds were like wolves. It was madness. I never believed that people could act like that. They were the people I had lived among all my life . . . sane and orderly people. Then, in a moment, they are insane. Like a people possessed. Our Koran tells us that we are to think not of those who are slain in the way of Allah as dead . . . they are living. But right now that doesn't soothe my heart when I think of my beautiful sister . . . my father . . . my mother. I have nothing but bitterness for those who did it.'

'I understand, friend. I lost my cousin and all my uncles and aunts. They were the only friends I had. I too am like you . . . so we must stay together.'

They walked for two nights together, stopping only when they could feel the warm rays of the sun on their necks and when they would search for enough food to keep them for another day. They were in maize country and there was no shortage of the big juicy sweetcorns, and there were nut plantations and fruit orchards in the shade of whose trees they rested and slept throughout the day.

Because both were still reflecting on the horrors of what they had experienced, they had spoken only a little to each other and it wasn't till the morning of their third day together that Rasool had asked Javaid about his family.

'I never knew who my real parents were. I was adopted by a family and they called me Javaid. It means "alive . . . living". They told me the story when I was a young boy. You see I was a tribal. We came from the far north-west and every year when the cold winds came the families would trek south for the winter. They had been doing so for centuries. They would go all the way to near Karachi, down the Sehwani, as they called it, the road built for the pilgrims to Sehwan Sharif. The families were camped near a village about twenty miles from Karachi when my mother went into labour with me. Do you know the customs of the tribespeople when a child is due?'

'I'm afraid I don't, although there are some at the college from the north-west.'

'At Aitchison's. They must be the sons of chiefs. They would not be born our way. When the woman's time comes she must leave the camp and hide among the tall grass or in the bushes far enough away so that her wails and her cries are not heard. If they are heard, then that family would be disgraced. That may seem a very strange thing for city people to understand but it is the way of the hill people. Being born like this is very important to them, especially for a boy. For the child that is born in the wilderness will have the courage of a lion, the soul of a free bird. So they believe, anyway.'

Rasool was fascinated by Javaid's tale and for a while his own misfortunes were overlooked.

'That will account for your lighter skin then, Javaid . . . you being from the north-west. You'll be a Pathan.'

'That is so . . . but my story goes on. You see, I was not brought up by the tribespeople. When the woman goes out from the camp to have her child they leave her with a pitcher of water and sometimes even food if the other women say that she is to be long in labour. Well, anyway, my mother died just after I was born and I was discovered by a village woman. She was the wife of a small farmer. She had lost her only son in childbirth and discovering me, they said, was like a gift from Allah. They had thought my mother had been abandoned by the tribespeople and so they took me away. The old couple died when I was about eight. They had three girls and myself and we were split up among relatives who had been told the story of my birth and how I had been found and they re-counted it to me when I was older. The relatives were poor and old people, but they were kind to me. After some time with them I left to head for the north, hoping that one day I might eventually find the tribespeople from which I had come. I got all the way up to Lahore. There I lived in the Old City with a cousin of the old couple. It is quite a place. Life is lived there like it was in the beginning. Do you know the Old City, Rasool?'

'Of course. We used to go to political meetings at the Mochi Gate. And we used to wander through the Anarkali Bazaar and that leads up, I think, to the Mori Gate. And there's another gate nearby.'

'That's the Lahori Gate. That's near where I used to live. You'll remember the Lahori Gate, Rasool? That's the one where near the entrance you have all the shops selling the wedding money-garlands. Well, if you went through the gate, past the stall where they make chewing pan, then a raffia seller, the yoghurt maker, a herbalist, the sweet oil merchant, the butcher who sells skinned goats' heads, the stall for hookahs, tobacco and charcoal and just before the little mosque at the first corner on the right, there's a tiny alleyway. Well, my cousins had a room in there which we shared. But it was so small and there were so many of us we could not all sleep at the one time. But we managed. You have to manage in the Old City.'

'I don't know how people manage there, Javaid. It's like turning the clock back a thousand years.'

'Yes, but I learned more there, *yaar*, in one year, than all my life put together. Living like that, Rasool, you first of all learn tolerance . . . for you have to be tolerant when you are living, thousands upon thousands of you, in such a small area. And you learn too to trade more competitively than they do anywhere in all the world.'

'Not *all* the world, Javaid.'

'Well, all my world, and I have been in many towns on my long trip from Karachi to Lahore. You have to know what to make, where to sell it, when to sell it, how to sell it; for if you don't sell, you can't pay your rent or buy your food. Every day, a great new challenge. I was about eleven years of age when I went out to make a living on my own there, which was older than many of the others, for they begin selling in the streets just as little children, sometimes at four with an older brother who is maybe eight or nine.

'My first job was with the street traders, turning the press of the juice extractor at the pomegranate stall. Then when my muscles got bigger I was able to work on the big sugarcane juice presses. After that I teamed with another boy and we got a little charcoal pot and cooked poppadoms for the Friday and Sunday strollers in the Shalimar Gardens.

'And on the days when there was no one in the gardens and parks I sold cage birds at the bazaar . . . sparrows, tota, kabutar and the like. If I sold five sparrows in a day that made me enough money for my dinner. Two of the more colourful birds, like the tota, would give me enough profit for a day's rent.

'For a while I was a grease boy with the motor mechanics; you know, all the ones who have stalls on the MacLeod Road. Very dirty work, Rasool. Covered in oil and dirt every night. But it made me learn about cars and engines. After that I was a kitchen boy in the Mussarat Gah restaurant just off the Dil Mohammad. Rasool, I have done everything, which is what you must do just to live in the Old City,'

'And now you're like me, Javaid. A refugee. What will you do when you get back to Lahore?'

'Oh, I will not starve, Rasool. What . . . with all my trades! And I can always get a bed somewhere for I know lots of people around the Mori, Lahori and Bhati Gate areas. What about yourself, Rasool?'

'Oh, I have some uncles. I will be all right. And, like my father, they are quite wealthy. Even if they were not, they would look after me till I found something to do. I got a good degree from university . . . History, French, English and Persian. I was going to go into the Civil Service like my father . . . but now I don't know, I really don't know. Anyway, who knows what's ahead now? Independence and the Partition have brought ruin to our country. The Hindus dominated in the Civil Service, in the learning institutions and the banks and in commerce. Now they have all fled to their India. It will be chaos . . . I'm telling you. I fear for . . .' Rasool broke off suddenly. 'What's that noise? It's like voices.'

They had been resting in a small orange grove since daylight that morning, unaware that the main trunk road, in whose direction they had been heading, was just 200 yards away. The sight before their eyes amazed them. A slow-moving biblical column trudged towards the west and stretched as far back as they could see, at which point it merged into a dusty mist.

'God, Javaid. It's like a whole city. No . . . a whole country on the move. Have you ever seen so many people? I can hardly believe my eyes.'

'We're safe now, Rasool . . . they're our people. Muslim people. Our Pakistani people.'

At that he stood up and shouted the word. 'Pakistanis.' And Rasool stood up and they started running together in the direction of the column shouting the word more loudly each time they said it . . . 'Pakistanis . . . Pakistanis . . . Pakistanis . . .'

It had been Maqbul who had stopped, as the column continued its slow trudge towards the west, grinning broadly at the two strangers running towards them shouting the name of their countrymen. 'Welcome, *yaar*. A thousand welcomes. From where have you come?'

They gushed out some of their story, between the big draughts of water which Maqbul had got for them.

'Are we near the border? How far have we got to go? Which town are you headed for? How long have you been on the march?'

'Easy, *yaar*. Easy. One question at a time,' said Maqbul. 'The border is near. We will cross it today. The soldiers with us are from the Pakistani Army. They're the Punjabi Regiment. They're from the cantonment at Sialkot and joined us yesterday so we are safe now. And they have brought us food . . . the Indians would give us nothing. The soldiers are taking us to a big camp near Gujranwala . . . it will take us three or four more days.'

'But we're going to Lahore,' said Javaid.

'Best you stay with us for your safety,' Maqbul advised. 'Anyway, I need some able men like you to help the group I am with . . . there's the sick and the old. Come with us to the camp at Gujranwala, then you can head south to Lahore. From there it will only take you a day, two at the most.'

As it turned out Rasool and Javaid spent six weeks with their new friend, on the long march from India then helping the soldiers to establish the big camp.

Rasool would have scoffed had he been told a couple of months previously that he could have enjoyed the company of a peasant farmer's son and a boy from the Old City who lived in a shared room up an alleyway past the yoghurt maker, the hookah seller and the butcher with the skinned goats' heads. They were so unlike many of his privileged friends from Aitchison's and university, the only kind of friends he had known. But they were admirable companions. One was of the earth, both were of the earthy, their culture forged of the struggle that was life and how to survive it, one by sinew and seed, the other by guile and graft. They were honest men who could speak about ambition without a hint of covetousness or envy. They were without, yet had so much and had made Rasool reflect on his own life which had been with so much and all of which had been taken for granted; as though it was a right; that it was the way it had always been and should be. Maqbul's ability to inspire and cheer the refugees had been the very epitome of the courage and inspiration they had tried to teach them – the English way, as they knew – at Aitchison's. The games ethic, as it was known. Yet here he was, this man of the soil with no formal education, except that of his father and his father's father and all their forebears in the husbandry of the earth, demonstrating all the stability and dignity of the noble spirit at a time of great trial and tribulation.

It would be a lesson he would remember for the rest of his life.

Maqbul was fevered that last morning when Rasool and Javaid made to leave the big refugee camp for the journey south to Lahore. 'It's the mosquitoes,' he said. 'I am not used to them. Where I come from is a dry area . . . not like this rice country.'

'Gujranwala rice,' exclaimed Javaid. 'Finest rice in all the world they say.'

Maqbul smiled at Javaid's efforts to cheer him.

'Nothing feels fine, my *yaar*, when you have the malaria coming on you.'

He lay on a rickety litter, barely able to support his weight, as they shook his hand and made their farewell. 'You've been good and trusting travelling companions,' he said, the usual exuberance and cheer missing from his voice. 'I wish you well in Lahore. When I am better I will go with my family to Gujrat. My father has a brother and two cousins there. One needs family in trying times like this. May God be with you.'

'God be with you, Maqbul.'

Rasool and Javaid walked towards the roadway and in an instant they were lost among the crowds of refugees who, like them, were heading for the capital of their state, Lahore.

BOOK I

1

In the 'Shields

Janice was the kind of woman whose mind figured other people's personalities like a ready reckoner, indexing, cross-indexing, referring, re-referring as it peeled off frontal layers like a painter blowtorching a ten-coat door. She preferred those who would give her a challenge, masquerading behind their defects like a leapfrog game, camouflaging one when it was under threat of exposure, hiding behind another if the subtleties of the conversation posed a threat of baring a hidden truth. If necessary and if she was really challenged her sharp mind could fillet out someone's real character, leaving it as exposed as a cleaned haddock on a fish-shop slab. It was all much of a game with her really. She would often toy with the others of her weekly coffee crowd in Pollokshields in order to elicit some new aspect of their true self. There weren't many other challenges for Janice, living as she did in one of the grandest houses in the 'Shields, as they fondly called their area, wearing the word as though it had been passed to them in the Honour's List.

It was Janice's turn to host the coffee morning that early spring day in 1951. The previous week, at Sandra's place, they had had a brief discussion about the guest Janice had said she had invited to meet the girls, as they liked to call themselves, their ages ranging from the late thirties to early fifties.

'Well . . . I thought at first she was his new mistress. There was another woman, you know, after his wife died,' said one of them, in the obligatory twin-set, pearls and brogues. 'Anyway,' she went on, stretching the word out for emphasis, 'it turns out that she's his niece . . . at least that's what Sandy Rankine the newsagent tells me. Good-looking girl, mind you. Lovely figure.'

There were nods of concurrence.

'I met her down at the Maxwell Road shops,' said Jane, wife of one of the senior executives with Lorrens, the big builders. 'We were in the butcher's together. God . . . changed days, having to do your own shopping. That war did none of us any good. People don't want to work as staff any more.'

Janice gave a wry smile at the remark, thinking that she would have been almost disappointed had she not said it.

'What was I saying? Oh yes, the girl. Anyway, all she bought was a cheap cut of stewing meat.'

'Maybe she's vegetarian and it was for the dog,' said Janice, smiling with some of the others at her aside.

'Oh you never know these days . . . do you?'

'What does her uncle do anyway?' asked Shirley, the newest of the *nouveaux riches* to have recently graduated to the 'Shields, her husband just having made one fortune in the new golden trade, the demolition business.

'Bit of a mystery about him,' came a reply. 'They've lived here for a few years now and in that big house too . . . Sammar isn't it? Sounds Russian. There was a rumour that he was a spiv during the war. Black market, you know. Imagine a spiv living in Pollokshields.'

'I could tell you about quite a few,' Janice came in. 'Only they put on such a good front you could never tell.'

Shirley continued again. 'You know his wife died an alcoholic. That was when his niece and her mother came to live with him.'

'Was she his sister . . . the mother?' asked someone.

'No,' said Shirley, who appeared to know most about them. 'She was a sister-in-law apparently. But there was some talk . . . you know . . . about him and her. However, she wasn't there all that long until she died too. They say she was a dipsomaniac as well. Imagine that, two from the one family.'

'God, I wouldn't like to think how many we had in our family,' quipped Janice. 'Uncle Harry, a millionaire from his chain of grocer's shops, sozzled every night. Aunt Lottie, his wife, is the same. And so's my father, eighty-one last week and can still do the best part of a bottle of Teacher's every day.'

They laughed and shook their heads at Janice's frankness. 'It's the money,' they whispered at meetings when Janice hadn't been there. 'That's what gives her the freedom to be so frank. Everywhere she looks there's money . . . her father . . . her husband . . . her husband's family.'

'How did they know,' a question went up, 'about the other woman being a dipsomaniac?'

'Didn't you hear?' said Shirley, surprised. 'Sure, did they not find her lying at the foot of Dr Samson's monkey puzzle tree one morning half dead with the cold and only living because she had been so pickled the night before.'

'Well, for someone we don't know much about, that's not a bad start. Anyway, you can find out as much as you want very shortly for I've just seen her coming through our front gate.'

They walked together into the big drawing room, having chatted for a few minutes in the handsome light-oak-panelled hallway. 'Girls,' said Janice, a dominie ring in her voice, 'I would like you to meet our guest, Miss Nelson from up the road. And her first name is Star . . . Isn't that a lovely name . . . and I must say most fitting for you, dear.'

'I'm flattered,' she smiled.

'We met in the butcher's,' said Jane as they shook hands. 'And Star, is it? What an unusual name. Your father wasn't in showbusiness by any chance?'

'No . . . he was very well known, apparently. But . . . eh . . . it was another line he was in. He died when I was very young.'

'Oh, I'm so sorry.'

'Please don't worry. I never ever knew him.'

'Do you like living in the 'Shields?' came in Shirley, anxious to learn more about her.

'Yes, it's lovely. It's been two years now, actually. Living here you tend to forget how cruel and hard life can be in so many other parts of Glasgow.'

That was an unusual tack for the coffee morning crowd and Janice eagerly looked round the faces for reaction.

'But we've lots of lovely areas in Glasgow,' came a twin-set, pearls and brogues. 'There's Newlands and Giffnock and Whitecraigs and even Clarkston. Lots of lovely places on the south side.'

'That's funny,' smiled Star. 'The words south side. Where I came from south side only meant one thing.'

'And what was that?'

'The Gorbals, of course. That's what we called it. The south side.'

Janice couldn't remember when there had been a longer hush at their morning and she sat forward in her seat studying the responses, the predictable, the unpredictable, another little bit of character revealed. She enjoyed that.

Star too knew what effect the statement would have on the women. She knew her Glasgow. She knew the first two things people wanted to know about you were which school you had attended and where you lived, the answers to which were the most vital items of information in making any kind of assessment of a person in the city, one revealing religion, whether you were Protestant or Catholic, the other status. Was there any more you needed to know about someone in Glasgow? Sometimes it didn't really matter about the answers, more often it did; but they always wanted to know. They always needed to put the religious label on you in order to satisfy conditioned minds. The Catholics had their attitudes about the Protestants, the Protestants theirs about the Catholics and these ranged from contempt to concern, from scorn to suspicion, fear to phobia to hatred. And whether or not the religious label suited, they still wanted your worth, pinpointing your precise address so that they could almost fill in the blanks by themselves, like the status of your parents and the kind of people who lived around you.

And you didn't have to be all that good at address assessments to know that Pollokshields was for the Brahmins, the Gorbals for the Untouchables.

Janice took an instant liking to Star for the bold and obviously proud way she had almost volunteered her background. It could have been so easy to disguise, particularly with her not having the kind of raw accent which was a castemark of the Gorbals. Instead there was an air of defiance as she calmly looked around at the 'girls' in the hiatus of embarrassed silence which had been their reaction to Star's pronouncement, one staring at her unashamedly open-mouthed, another coughing and searching for a pair of eyes to give her comfort.

'Do you know, I'm ashamed to say I've never been in the Gorbals,' said Janice, the first to speak.

'It's quite historic, when you've made a study of it, that is,' said Star. 'I'll take you for a walk round it one day. See how the other half live.'

'Which half?' queried Janice.

'I didn't say,' smiled back Star.

'I wasn't suggesting . . .'

'Neither was I . . .'

'But you have your thoughts . . .'

'Yes . . . I do. The Gorbals half are neither the bottom nor the top. They're the "other" half. The half that have not. And what you lucky ladies here represent is the half that have. It's an ill-divided world. But that's the way of it. Everyone seems to have a remedy . . . and do you know one that has worked?'

'Bravo, Star. Well said.' And with that Janice ran her eyes around the room. There were reactions to be studied.

'Gawd,' sighed Jane, 'is that us into politics?'

'Nonsense,' retorted Janice. 'Star is perfectly correct. We *are* an ill-divided world.'

'If your husband Harold could only hear you . . . my God, you're sounding like one of those Socialists.'

'Jane, darling . . . hubby Harold doesn't have time to think like that. It would get in the way of making more money. As far as being a Socialist . . . poppycock. I'm a Winston Churchill girl through and through. You know that. But it's still an ill-divided world.'

'Right then, girls,' said a jolly, plump woman, helping herself to another piece of the cream sponge cake. 'Enough of all that serious blarney. Let's get down to what matters . . . what's the latest scandal?'

'There was a burglary at the Murrays the other night.'

'Goodness, that's the second they've had.'

'I know. And you know why! He's a turf agent or turf accountant or whatever they call themselves . . .'

'You mean a bookie,' smiled Janice.

'All right, a bookie then. They mix with all sorts, you know. And you know about them and the banks? They don't trust them.'

'It's not trust . . . it's the Inland Revenue. They don't want the tax man to know how much they earn. So they have little shoeboxes bung full of the stuff beneath the bed.'

'Well, the burglars seem to know all about them. That's why

they came back a second time. And do you know, they don't even call the police.'

'How did you get to know?' asked Shirley.

'My cleaning woman, you know Lizzie from Eglinton Street? Well her neighbour is the Murrays' cleaning woman. And she tells her everything. Apparently they were very upset. According to her they got away with thousands . . . and some of Mrs Murray's jewellery too.'

'Well, that's what happens when you don't trust banks.'

Another was anxious to give her item, which she posed as a question in the hope that someone else might have some more information than the scant details she had.

'What about the new people in Nithsdale Road?'

No one responded.

'Oh . . . haven't you heard? They're in the big red sandstone . . . the one Dr McLaren left. Well . . . they're black.'

'Never.'

'Seen them myself.'

'Maybe they're visitors.'

'I saw them supervising a gardener. It was old Jock, you know the one who used to do for the doctor?'

'Gracious, what's the world coming to!'

'Could affect our valuations you know.'

'Wouldn't like them living next door to me.'

Janice was shaking her head. 'You're havering the lot of you. We had the lovely Mr Ahmed who lived in St Andrew's Drive for years. Perfect gentleman and what a lovely family.'

'Yes, but Mr Ahmed was a surgeon. One of the best at the Victoria they said. This one is no surgeon.'

'How do you know?'

'He's got a little van . . . full of goods and things. I think he's a pedlar.'

'You mean an Indian Johnny? You're joking. They couldn't afford to live in the 'Shields.'

'Does he wear a turban?'

'Are you being funny, Shirley?'

'Not really. Some of the pedlars do, you know.'

'He won't be all that black if he's Indian.'

'No . . . he's not really. He's got quite a European face, actually. But he's not white.'

'He could be a Pakistani.'

'Oh Janice, you always have to complicate things. Does it matter what he is? He's a different colour and he's living in Pollokshields. And the next thing he'll have all his cousins coming here from Rangoon and smelling us out with their curries.'

'Rangoon's in Burma, darling.'

Another was anxious to speak. 'Did you hear the McLean girl has got engaged . . . to a chap she met at Oxford? Going to live down south I heard.'

There was no further mention of the new neighbour from somewhere overseas.

Janice walked down the long front path with Star as the women began dispersing from the 'morning'.

'I do hope we'll be seeing you again, Star,' and without waiting for an answer gripped her by the arm and smiled. 'I must say you handled yourself so well with the girls. It can be a bit daunting being with that lot for the first time and you being so much younger. They can be a real snobby bunch at times. I suppose I'm one myself. The difference is I know it. It's when you don't realise you're one that's the terrible thing about snobbery.

'But I try not to think too deeply about the girls. Despite their faults they're quite a jolly bunch really and we have some good laughs together. You're going to work for your uncle, you were saying, so you won't be one of our regulars?'

'I'm afraid not, but it was nice to meet you all. I've finished my business administration course now and Sammy, Uncle Sammy that is, wants me to get into his company right away. He needs organising, he says.'

'What about his son . . . isn't he thinking of going into the business?'

'John, you mean? No. He's dedicated to law. Lives in Edinburgh now. Serving his apprenticeship to be an advocate . . . or devilling as they call it.'

'Good for him. You'll think me a real nosey parker, but what line of business is your uncle in?'

'Well, at the moment he's got a public house and he owns the

Pantheon . . . it's an old cinema in the Gorbals. But I don't think either are doing well and he wants to use what I've learned at college to help him straighten a few things out. I'm really looking forward to going to work again.'

'Work . . . Star,' Janice exclaimed. 'Pollokshields ladies don't work. They go out to business.'

They laughed together, stopping at the tall stone-pillared gateway to the house. 'Star, dear,' said Janice holding out her hand. 'How lovely to meet you. You seem a very nice person and I really hope everything goes well for you in your uncle's business. It can be a tough and ruthless old world, you know . . . especially business in Glasgow. If ever you need any help or advice, my husband Harold has got lots of good connections. Very good connections. Don't hesitate. Now I'll have to dash back to the house. Cook is waiting for me to tell her what we want for dinner. Oh, the problems of being the other half.'

2

That's Pub Life

Sammy Nelson was a fit-looking 51-year-old and despite his
greying hair could easily pass for a man ten years younger. He
said it was the walking that did it, by that meaning the regular
walk to and from the Gorbals, the centre of many of his activities.
It was in the Gorbals that he could meet old friends, relax in the
patois, relish the patter, the banter. He lived in Pollokshields,
but he was living when he was in the Gorbals. The Gorbals was
still like home. He knew them in the 'Shields, he understood
them in the Gorbals. The people he called acquaintances in the
'Shields he called friends in the Gorbals. Where he lived he was
known as Mr Nelson, plain anonymous Mr Nelson, the owner of
Sammar, the big house at the corner of St Andrew's and
Nithsdale, businessman and gentleman – well, he had to be that
for he was one of them if he lived there. Where he did his living
he was Sammy, the same Sammy that owned Sammy's Bar and
the Pantheon, Sammy Nelson of the famous Nelson family, and
God wasn't that a name to reckon with in the Gorbals, him being
the brother of the man they still spoke about and remembered as
Jamesie, dead now for twenty-four years and a bigger legend
than ever, for wasn't he the hardest of all the hard men in the
area? And there was Sammy, good old Sammy, his very own
brother, 'a real Nelson and doing well, the boy, isn't he?', as they
would say. They didn't think things like that about him in the
'Shields.

Sammy wore the philosophy of his life like his Crombie. One
was tailor-made, bespoke no less, the other ready-made, available for the occasion, a movable feast. One was about warmth
and wealth, the other about soul and self. The Crombie was real
and about achievement; the philosophy about reality and atone-
ment.

They said everyone had a conscience, but usually it only
worked when they were right or when they were at confessions.

For Sammy, conscience was a crutch he couldn't do without; true, it often blurred what was right and what was wrong, but at least he tried to obey it and on that account he considered he led a principled life. Even his activities as a wartime black marketeer and slum landlord could be squared by his conscience. He had reasoned that making his fortune in such a manner wasn't really all that bad. In fact, it wasn't bad at all, for he was doing more good than bad. Wasn't he? Of course he was, said his conscience. So, then, what did it matter if some laws were broken, the occasional toe trodden on? But eventually even Sammy's conscience began to see that these might be considered to be errant ways and he had promised his dear and faithful wife Margaret, he fondly called Peggy, before she died that he would be for evermore on the straightest path in life. Conscience permitting that is.

Sammy discussed with Star how he thought she could help in his businesses at the public house called Sammy's Bar in Ballater Street and the old Pantheon Picture House in Caledonia Road, two operations which ran virtually without any supervision from Sammy, apart from a regular weekly visit . . . 'Just to let them know I'm the gaffer.'

'Absolutely incredible,' said Star.

'I know. I know. Incompetence . . . call it what you like,' he said, visibly squirming when he revealed that he merely collected a brown envelope each week which contained what his manager said were the profits. As for yearly profits, reinvestment, working capital, maintenance costs, taxes . . . 'The accountant does all that. They, the managers, send him returns and he sorts out the books.'

'How on earth did you ever make money?'

'Ah, that's another story, Star. You see I always did it on my own. I knew everything that was going on . . . that was when I was trading during the war. Then I had some houses, but I had two good men looking after that side of the business, and we always kept things right. Then, to please Peggy before she died, I went completely legit . . . I mean, I wasn't really not legit before that, just sort of, well, what you would say? Taking risks, . . . cutting corners . . . that sort of thing.'

'You sound like you've been a right old rascal.'

'Not really, Star. Never did anything I couldn't square with my conscience.'

'Yes . . . but you know what you can do with consciences,' she smiled.

'Anyway, I'm really looking forward to you coming into the business. I think if things were organised we could go places. Your enterprise, my money.'

'How do you know I've got enterprise? It was only a business administration course I did.'

'Star, in the Gorbals that's enterprise. Now you take the Jews. They know how to go about business. It's in their blood. Same with the other boys that are arriving, Indians and Pakistanis. They're all traders. But see us? We think if you're in business there's a bit of the gypsy or the tink in you. And right enough when you see how some of them work, they're not far wrong. But the Jews and them, they're not amateurs. See, once they get you as a customer, they want to keep you. Give you a deal and that. They make you think when you walk out of their shops that you've knocked it off. That you've got a right good bargain.

'So you remember and you go back to them again for another bargain. But see us? It's take it or leave it. Treat customers like they're a nuisance, so we do. We're just not business-minded like the Jews and the others. I'm the same. I'm not making what I should of what I've got. That's how I need you and all that training you've had.'

'Well . . . where do you want me to start?'

'I've been thinking about that. What I'd like you to do is get some practical experience.'

'You mean do my usherette at the Pantheon . . . and spray that terrible stuff they're always using there. What is it anyway?'

'I call it flea killer . . . but I don't know what it is. Anyway, we'll leave the Pantheon for the moment. I'd rather you get experience in the licensed trade. I'd like you to work in a pub first . . . get to know the ropes. You see the pub trade is full of . . . what shall I say?'

'Cutting corners . . . taking risks . . .'

'You've got it. And there's only one way you'll learn. That's from somone who knows all the risks, all the corners. I've got this pal Jimmy McLean . . . we call him Claney. Great character.

31

Was in the war and that. Mine-lifting with the Engineers. He'd a terrible time. Then he used to help me when I ran the houses. Like a rent collector; know what I mean? After that he went into the licensed business and he hasn't looked back. I was going to get him to come in with me. But see Claney now, Star? I couldn't afford him. He's the manager of the Nevis Bar in St Enoch Square.

'The Nevis is a brewer's place, you know, owned by one of the big brewery companies in Edinburgh . . . they're all run by Lord This and Lord That. Well, Claney drives a bigger car than the Lord This that owns the brewery. And he's bought himself a smart house out in Clarkston. And his wages are less than a tenner a week! Claney knows every trick in the business. Just as well he didn't come with me . . . he'd have done me rotten. But we're the best of pals and I'll get him to fix it so that you get a job and he shows you the ropes and that. Got to start from the bottom, Star.'

The great public house revolution had begun to happen about the same time that Sammy Nelson bought his first pub in Ballater Street, Gorbals, in 1948. A whole generation of men had been off to a war that had most of them seeing the world away from Scotland for the first time. The Glasgow pub was all they had known before 1939. They knew a lot better in 1945. The Glasgow pub was mainly a result of Calvin and the Corporation, one being about the total depravity of natural man, the other about the subjectivity of the voting man. Man could achieve nothing without God, preached the man from Geneva. Man could achieve nothing without a Councillor, preached the men from the City Chambers. Joyless salvation, said one. Joyless salutation said the other. And the public house was their shop window. Enjoy yourself lads, but don't dare show it. While the brewer barons took their honours for giving them their drink, the drinkers took their rations within the terms of the joyless licensing laws in their functionally cheerless drinking shops, each one a post-graduate centre in the study of the morose.

And when they had got their fill of drink or else their meagre funds were exhausted they were cast out, like tribesmen who had been collecting their liquid gewgaws, patted on the head and despatched back to the *kraal*. Drink and degradation went together which was why the pubs were the way they were: surgeries for dispensing momentary cures from life in the bleak and blighted barracks they called the tenements. The men and women just back from the war wanted better. And slowly they were getting it. The law said there had to be no singing or music, not even a folksy fiddler or a jolly jew's harpist. You weren't to play darts and they even frowned on dominoes and preferred you stood for your sups rather than sat. Sitting was enjoyment; standing was not.

Jimmy McLean, Sammy's friend, manager of the Nevis, a rumbustious and bustling city-centre bar near the draughty St Enoch Station, described his customers as a 'mixed clientèle'. There were bowler hats for large ones or polite gin-and-tonics elbowing it with homburgs and trilbies for sweet stouts or bottled lager and bonnets and mufflers for half-and-halfs or big bubbling pints; punters and patter men, some on the make, others on the take; shiny-suit clerks counting their pennies and gents in nap coats who didn't even check their change; and behind an opaque glass partition a family department with waitress service for women customers or mixed company.

It was owned by one of the Edinburgh brewers and McLean had been one of their most successful managers: successful for them; successful for himself, the twin success being based on the fact he had perfected the ideal formula for deceiving the brewers and getting away with it. His immediate predecessor at the Nevis had been dismissed together with the entire staff after a spot check had caught him cheating. Claney not only increased the profits but boosted them to their highest ever, making the bar one of the jewels in the group, and putting him above suspicion in the eyes of his supervisors.

'That's how I can get away with so much,' he had told Sammy. 'They don't think I'm at it and there's me with the new Humber and a cracking Johnny Lawrence out at Clarkston. You've got to be real fly at this game, Sammy.'

Claney *was* real fly. He was a consummate professional in the range of ruses and subterfuges, about which there was more to be learned than the actual trade itself, and which were practised by bar staffs in order to supplement meagre wages; pittances that helped make palaces for masters.

'Your niece Star . . . eh,' said Claney when Sammy had gone to see him at the Nevis. 'Jamesie's daughter!'

'Aye.'

'That's going back a bit. She's the girl that Snakey Holden tried to murder.'

'Aye . . . but she never knew anything about that. Nor did anybody, Claney.'

The two men looked at each other and a whole past, a catalogue of events, some terrible, others tragic, many nostalgic, flitted between their thoughts in a silent, unspoken empathy which marked their long friendship. Little exchanges like 'changed days' and 'it wasn't yesterday' summed up years of experiences they had shared as younger men in the Gorbals before and during the war years.

'So you want Star to learn the trade? No problem. I'll fix her up with a job. And what she doesn't learn here . . . not worth knowing, Sammy.'

Sammy smiled. 'I know you, Claney.'

'Aye . . . as well as I know you, Sammy.'

And another flood of memories cascaded through their minds.

'How's your bar, Sammy? Still spit and sawdust?'

'That's right. But I'm thinking of making changes.'

'Get into the lounge game quick, Sammy. Carpets, couches and ye olde oak beams faked wi' three-ply wood and you'll stow the place out. The day's coming when you'll no' be able to sell them a pint if it's at an old shop. Even the word shop . . . that sums up the old pubs, Sammy. Ye'd get a better welcome at the unemployment bureau. The young ones are different now, Sammy. They're all jumping about going for bus tour holidays to Blankenberg and Knokke. They're wanting drinks to match the carpets, you know, Cointreaus and cocktails and Tia Marias. See a Cointreau, Sammy! I can make more skin off of one than selling five pints. And as for cocktails . . . they'll make me twice what a Cointreau does. The world's all changing, Sammy. And, as the conductress says . . . you either get on . . . or get aff. What would you like to drink?'

Life as a waitress at the Nevis Bar came as something of a shock to Star Nelson. She knew the basics of Glasgow life. Apart from her years as a wartime evacuee in the country where she had learned other values, she had been born and spent most of her twenty-four years in the Gorbals. She had known and coped with the life of a working factory girl at Gordon's the big clothing manufacturer. But working life in a busy public house was another university. A city pub like the Nevis was a junction place of Glasgow humanity, a Freudian warehouse where inhibitions could be and often were left at the entrance, some being collected when they went out again, others being exchanged for another set, some leaving without any.

Unlike many of her friends Star hadn't really known pub life. She had been, of course, to the occasional night out with the girls when she had worked at the factory and later from the commercial college. But they were evenings with a slow, sweet sherry in the art deco of the Whitehall lounge bar and the like. The Nevis was a new experience.

'You'll pick it up from the rest of the girls,' Claney told her when she started as one of the waitresses. 'They'll teach you the various fiddles they get up to. Once you've learned that I'll give you a degree course on the real tricks of the trade.'

The bar staff's principles, like the customers' inhibitions, went the same way at the Nevis. You either abandoned them or changed them. There was Effy, for instance. Sang in the church choir, so she did, the Candlish Memorial in Govanhill at that. Effy was an expert at knowing at precisely what stage a drinker would get to when you could start short-changing them. 'Keep your eyes on them and count the drinks they've had. If they've come from another pub, and you can always tell, start calling you hen and darling and that, well, you can do them quicker. You can take anything you like from some of them and they wouldn't know. I heard a programme on the wireless about it once. It was about character study. That's what working in a pub is about. Character study. Never worked in a pub before, dear? Oh, you'll soon learn. Take that one over there, for instance. Three whiskies and pint chasers. I'll get his next order. There'll be two bob at least in it for the tronc. A bob skin and a bob tip . . . or bob's your uncle as they say, Star.'

She noted the disdainful look on Star's face as she spoke about the customers as if they were commodities, items which continually appeared and were the source of revenue for her. 'God looks after those that looks after themself, dear. What church d'ye go to?'

When Star queried her on the propriety of her actions, Effy's defence had been that it was the done thing in the trade. 'Everyone does it, Star. I do it my way, Harry and Jack and the other barmen have their way, the cellarman has his way, and Claney the boss is better than any of us. He's even got a special key to fiddle the cash register. I also know he's in cahoots with one of the supervisors that comes from the brewery to check on him. And I'm frightened to even imagine some of the tricks the brewers themselves get up to making the stuff. God has certainly looked after them very well.'

Jim 'Claney' McLean liked to think of himself as the true professional in the licensed trade. Apart from the time he spent as one of Sammy Nelson's rent collectors and his service during the war with the Royal Engineers, he had been in the liquor industry all his life. As a boy he had worked in a whisky bottling plant, then started an apprenticeship, or serving his time, as they called it, in Tennent's brewery, but hadn't returned 'because of a wee problem', as he put it, with the Military Police. That was when he started working in the bar circuit. He reckoned he was so experienced he could spot watered beer at a dozen yards and tell an adulterated whisky at a glance.

He had worked as a cellarman in the days when all the beer came in 36-, 22- and 18-gallon barrels, newly brewed and still 'live', the yeast hard at work fermenting the sugars into a bubbling alcoholic froth. They had to ease the heavy wooden casks on to their stillages and then vent them at the precise moment of the carbon-dioxide build-up, replugging with a softwood peg so that it would continue to fret. When that stage had been completed and it was in condition, they were replugged again with a hardwood peg until it was time to tap the barrel and fix it to the house's pumping system for delivery upstairs to the bar.

Claney knew his beer. He knew his whisky too, for it used to be delivered in bulk, also in barrels, and it was part of the cellarman's duties to bottle it, 21 quarter-gill measures to the bottle, or if they were working in fifths, 26 and two-fifth measures to the bottle. The cellarman had to have muscles for his barrels, timing for his beer, and precision with his whisky. Claney had them all.

'This is a trade that's a profession,' Claney explained to Star. 'There's two sides to this trade, Star. There's the bit that you're supposed to know and the bit you're not supposed to know. Some master a bit of the first and a lot of the second, and with others it's the opposite way round. Master them both and it's no longer a trade. It's a profession. You aim at being a professional, Star. It's the only way if you really want to know this business.

'Right, we'll do glasses today. I bet you thought there was just wee glasses and big glasses? Well, there's a lot more to just ordinary glasses than you would think. Take the ones we've got here. It's Ravenhead, Shardley and Nonik's we use . . . they're the manufacturers, like.'

He arranged a long, military line of them on the bar, varying from the smallest to the largest. 'There they are, best glasses in the business, at least so the trade papers keep telling us. Every one for a purpose. The big one, for instance. That's the one-pint Nonik. You can get them with the Government stamp on them and without. I always get them with. There's the occasional smart alec who'll complain it's not an official pint because there isn't a stamp on it. So it saves bother. Then there's the 12-ounce Pilsener, use that for the bottled beers, or the 12-ounce Worthington, good for the family department or the new lounge bars. Bit more class about it . . . looks like a giant sherry glass. Next is the half-pint Nonik and the 12-ounce Nonik, good everyday kind of stuff for the men. That's all the beer ones. The rest are for spirits and sherries. That's a one-tenth quart Pilsener, I use them in the men's bar for their whisky. They look like the ones they serve in the cowboy bars in the pictures and the men like them. Three of them, Star, and they start talking to you like the Lone Ranger. The one next to it is the club goblet, then there's the one-fifth quart Lyric, the club sherry and the club cocktail. The big future is in the last two. See sherries and cocktails, Star. There's a fortune to be made in them. You see, it's what all these daft lassies – no harm meant, like – are drinking. They all want something new. Everything's got to be contemporary . . . you know, like that furniture that's all the rage . . . skinny legs, fancy lines and made wi' orange boxes. Contemporary is in. The traditional is out. Same with the drinks. It's got to be new to them . . . Harvey's Bristol Cream, Sweet Martini, Pimm's No.1, and this new beer they're all raving about, Carlsberg Special. And you should see what three of them does to a woman! Anyway, that's glasses for you. You'll get the hang of them eventually.'

Putting the glasses back on their racks, McLean walked to the centre of the bar and stopped. 'And here, Star, we have the source of all wealth in a public house – or a lounge. This is where life begins and ends. It's the centre of attraction, the focus of attention, the star of the show . . . the till. This is what they all want to get into, for one kind of fiddle or another. If you can keep them out of this, then you're on a winner.'

She remembered the woman Effy's story and smiled to herself.

'Once they get access to the till they can operate all sorts of flankers, under-ringing so that they can take their own profit out, or else not ringing up at all. You'll hear barmen and waitresses shouting, "Catch that order." They say they do it because they over-rang a previous order or else there'll be another excuse. But the fact is, when they shout "catch that order" it means they have worked some kind of dodge with the stock, maybe bringing cheap stuff in, and that gives them an excess in money. They can then take that money out of the till and keep the account for the night square by not ringing up the appropriate amount.'

Star said she was puzzled, especially about them bringing supplies into the pub.

'I'll explain it. You see, whisky, sherry and that is a lot cheaper at the licensed grocer than it is when we sell it in the pub . . . for we add on profit, etc. Now if you, say, bring two bottles of whisky into the pub that will cost you £3 10/- . . . 35/- each, right? But then you sell it at the pub price which is more than twice that so that means you've made yourself more than 100 per cent profit . . . for just walking into the bar with a couple of bottles of whisky. That's almost a week's wages . . . for just one night of the week. And that's just one of the tricks. Take that cheap Cyprus sherry . . . it's about twelve bob a bottle. Harvey's is nearly a quid. Now, see, after a few sherries, some of them wouldn't know whether they were in Bristol or Famagusta . . . so you can give it to them mixed and once they've had a few more you can even swap the Cyprus for the cream.

'And once again you take the difference out of the till. Nothing's ever written down. They can remember how much to under-ring, how much to take out, which is simple enough if you're just running the one fiddle, say with a bottle of whisky, or sherry, but they can do it with a whole variety of fiddles being run and make their till and their stock square with each other at the end of the week. That's the difference in it being a trade and a profession.'

Star looked incredulous as McLean warmed to his subject, his pupil transfixed in rapt attention. 'Fiddles, Star . . . the trade is one giant fiddle. And most of them go on in places like this . . . brewers' shops we call them. You know, owned by one of the big brewing companies. They pay their staff terrible wages, poorer than labourers even. And that applies to managers like me. I think the philosophy is that the brewers reckon they'll be done even though they paid decent wages, so best to give them as little as possible. Not much of a philosophy, is it? Anyway, most managers have got it quite well organised . . . for themselves that is.' At which he gave a knowing wink. 'Of course, they get regular visits from stocktakers, supervisors and area managers, but you can even get them in on the rackets. Sometimes they'll do spot checks with men they send out from the brewers but if you've got the right contacts, you'll get a telephone call beforehand. Often you might find yourself short of stock when the stocktaker's due. You get round that by borrowing what you're short of from the bar up the street. I've known them to race supplies from one bar to another and then to another, to keep one step ahead of the stocktaker. And as soon as he's finished, it gets raced back again to the other bar. You can even get the same stocktaker counting some of the same stock in three different bars in the one day! I'm telling you, there's more laughs at this game than you get at the circus. We've got more fiddlers than you would get at one of those teuchter Mod things.'

Star shook her head in disbelief. 'Claney . . . it's all too much for me. I'm utterly amazed at what goes on. It's unbelievable . . . staggering . . . I'm stuck for words.'

'That's because you're sweet and innocent, Star. The world of the drinks trade is not like that. Unlike some other games, it's not who you know, but what you know. And the more you know, the more you make.'

'That apply to you, Claney?'

'Of course it does, Star, I'm in the business for just one reason. To make my pile. No different a reason from the brewers themselves. And when I've made enough, I'll be off from here and have a place of my own.'

'Then you'll be a victim of all the fiddlers.'

'You're forgetting something, Star. I'll be running it.'

Star could hardly wait till that Sunday, her first day off since starting work at the Nevis, when she would have the chance to have a long talk with Sammy about what she had learned that week. They sat together at the head of the long Regency table in the dining room after lunch, Star recounting the deceits and the deceivers, the fiddles and the fiddlers, the dodges and the dodgers.

'And do you know they even re-use all the slops from the men's glasses at night? True. All the lager and the special beer goes back into the light beer barrel. Do you know why that is?'

Sammy sat bemused at the thought of Star telling him, Sammy Nelson, the fly man of fly men, such things. Then, sheepishly, he had to admit that he didn't know why the slops went into the light beer barrel.

'Because it's the darkest-coloured beer. They put lager, special, stout . . . everything back into it and it doesn't show. Same with the spirit leftovers . . . and you'd be amazed what they leave at closing time. Well, they put all that back into the dark rum bottle. They measure it out first and if they put five measures of mixed spirits into the rum, they can then take the price of five rums out of the till.'

Sammy, wide-eyed, was taking an intense interest in Star's account of the week. 'Gees, Star, there's me been drinking in pubs all my life and never thought they would be up to tricks like that. Right enough, we used to get up to a few little capers during the war, making substitute whisky and things like that, but that's another story. That was a service we were doing. What you're telling me they're doing . . . that's like daylight robbery.'

'And there's other things. One of the barmen has this measure and it has a coin soldered to the base inside it. He reckons he can get nearly two measures for himself out of one bottle by using it. Think of the money that's making him.'

'Aye, and more important, think of the whisky that some people are no' getting.'

'What about the Steeds that look after your bar?'

'Of course, they're at it, Star. Everybody's at it. I just trust them no' to do me rotten. There's a difference, like. You can get done . . . and you can get done rotten. The Steeds will do one, not the other.'

'You hope.'

'I trust them, Star.'

'Maybe the same is going on at the cinema.'

'What?'

'Fiddling.'

'How can you fiddle the price of a picture seat?'

'How can you fiddle a pint of beer? I've certainly had my eyes opened to what's going on. It's terrible to say it, but it makes you lose trust in people. It's all so immoral.'

'Star, dear. It's a business you're going into. Not a church. Is it moral to make a profit out of another man's luck? If you think about that too much you'd end up a nun. Listen, in my day I've been up to a few . . . wee tricks, shall we say? But I never ever thought about them as being immoral. I never hurt anyone. I always gave people a service. In fact, you could say I did more good than bad. I thought it all out when I was younger, Star. Morals, to me, are about what is accepted. It's accepted that you can give a man a tenner a week and that man makes thirty or forty quid for you and you haven't lifted a finger. It's accepted that you can buy a bottle of whisky at one price then pour it into wee tumblers in a shop and sell it at double that price. And it's very accepted that if you make thousands of gallons of the stuff you'll make yourself a fortune, live in a Highland castle and get a medal from the king.'

'Therefore you're saying it's acceptable to fiddle?'

'Aye . . . I suppose so. As long as you do it in an acceptable way.'

'Uncle . . . you can find a way round anything.'

Sammy smiled. 'Star, I've had to come to terms with this world. There's an awful lot that's not right about it . . . like the poor buggers that live ten to a room in the Gorbals with their TB and rickets and all that mob at Buckingham Palace and the like. It's not right, Star.'

'Oh, dear . . . we have wandered a bit from putting the slops back in the beer and the black rum bottle. Now how does that fit in with your morals?'

'That's no' morality, Star. That's just bloody dirty. And greedy.'

3

The Steeds

There were families and there were families but when it came to
the Steeds, they were a family's family. If you were against one,
you were against all; if you were for or of one, they were for and
of you. Some loved them, others hated them. They loved and
they hated. Hate could be for others; love was only for them.
Nothing in the world was more important to the Steeds than the
Steeds. Not even the King and all his family was more important
than a Steed to a Steed. And that *was* important for they were the
staunchest of Orange people, Bridgeton Orange people, and you
had to go to the Sandy Row to get Orange people as good as that.
Had the Steeds been Sicilians, they would have been *Cosa
Nostra*. But they were Glaswegians and Our Thing was *them*.

Head of the family was old Tommy, but he was retired, an
expression which he had meant to indicate that he was no longer
working, the fact being that he had never really worked, not in
the employee-employer sense. His work always had been, as he
would say, 'this and that'; 'this' being a sometime steward at
Gilmour's boxing promotions at the National Sporting Club or a
part-time official at the Hamilton races; 'that' being an occasional
professional punter or a betting line lifter for Bill Duncan, the
illegal Dalmarnock Road bookie, or, when the occasion demanded, negotiating bribe money to the police for keeping away from
a betting pitch or for tip-offs of a likely raid, in which case
Tommy would arrange the hire of stand-in staff, none with
previous convictions, so that they would get lighter fines from
Stipendiary Magistrate Shortwood and thus save bookie Duncan
money. Nowadays he confined his activities to a little bit of the
'that' but could mainly be found with the other men who would
spend their days in idle street corner chat, a Bridgeton Cross
boulevardier. And Tommy, being a Steed, was one of the best
known of them. During the war he had been one of Sammy
Nelson's helpers, or agents, as he had preferred to call them, in

the black-market operations in which he had been involved. The Steeds would collect food and clothing coupons for him. They were paid for these and, in turn, Sammy added a 25 per cent profit. As Sammy always said, there was no harm in that – the coupons were just like currency and, therefore, he was just like a broker or a merchant banker. They had got to know each other well and when Sammy had mentioned he was thinking of going into the licensed trade, it had been Tommy who said he could get him staff. 'Genuine eighteen-carat staff . . . will do you a real turn and there'll be none of the hey-diddle-diddles.'

'Who?'

'The family, of course. They've been in the trade for a while now. They move around, like. Big Bert's not working at the moment, taking a rest, like, and the girls are part-time up town.'

Sammy like the idea. At least he knew them, he thought, and that in itself, he hoped, would ensure he would get his profits all right; well, most of them.

Sammy's Bar was the greatest thing to have happened to the Steeds. It was virtually a pub of their own which they could run without supervision or control. They gave what they considered was a good profit to Sammy and he was happy. And from what they were able to make for themselves, they were very happy.

Bert, or Big Bert as he was always called, was Tommy's son and had been a manager with the brewer's until a snap visit by the stocktakers. He had no answer to why so much of his stock was missing and before they had even completed their count he had pegged his apron and bid them, 'Goodnight gentlemen. Get the head office to send on my cards.'

That bar had done Big Bert well and the profits he was able to extract from it in a variety of ways had bought him one of the best houses in Main Street and filled his wardrobe with the best of Benson. Bert, like his father Tommy, viewed life on a day-to-day basis; something would always turn up for them and if it didn't today, it would tomorrow. The fools of this life were those who committed themselves to a gaffer, who clocked on in the morning and off at night and who were headlong into the predictability of life since the day they left school at fourteen; one day a boy, the next a predestined man, their future fully declared, chapter and verse, never to deviate from the script.

The fact that one brewer had found Bert out meant little to him. There were other brewers, other bars; other golden chances in life that would come his way.

Betty, his wife, and Margaret, his sister, worked as part-time waitresses together with Margaret's husband George at the Two Four Two, a city restaurant and cocktail bar, the kind of place where, as they would tell you, only the 'awful nice people' went. 'You know what I mean,' Margaret would elaborate, 'big-time people. Lawyers, doctors, what you call professional people. Real toffs.' Nevertheless, the big-time people, lawyers or no, were all victims of a family operation which they ran as a matter of course with never a hint of malice towards their customers, the regulars whom they genuinely treated and were themselves treated in turn like long-lost friends. They had learned their little 'tricks of the trade', as they thought of them, from others who had done it before them and who, in turn, had been tutored by others before them. Their graft was a craft, a sort of under-the-counter heritage; an inheritance which was there as a right of the job.

Each of them could make more than their night's wages of fifteen shillings with just one of their variations of the sherry trick. Once a fortnight they would buy a case of Harvey's Bristol Cream sherry and another case of cheap Cyprus sherry, both at discount price from Crosgrove's, the licensed grocer. It was Bert who had shown them the trick. He would hold the Harvey's bottle upside down in a pot of hot water until the seal softened sufficiently to be slipped off. Half would be decanted and the bottle filled with the other sherry and the unbroken seal slipped back on again. The women would take a bottle each with them every night to work. Bert called it 'the big double kill' – not only could they take the bar's profit on the dear sherry, but by introducing the cheaper sherry into it, they were reducing the buying cost. And no one ever knew. In fact, it was Mrs Calvert, the lawyer's wife from the West End, one of the 'awful nice people', who would often say to Margaret when she served her, 'You know, the Two Four Two's cream sherry is the best in town.' And Margaret would invariably look round the other customers at the table with a knowing nod. 'It's a special line the manager buys. Nothing but the best for the Two Four Two's customers, you know. How are the children, Mrs Calvert?'

George, Margaret's husband, was behind the bar and looked after the till, the source of their profit. He also made the cocktails, which had always been a feature of the premises. A customer who ordered a cocktail always got an extra smile. 'One Harvey Wallbanger. Certainly, Mr Calvert.' And there was an even bigger smile from George when he, in turn, said, 'One Harvey Wallbanger, Mag'ret.' Mag'ret being their glottal-stop way of saying Margaret.

George was something of an expert at cocktails . . . Tom Collinses, Manhattans, Rob Roys, Sidecars, Rusty Nails. If there was a name to it, George could make it. He knew too that every time one was ordered, he could under-ring another shilling on the till and pocket it with their other profits when he did his tally at closing time. As he told his brother-in-law Bert, 'See, once you fill a glass up wi' orange juice, they haven't a bloody clue how much vodka or cointreau they've got in their cocktail. Harvey Wallbanger! Huh . . . you'd have to be a Harvey Headbanger to drink them.'

Together in Sammy's Bar, they were quite an operation. They could operate every racket in the book if they wished, such was the freedom which Sammy gave them to run the business. 'He's our sleeping partner,' they would joke, although among themselves they would declare their brand of honesty for Sammy's interests with such vows as, 'We'll see Sammy all right. We'll make Sammy the best of profits. He's done us a turn, so we'll do him a turn.' Anyway, they had been warned by old Tommy when he had got them the job that they were not to fleece his friend. 'Keep the heid . . . know what I mean, like,' he had said. They knew what he meant, like.

And, in a code of their ways, protecting Sammy's interests was their policy. Returning spirit slops to the black rum bottle and beers to the light beer cask wasn't robbing Sammy, was it? That was economising, said Bert when he discussed it with his father one night. 'Sammy doesn't lose a penny when we do that.'

'But what about the bottles of whisky you've been taking into the shop?' Tommy asked.

'That's all right, Da. You see, you don't understand the trade. Now, if I was like any other manager, I'd be taking in about four times that amount. You see, I don't push it. Anyway, I'm doing all right out of the beer.'

'Are you watering it?'

Bert was shocked at the suggestion. 'C'mon, Da. Watering the beer! I think managers that do that should be strung up. No kidding. No, I've got a wee thing going with Big Dunkie the drayman. D'ye know Dunkie? Looks like Lon Chaney Junior did in that *Mice and Men* picture. I usually get a barrel a week from him . . . extra like. And the profit's mine.'

'How do you mean an extra barrel?'

'Dunkie can get them . . . half price, like.'

'What, does he knock them out of the brewery?'

'No . . . no chance there. They count them at the gate. He gets them by short-delivering. You go to some of the busy pubs with big cellars and they've got barrels all over the place. Some of these old cellarmen haven't a clue what they've got in the place, half-drunk some of them on the whisky and beer they knock off. Dunkie knows the ones. They'll ask for six and he puts five in and moves one of the cellar's stock barrels beside the delivery to make it look like he's just unloaded it. That means he's got a free barrel on his load, and I get it at half price. I'm not doing Sammy, for it's my beer, isn't it?'

Tommy nodded in agreement. Their code of honesty had been maintained and his friend Sammy was, he felt assured, getting a fair deal.

'By the way, Bert. I met Sammy yesterday. He came to see me at the Cross. Tells me there's a lassie he knows that's asked him for a job. He says you've to give her a start, even if it's just part-time. She'll be into the bar one day this week. Neeson's her name. Star Neeson.'

'Neeson, you say?'

'Aye, Neeson.'

4

Disillusion

Javaid never was to find the tribespeople from whom he had his
Moses beginnings. When he returned to Lahore in the company
of Rasool, his companion of the long march, he had gone back to
the Old City to try to make a living of some kind. The displaced
refugees had poured into Lahore in their tens of thousands. They
were villagers and peasant farmers; the poor and the penniless;
the flotsam of an emasculated empire. The crowded Old City,
where arms-breadth streets daily thronged with medieval mobs,
took on a further burden of merchants and mendicants, traders
and touts, each with a service, an item for sale and a chance to
provide for himself and those who depended on him the meal
that would make another day possible. And tomorrow, under
another furnace sun, they would be doing the same again. They
accepted their daily struggle without despair, helped by the fact
that they were all Muslims and what Allah, their God, had in
store for them must be: 'Whoever provides the teeth, will also
provide the bread.'

Rasool and Javaid had walked together with the other refugees
into the city and at that point where the Grand Trunk Road
meets the Circular Road not far from the railway station they
stopped. 'This is where we part then, Javaid. I will go to my
uncle's at Samanabad and give his family the terrible news about
my parents and sister. They will look after me. I take it you will
be going to the Old City?'

'Yes, Rasool . . . To the Lahori Gate area. You will find me
there anytime. I will be working at something.'

Rasool held his hand firmly as he spoke. 'Maqbul and yourself
were great friends to me. You made me see another way of life, a
way of life I knew existed but never in my wildest dreams
thought I would experience. You both helped me through a very
trying period of my life. Without your help . . . I really don't
know how I would have fared. You saved my life that first day

48

for I would probably have run into a Hindu mob.'

Then they made their farewells, Rasool saying the Punjabi *Rab Rakha*, God take care of you, Punjabi being Javaid's first language, and Javaid replying in the Urdu, Rasool's first language, *Khuda Hafiz*, may the Saviour take care of you.

'We'll meet again, Javaid . . . I promise to come and see you.'

Rasool kept his promise. He went twice to the maze of alleyways around the Lahori Gate, each time finding the yoghurt and the hookah man and the goats' head butcher but never seeing Javaid. 'He has gone,' said a man who knew of him. 'He went up north,' said another.

It was to be three years before they were to meet again. Rasool had been strolling in the restful Bagh-e-Jinnah, the Jinnah Park. He stopped near a *chai* stall and took a seat on a bench beneath a magnificent pipal tree to read the book he had been carrying. After a while he heard the unmistakable sounds of a perfume seller. The perfume sellers would swing their bottles of scented oils in their chromed cages, like huge condiment sets, and the bottles would tinkle against the metal like little bells. Some sellers, like the one approaching, would twist their wrists as they swung the bottle cage, making an even louder noise.

'Here,' summoned Rasool, and the seller soaked a dab of cotton wool from one of the oils without looking directly at the man who had called him and who continued to read his book. It was when he handed over the perfume-soaked swab that their eyes met. The man on the bench dropped his book in surprise. 'Javaid . . . Javaid.' Javaid recognised Rasool immediately and they shook hands warmly.

'I did come to look for you in the Old City, Javaid. And when I returned a second time they said you had gone away.'

'I did go away,' said Javaid. 'Life was very hard when I returned at first. So after a while I left . . . you remember I wanted to find my own people in the north. Anyway, I stopped at Gujrat where I have a cousin and helped him on his little farm. I was there for nearly two years.'

'That's where Maqbul went, was it not?'

'That's right. We saw each other often. He had been very ill with the malaria after we had left him and he nearly died. But he fought through. And now he's away in England.'

'He's gone to England!' Rasool repeated in surprise. 'Why, I'm off there myself next week. Do you know where Maqbul went?'

'The place they call Birmingham. Is that where you are going?'

'No. Another place. It's called Glasgow.'

'You are lucky, Rasool, to be going to England. But why? You have no need. I mean, you are rich.'

'Yes, I know I have no need, as you say. Despite everything, life has been good for me since Independence. I got a good job in the Civil Service. I have a car supplied and a bungalow with a cook and staff.'

'And a wife and family?'

'I lost them, Javaid. She died in childbirth last year. The baby was lost too . . . a son, no less.'

'Oh . . . I'm so sorry. Poor Rasool . . . you have been so unlucky.'

'Maybe that's one of the reasons I need to get away. But I never was happy in the Civil Service. Life is so predictable. Next year I will be on a higher grade and five years after that a higher one again and so on.'

'I wish my life was predictable like that, Rasool. All I can predict at this moment is that if I sell enough perfume today and there are plenty of customers at my other job in the karahi tikka restaurant tonight I will have half of my rent money. What will you do in England, Rasool? Not their Civil Service?'

'No . . . no more Civil Service. I need a challenge in life, Javaid. We have lots of good manufacturers here and I am going to represent some of them in England and sell their goods for them. If I can sell well for them then I will be as well off as I am in the Civil Service. In fact, I can even make more money if I am successful and I will have a lot more freedom to move around. Well, going to England for a start is something different for me. But tell me about yourself, Javaid?'

'Well, as I said, I stayed in Gujrat for a while. I worked for a time at the pottery . . . even learned to become quite a good potter. And before that I had been helping my cousin on his little farm. The pottery work was much better. All that happens on the farm is you end up with a broken back and a face blackened with the sun. I came back to Lahore a year ago.

'Things have improved since 1947 and '48. My God those were terrible years for us. But ever since this war in Korea everything has been better. There's a shortage of the kind of raw materials that we produce and everyone seems to want them, at least so the others tell me. With my two jobs, the restaurant at night and selling the perfume by day, I make enough . . . I can even save a little, Rasool. That is the first time in my life I have saved some rupees. Why don't you come to the karahi tikka restaurant where I work and we can have a longer talk? It's Friday and there are lots of people in the park today and with all this sunshine they are wanting my perfume to freshen themselves.'

'A karahi tikka . . . oh, I haven't had one of those for years; since I was at university. Where is the restaurant?'

'Do you know the junction of McLeod Road and Nicholson Road?'

'Yes, I know it well. Just opposite the Orient Hotel. It's almost as bad as the Circular Road junctions for traffic.'

'Then come tonight, Rasool. I'll be there and I'll get cook to prepare a special dish for you. Nothing but the very best for you, Rasool.'

'Yes . . . why not? I'll be there. A karahi tikka, eh? What magic taste . . . and all from offal. I don't suppose I'll get one in England.'

The karahi tikka cooks would appear at nightfall along the roadway between the minaret calls for the *asar* and *maghrib* prayers. From overhead verandahs and backroom stores and little courtyards and dark alleyways men and boys would appear carrying all the accoutrements of a pavement café – tables and chairs, utensils and appliances, and pieces that when put together made up a stove and cooking range, together with boxes containing all manner of things which would be necessary for the working of a complete restaurant.

It was one of the magical sights of Lahore; a daily gastronomical version of the circus came to town as the porters and handlers lowered their props, started their oil-drum stove fires and produced supplies of the offal and herbs and salads and breads for another night's cooking in the impromptu roadside restaurants.

Within minutes their charcoal fires would be burning inside the big blackened oil-drums and when the kindling smoke from them had gone and the coals had merged into a brilliant glow, more helpers would come running from the same somewhere that the rest of the equipment had come. They would be carrying heavy iron discs, big as an ox-cart wheel, so big that they couldn't be held at their widest circumference. And when they got to the readied stoves another helper would assist them to place the discs on top of the oil-drums. They were the karahi pans, the big griddles for which the establishments were named. And with them in place, the restaurants were ready for business.

Their speciality at McLeod and Nicholson Road was sheep and goat offal, mounds of which they would arrange on trays around the cook, squatting high on a stool beside his enormous pan waiting for his first order. The customers would choose the pieces of innards which appealed to them with a pinch and a touch and a feel and a poke. They had everything from within the animal to choose from, including the whitest pieces, the ones which were ivory smooth and glistened like giant pearls; gourmet jewels they called *kapoora* . . . the testicles. With a splat of *ghee* on the big girdle, the cook went to work with all the fervour and clangour of an old-fashioned Clydeside riveter as his two-handled chopping knife cut and chopped and decimated the ingredients, scooping and piling and mixing them with flavourings of tomato and onion and a confetti of fresh chillis and six-spice *garam masala*, chopping and scooping and piling and mixing them again and at the same time arranging a layer of *nan* bread to warm on the rim of the huge pan. And when it was ready, which took only minutes, he would trowel the steaming dish on to the customer's plate, decorate it with some salad and cover it with the warm bread so that none of the exotic flavours and aromas would be missed. And together with a tall glass of satin-red pomegranate juice there was a meal worthy of a mogul.

'Steamed brains, *yaar*? Of course, *yaar* . . . one steamed brains coming up.' Steamed brains from a glowing griddle pan? It was no problem for these roadside chefs. Into some of the exquisite juices from the previous meal they had cooked, scraping only the burnt fragments away, they would plop a pulped tomato, deftly rendered by holding it in the palm of their hands and then sharply clenching their fist. The brains were then placed into this steaming sauce, chopped neatly once they had firmed, dressed with herbs, a spot of *ghee*, then covered with an upturned basin splashed with cold water so that it created a cauldron of steam, the intensity of which rapidly produced the dish they called *maghaz*.

Rasool went that night to the busy junction and wandered past the various pavement kitchens until finding the one where Javaid was working as an assistant to one of the cooks. Javaid waved and smiled when he saw him. 'Let me choose the pieces for your meal, Rasool. Some of these bits are days old . . . you would need a strong stomach for them. I know the ones that are fresh.'

When he had finished the meal, Rasool wiped his plate clean with a big piece of the soft, pear-shaped *nan*. 'Well, that's what I thought of that, Javaid,' he said showing him the plate with not as much as a grease mark on it. 'Absolutely divine.'

'The cook is from Murree, up in the north, and he does many things the Kashmiri way. But tell me about your trip to England. You leave in a week, you say?'

'That's right. I know I am giving up a lot here, but I'm convinced I can really be successful as an agent. I will try it for a few years anyway. I am looking forward to it greatly.' At that he changed the subject. 'You work hard, Javaid. Here all night in the kitchens and during the day with your perfume.'

'But not every day, Rasool. I do take days off occasionally if I have enough money to keep me. Allah has not been unkind to me. I never starve.'

'Would you like to go to England?'

'Of course. I would like to live in paradise too, but neither is possible.'

'Supposing I was to make it possible, Javaid? I can loan you the money for your fare to England.'

'But I could never repay you, Rasool.'

'You could with the money you would earn in England. And do you know, they even pay you there if you cannot find work.'

'You are joking with me, Rasool. How can a man be paid if he does no work?'

'That is the way of it, Javaid. I can assure you of that. And if you are sick the doctor is free and so are the hospitals.'

'England must really be paradise, Rasool.'

'Well, would you go if I arranged the fare?'

'Of course, Rasool. A man cannot say no to paradise, can he?'

'Then I will arrange a ticket for you. Do you know the big Habib Bank in the Mall? That is my bank. The manager there knows me well as he did my father. I will need some time to settle and make all the various arrangements for my agency when I arrive. Give me three months. Today is the third day of *Rajab*. If you go to the bank on the second day of *Shawwal* and ask for the manager, he's a Mr Khaled, then he should have some news for you. I will speak to him before I leave.'

'Rasool, I will forever be in your debt.'

5

Sharp Knives

It had been at Star's insistence that she take a job at Sammy's Bar. She had worked at the Nevis for nearly six weeks, applying her stocktaking training to some practical work with the help of Sammy's friend Claney who also taught her the legitimate ways of running a bar and, what appeared to her to be more important in the trade, all the illegitimate ways.

'I'm going to learn everything . . . and I mean everything,' she said as she spoke with Sammy that first Sunday after starting work at the Nevis Bar. 'I'd heard all the stories about what some staff can get up to in bars, but wouldn't have believed it until seeing it with my own eyes.'

'How come you know so much about bars with you never having gone about them?'

'Remember . . . I used to work in Gordon's at the machining. Well, like bars, you get all types in a clothing factory. And a girl at the next machine to me worked in a bar part-time at night. Her boyfriend was the manager. Well, the things she told us were absolutely incredible. So much so that I thought she was making them up. They reminded me of Orwell's account of life below stairs in the restaurants of Paris. Have you read Orwell, Uncle Sammy?'

'Star, dearie. I read the *Noon Record* and Garry Owen the tipster is my favourite writer.'

She laughed. 'Well, Orwell, the writer, worked in these restaurants and if they dropped anything on the floor, say even a chicken, well they would pick it up, apologise profusely to the customer, rush through to the kitchen, plop it on a different plate and return again, the customer thinking he'd got a fresh meal. And do you know what the biggest deception was? Sharp knives.'

'Sharp knives?' Sammy was puzzled.

'Yes, sharp knives. That's the secret of a good restaurant. You can then use inferior meats but the knives cut it just like it was the best-quality stuff. It's a trick. A confidence trick. And clever.'

'Heh . . . that's good, Star. Some right fly men in Paris, then. But what's that got to do with Glasgow pubs?'

'It's exactly the same. What the customer doesn't know. It's obviously the basis of the way they work, changing drinks in bottles, slops in the beer, water in the beer, water in the whisky, false measures, goodness, they're at everything. I think it's all rather terrible.'

'I've never had to complain about what goes on at Sammy's Bar.'

'You mean you've never caught them. What about your profit?'

'They're honest as the day is long, Star.'

'How do you know?'

''Cos I saw the books before I bought the pub. Went over them with the accountant . . . turnover, profit, and all that kind of stuff. And they're giving me more profit. So there's the proof that they're not at it.'

'But they could be making twice the profit of the last manager, but only giving you a small percentage of an increase. That's logical, isn't it?'

'C'mon, Star. They're Tommy Steed's family. Good people. Wee Mag'ret, that's Mrs Steed. She's in the Eastern Star and used to sing in the choir of the Old Church in Dalmarnock Road.'

'Don't tell me about women who sing in church choirs and work in bars.'

'Star, you've got to have some trust.'

'I couldn't agree with you more, uncle . . . about trust, that is. I'm all for trust and trusting people and having people trust me. Life would be unbearable without trust. But I'm also a realist and since working at the Nevis I'm much more of a realist than ever. Money . . . the drinks trade . . . and trust are a very unlikely trinity it would appear. Tell me, Uncle Sammy, who does your stocktaking?'

'Bert. You know, Big Bert, Tommy Steed's son. He's the manager. His brother-in-law George is the barman, then there's the two girls, Margret and Betty, both Steeds, like, and they also get the odd part-timers in at the weekends.'

'And how often does he stocktake?'

'I think it's every month.'

'And who checks his results?'

'Well, nobody really. He shows me the books and tells me the profit and it's usually the same, sometimes a wee bit up.'

'Can you understand the books?'

'Not really. But he doesn't know that.'

'Uncle Sammy, you amaze me. How you made the money you have I'll never know. Don't you realise you're giving him licence to do anything he likes. If no one is checking the stock apart from him that means he can get off with anything. Write his own cheque, as it were.'

'But I've got no complaints, Star.'

'Well, I have. When you brought my mother and me here from the Gorbals and then paid my fees at Skerries Commercial College with the prospect of helping you in business, you gave me the most wonderful chance in life. I appreciate that more than you think and now I'm out to repay my gratitude for everything you did for me and mum while she was alive. The only way I can do that with the knowledge that I have is to look after your business interests. And not only that, there's something else just as important to me. I'm needing a challenge in life. I'm needing that very badly. My life so far has been . . .' At this point she paused, knowing that she couldn't really tell her uncle about her true feelings. She couldn't tell him that her life, through circumstances which had been none of her doing, was so unfulfilled; that despite being lovely and loving, she had never loved or been loved.

'Your life has been what, Star?'

'My life has been waiting for this great chance,' she countered quickly to cover the hesitation. 'And I won't get it by merely working for you and letting your business just tick over the way it is. You've got capital tied up. What's obviously needed is some kind of expansion programme. The war's over now, there's plenty of work and people are looking forward to the good times. We should be making a study of the licensed trade and see where the future lies in it. From what I can see they're a pretty complacent bunch that runs it. They know they've got the customers no matter what kind of conditions they serve the stuff up to them in. I'm sure they rig the prices to suit themselves too. I've been looking around at the conditions in some pubs. They're absolutely disgusting. Treat people like pigs and you'll get them behaving like them. Put them in single-end houses and you get single-end people. Shove them up a close and you get up-a-close minds together with up-a-close faces.'

'Gees, Star, you make me feel like applauding. I used to sound like that when I formed the union at Myer's Store and led the strike. I used to read then, Star. Read Karl Marx, Engels, the *Manifesto* . . . all that Bolshie stuff. Exciting, so it was.'

'What about the strike then?'

'Most of us got the sack . . . including me. Best thing that ever happened to me. And I've been a capitalist ever since,' he added laughing. 'Even ended up living in the same road as the old bastard Myer that sacked me. Oh, sorry, Star. That just slipped out there. You were talking about the business. Sounds great to me. I'm not without ideas myself. I've just lacked the push since my wife Peggy died followed by your own mother.'

'Then you're like me in a way, Sammy. There's a void in your life. Getting the business really going could be good for you as well.'

'Aye, maybe you're right, Star. Gees, you've a wise head on you for a lassie.'

'Right then. So you've told them a Miss Neeson is starting in your bar. Well, we'll see what Miss Neeson finds out . . . won't we?'

'Now you've got me worried, Star! Touch of they Frenchmen's sharp knives about that.'

6

Caught in the Act

They never suspected that Star Neeson was in fact Star Nelson. And quite openly they would bring in bottles of the same Bristol Cream and Cyprus sherry mix which Bert and George had made up for the Two Four Two. Very quickly Star assessed they were running the full gamut of the usual malpractices, under-ringing, 'Catch that order Bert,' short measuring, re-using leftovers. 'If you're short of cigarettes anytime, you can always take a packet from stock. Perk of the trade, as it were,' said Betty on Star's first night at 'Sammy's'.

She waited till the end of the first week working at the bar before reporting to her uncle.

'Do you know you are being done right, left and centre? Really, they couldn't be at more if they tried. See Big Bert. What a confidence trickster he is. The customers love him for he's got all the patter. Know what he does with pensioners? He pours their whiskies out in front of them so that everyone can see he fills the measure to overflowing and there they are all smiling and nodding saying, "Some guy, Big Bert. Heart of gold so he has." And all the time he's using a measure with a big brass washer inside it so all they are really getting when he overflows it is the proper amount. What a rascal! Yet they're all such nice people and I can't help liking them. They really like the customers too and never call them mugs or anything like that behind their backs. You get the impression that it's just like a big game to them and that the fool is the one who doesn't play it. There was a manager from another bar in the other day. He was short of stock so Bert loaned him a case of whisky for the day. They were discussing stocktaking and I overheard Bert tell him that you never troubled about stock so he didn't bother with it either. And they were winking and laughing with each other when they spoke about the regular profit the bar was making. Well, they're in for a big shock. Claney is coming over this Sunday to help me do a complete stocktaking. We'll repeat it after a fortnight and compare it with the profit level you get. I think the results could be interesting.'

The stocktaking routine varied little in the trade. They counted the cases of bottled beer, soft drinks, sherries, gins, brandy, fortified wine and tobacco, used big dipsticks to measure what beer remained in the tapped 36-, 22- and 18-gallon barrels, noted the untapped barrels, checked the working gantry bottles calculating their contents in tenths – 'You'll be able to spot a three-tenths bottle at a hundred yards after a while,' said Claney – then listed all the invoices. To get the full accuracy of the worth of the bar they would have to cross-check all their figures with the second stocktaking, comparing the invoices and the till takings in order to subtract the cost figure from the retail figure, dividing the difference by the retail figure to arrive at the gross profit.

To get the details of these, Bert would have to be told.

They could have waited and let Sammy ask for the invoices and till figures to know precisely how much of the profit Sammy wasn't receiving. But Star had all the evidence she required to give her an approximation. And, anyway, she had other plans, she told her uncle.

Star had changed a lot since she had come to live with Sammy Nelson in Pollokshields and as she detailed how they should proceed, Sammy reflected on how she had matured in that time. When he had first seen her at the little single-end house she had shared with her mother in Florence Street, she had hauntingly reminded him of her father Jamesie, the brother he had so revered, her strong and confident face a contradiction with her alluring feminine manner and walk. She had blushed easily and there was a reserved shyness about her, yet she was without the withdrawn surliness of some Gorbals girls and he had been surprised at her voice, broad Scottish but without the local coarseness of the lazy glottal stop.

Jamesie had been Gorbals, but everything about him had been different. He could turn the heads of those who knew him for what he was, he could turn the heads of those who did not know him for the way he was. Many tried it with bravado gaits, the gallus walk, play-actors on an asphalt and slate-slab stage.

Jamesie Nelson never had to act. Jamesie Nelson was presence. And so, by God, thought Sammy, was this girl Star as she was now. The initial shyness had gone, slowly gone, and been replaced by a rare confidence, not the sort that had to manifest itself in order to let the world know about it and which was often either sham or pseud, but one which emanated a wave of composed determination. Just being in her presence made Sammy feel somehow safe and secure, the very same way he used to feel in Jamesie's company; the psyche transcended the physical. And her aura of assuredness was in full flower when, with Sammy, she had gone to the bar that Monday morning to open it before Bert and the staff arrived.

'God, I thought for a minute we had been burgled there,' said Bert when he discovered the main door unlocked and the lights on.

'I'll speak,' Star said to Sammy when Bert, confused, tried to work out the calculation which might give him a reason for the strange scenario in which he found himself when he entered the bar. He knew there was something that he should be suspicious about . . . well, Sammy's face for a start gave something away; the kind of look that only meant bad news.

Star stood behind the bar, dressed in an expensive light Burberry, the stylish kind that you didn't associate with the Gorbals. 'Take a seat, Bert. We've something to tell you . . . at least, I've something to tell you. First of all an apology. I'm afraid I've had to deceive you these past few weeks. My name is not Neeson. It's Nelson. Star Nelson. Sammy here is my uncle . . . my father's brother. I'm in business with him. And I mean business in the proper and best sense of the word. We have capital invested, it works, it produces profit, the profit is taken and a good share is ploughed back into the business again in the hope that more profit is made. At least, that's the way it should be. But it's not working for us efficiently here. Is it, Bert?'

'Orright, Star . . . hen. I've got the message. Ta ta, Bella. And send my cards on,' said Bert as he rose to walk away.

'Don't get up,' Star commanded. And somehow Bert found himself rooted to the seat, without a thought of questioning the order.

'I'm not here to conduct a court of inquiry, Bert.'

He liked the way she had said Bert. It was as though there was some respect for him.

'I'm here to, let's say . . . to impart some information. First of all, Sammy and I know everything that's been going on. Everything. I've done two stocktakings and although I haven't got the full picture, it would appear that you've been working as if you were a partner of my uncle instead of an employee.'

'Are you insinuating . . .?'

'Insinuating nothing, Bert. I'm telling. For I know. I haven't completed the stocktaking . . . as you'll know I need the full invoices and till takings, receipts . . . everything. If we're going to expand this business, I need to know its full worth.'

'What do you want me to do, Star? Hang around for a public execution? As I said you know where to send my cards.'

'And, as I said, I'm not finished yet. I do know what happens when a brewer comes across this situation at a stocktaking. The staff gets cleared out and they then move off to another bar where the same goes on again and the bar that's been cleared out gets another lot in who more than likely do exactly the same as the previous lot were doing. It's a vicious circle. None of which really makes sense, for you have the same people in the trade playing the same tricks as they get moved around the bars. Well, there's little point in me clearing you and your family out.'

Bert turned his head sideways slightly. What was this woman on about? Was she playing some elaborate game with him? Having a bit of fun with him? Maybe the Central Police's CID were hiding behind the counter and were about to leap out with the handcuffs! Who was she anyway, this Star Neeson turned Nelson? One minute she's a nice wee lassie that worked for him and did as she was told, now she's the boss and he's the one that's being told. It was like some bizarre dream and he was listening to himself as one of the principal characters in one of those Home Service afternoon radio plays into which he would regularly tune during the 2.30 till five o'clock closedown period of the pub. But this was neither fantasy nor fiction. There he was, Robert, for Robert the Bruce, William for his King William, Steed caught in the act, guilty as accused, the offender in the dock and the judge, a woman by God, and a one-man jury sitting before him and he was being told he was guilty but was getting admonished. And there was more to come.

'In fact,' went on Star, 'I propose to increase your wages. I know they're not the entire cause, but the poor wages the brewers pay their staffs is obviously one of the reasons why all these tricks originate in the first place. Apart from that, there's a place for you in our future plans. You see, I know your worth. I know what you did when you ran the bar . . . and I also know what you could have done. Obviously, there's going to be a lot of changes. There'll be regular stocktaking, full accountability of every transaction. Also the bar is going to be closed down for a week in order to be changed. It's to become a lounge bar . . . carpets, nice lighting, pictures on the wall, a new attitude from staff. And all under your supervision, Bert. Well, what do you think?'

'What do I think! 'Struth, I don't know what to think after that. Keeping us on! That's never happened in the trade before after . . . after a bad stocktaking. Wait till George and the girls hear. Will they . . .?'

'Yes, they'll be kept on . . . and their wages adjusted. But I'll have a talk with them first of all because I want to lay everything on the line, if you know what I mean. No grey areas. Everything cut and dry so that each of us knows what each other is about. I'm sure that's the way you'd want it. And, by the way, Bert. Tell Dunkie the drayman you'll not be needing any more of his surplus barrels.'

He shook his head and smiled. 'God, you don't miss a bloody trick. Sammy's Bar will never be the same again.'

'Oh . . . that's another thing. We can hardly call our new lounge Sammy's Bar. No offence, uncle, but the new identity should have no connection with the masculine past. I was thinking of a more female name.'

'Like Star,' said Sammy.

'I'm so glad you said it,' she laughed. 'Well, why not? Star's Lounge it will be. And now, gentlemen, you'll have to excuse me. There's a lot of business to be done . . . I've a picture house to go and assess now.'

7

Pantheon Ways

The Gorbals had a variety of legendary institutions, most of which were connected with some aspect of the enjoyment of the daily life of its inhabitants. There was Knott's Restaurant in Florence Street where before, during and after the war generations of families as well as immigrant Highland and Irish men without families got the kind of nourishment which, for one reason or another, they were incapable of providing in their own homes. For a shilling or two, and not many pennies more, they dined, as they told everyone, like kings and queens in their very own Knott's, with quart bowls of soup so thick and strong and full of nutrition they said you could dance on it; followed by servings in big delf catering plates of boiled bacon ribs, heavy with big chunks of glistening pink meat contrasting with the heap of spring cabbage, velvet green and tall as a haystack – just right for the kind of people who measured the worth of a meal by its size; then rounded off with slices of the house speciality, the renowned Knott's dumpling, big and round like the kind you saw in the pages of the *Dandy* and so famous, the story goes, that the Luftwaffe tried to bomb Knott's during the war in order to put an end to the dumplings and sap the morale of the Gorbals. So they said anyway. But had that been a fact, morale would indeed have been shattered. A Gorbals without its Knott's and a Knott's without its dumpling was inconceivable.

There were dancehalls like the Lochwood and the Parlour, as talked about through the generations as the Tripe dancehall itself, the legend of all dancehall legends, even though it was just outside the pale of the Gorbals boundary.

And there were pubs that were legendary too, places like Tommy Milligan's, he being the man who was a legend himself because of the night in 1927 at Olympia in London when he had stood up to the one and only Mickey Walker of America for the middleweight championship of the world and had all the Followers of the Fancy saying there would never be another fight like it. Maybe they were right, for few men ever showed as much courage as Tommy did that night and, sure, there he was, the very same man, to be seen in his own Gorbals pub any day you wanted. Then there was the Moy, at the corner of Florence Street and Cumberland Street, legendary because everyone knew the Moy with its big opaque windows etched with liquor advertisements, and everyone who was anyone went to the Moy at one time or another – even Benny Lynch himself, their very own world champion, had drunk in the Moy and that in itself was as good a reason as any to have a drink there.

Like many other things in life, the Gorbals had an abundance of picture houses. There was the Crownie, the Bees and the E.E.s, the Palace and Green's, the Ritz and the Bedford and the Collie. And the Pantheon. They all had their place in the folklore and legend of the district, but none was as special as the Pantheon. You spoke about the Pantheon like you would a member of the family. You wouldn't speak about the Collie, for instance, like that. The Collie, as they called the Coliseum, was tailor-made for entertainment, starting life as a music hall. A quarter of a century later they were still speaking about it as being the very place where they had shown the first talking picture in Scotland and if you had been one of those who had waited in the interminable queues to see and hear Al Jolson's historic words and songs then you could boast you really were something. Goodness, you were history itself!

The Collie with its huge screen and enormous golden drapes and tip-up seats and uniformed staff and epauletted doormen with white gloves they never wore and a manager in evening dress – now that was real showbusiness.

The Pantheon wasn't anything like that. The only history about the Pantheon was that those who were very old said they could remember the time when it was a church and that's why the seats were pews, the very ones they had used when it had audiences for a different kind of worship. Even in the fifties there was still the same kind of adventure about the Pantheon as there was going to your first magic-lantern show; it was of an era in the Gorbals that was about to pass.

It had been Sammy Nelson's aim when he had bought it that

together with his pub, it would fulfil the solemn promise he had made to his wife Peggy before she died that in future all his businesses would be completely legitimate; there would be no more enterprises – as there had been in the past – which could be classified as otherwise, although Sammy never really considered that any part of his past had been improper . . . as he saw life, that is. In view of that promise, he had allowed the Pantheon, just like the pub, to be operated . . . in trust. He chose a manager on the same basis he had got Tommy Steed's help with the pub: an 'old friend'. And you could put your faith in an old friend; that was Sammy's belief. At least he said it was. Star had other views.

Having sorted out the problems in the pub, which was now converted into a highly successful lounge bar making more than double the profit it had ever made before, Star, as she had vowed, decided it was time to turn her attention to the Pantheon.

'Do you think we'll find as much fiddling at your picture house as what was going on at your bar?' she had asked Sammy, who showed surprise at the suggestion.

'Come on, Star. How the hell can you fiddle in a picture house?'

'How can you fiddle in a pub?' she countered. 'You didn't know what was going on at your bar.'

'All right, dear . . . I know now. But I ask you . . . the flicks! I mean to say. What could be more innocent? And Billy Compton my manager! We went to school together. Been in the picture house business all his life. Started in the Majestic, you know up in Inglefield Street, the one they call the "Sticks", then went to the Cinerama and eventually made it to the big-time up town . . . the Regent, no less.'

'What was he there?'

Sammy hesitated before replying. 'He was at the door. A sort of assistant manager type. But he knows the whole business. Used to work in the projection box and all that. Very technical stuff in there, you know. Ever been in one? God, the smell of celluloid and that acetate stuff they use to join the films. Worse than you with your nail varnish.'

She gave him a smile before replying. 'In other words, uncle, your friend Mr Compton wasn't exactly executive status.'

'Who did you think I was gonnie get, Star, to run the Pantheon . . . J. Arthur Rank? Bill knows the tricks of the cinema industry and the business has been ticking over all right.'

'Well, I'll have a look, shall I?'

Star knew on her very first visit to the Pantheon that things weren't the 'all right' that her Uncle Sammy had imagined. She had stood in the street near the cashbox, where others would meet their partners on dates, pretending that she too was waiting on someone. The antics of the doorman caught her first suspicions. He was an old man wearing what had once been a colourful maroon and blue doorman's tunic. It was several sizes too big for him, the colours having faded so badly that the maroon almost merged with the blue, one as grease-stained as the other. One of the epaulettes had lost a button and it hung down the sleeve, limp as a banana skin. He was wearing the tunic with his ordinary suit trousers of baggy blue serge. Three times during her wait people approached him and passed something into his hand, upon which he nodded, then opened up an exit door for them to enter. The cashier was looking on as one of these transactions took place, but casually looked away again.

After having waited for about a quarter of an hour, Star decided to buy a ticket and go into the cinema. It was as she approached the cash desk that one of the usherettes came out and handed the cashier a small bundle, saying as she did, 'Another dozen, Annie.' The woman called Annie then replied, 'That should do us for the night, Ina.' The girl in the cash desk hadn't noticed Star approach and looked embarrassed as she placed the little bundle, which turned out to be tickets, beside the other tickets in front of her. 'Waste not . . . want not . . . balcony is it, love?' she said with a knowing smile. Then, when she handed Star her ticket she added, 'You'll like the big picture. Dead romantic so it is. See that Dana Andrews!'

Sammy had never known Star so furious. She had waited about ten days before giving him her findings, returning several times to the cinema in that time to make more notes and observations as well as speaking with one of the staff.

'This is really the limit,' she said. 'It's a downright scandal the way your money is being misappropriated and frankly, uncle, I think it's quite outrageous on your part that you've allowed what has been going on. I mean, it was bad enough at the bar, although it didn't come as too much of a shock to me after working for that spell at the Nevis. But what's going on at the Pantheon is a lot more than a happy family feathering their nest. From what I can see they're nothing but a gang of embezzlers, all doing their own little thing . . . and robbing you into the bargain.'

Sammy fingered his shirt collar nervously as he felt his neck go suddenly warm. It was an embarrassment he had never expected. Of course he had known all along that the Steeds at the bar and Compton and his staff at the picture house would be, as he would have put it himself, 'at the dip'. It was the way. It was the way all of them had had to live. It was society itself that had made them petty cheats; a society that expected so much of them, gave so little; a society with politicians of one leaning who would lecture them about the errors of the politicians of another leaning when in office and then would make the very same mistakes themselves when they got into power; a society in which the impoverished in so many ways were even more impoverished than they were in India and Pakistan, for there they were able to retain many of the original and lasting qualities of the pure and humble life – a contentment and a sereneness in their daily communion with that of nature, that of God. The society of Sammy's people had lost so much of that in the immense upheaval of industrialisation where so much was about greed and the greedy, and where a code of life was that if you didn't participate in one, you would be the victim of the other.

What embarrassed him was being told what he had known; what hurt him was that he had condoned but never condemned. Star was saying they were guilty; Sammy knew that their guilt was every bit as much his. Every detail about her latest findings pained him as she recounted them.

'The doorman gets his drink money by letting so many customers in every night through an exit door without tickets. The usherette who collects the tickets gives you a half-ticket in exchange, that half supposed to come from the ticket you give her. But instead of destroying the old half-tickets, they keep some of them. So a certain number of patrons every night get one of the old half-tickets in exchange for the ticket they have just bought and which the usherette retains intact. They then hand the whole ticket back to the girl at the cash desk and she issues it again. What a lovely little operation. And they can each make as much as their wages in one night . . . tax-free of course.'

Sammy visually winced with the mental torture he was undergoing when Star stressed, 'And don't think for a minute that's where it ends. The ice-cream girl buys cut-price ices from Gino's café and sells them alongside the ones she has supplied by Compton who doesn't even trouble to check what she's up to. She makes threepence on every one she brings in because Gino gives her a good deal on account of the regular number she buys from him. And your old schoolpal Bill Compton!'

Sammy closed his eyes. The pain of it all was getting too much; if only he could be spared the details. But there was no escape.

'He's got a good thing going for himself. He has teamed up with the agent for one of the big picture renters who operates some form of racket with cut-price films he buys and rents as a sideline to certain cinema managers. They work it through the books in some way that no one can find out and the proceeds are shared between them.'

At that Sammy felt he had to speak. 'Who did you have working for you, Star . . . Dick Barton, special agent?'

'No. I just applied myself to the situation in a logical fashion. It's amazing what you can find out on your own. As soon as I saw that doorman and the cashier up to their tricks I knew something was going on and that there must be collusion among all of them, particularly when the usherette came out with the bundle which turned out to be untorn tickets. When I went back for the third visit she remembered me and we got talking . . . well, I had to explain something being there so often and told her I was thinking of starting a Dana Andrews fan club and that I went to see all his films as many times as I could. That got us really chatting. Then I mentioned that I was on holiday for a week and that I too was an usherette . . . I worked at the Paramount, no less, I said. I also dropped the hint that we did the same trick as her with the tickets. Then I went back again and she was like an old friend, even asking me if there was any chance of a job at the

Paramount and I said I would try. After that I could hardly stop her from talking. It was as though she had known me for years. She confided everything to me. She hated Compton the manager. He kept drink in the office, she said, and entertained girlfriends there regularly, although she didn't use the word girlfriend. He had told her himself, one night he was drunk, about his pal, as he had said, from the renting company that fixed him up with cheap films. Apparently they're always switching programmes at the Pantheon and it has almost caused a couple of riots when customers have turned up and been shown a completely different film to what they had advertised in the evening papers.

'You know what they can be like around that part of the Gorbals! Because of this, audiences had been dropping which was another reason she didn't like Compton because falling audiences had meant a drop in the money she made on the side. What a vicious circle! Honestly, I don't know how you got mixed up in all this in the first place. What a terrible place it is, kids screaming and flicking orange peel into the projection beam or else trying to scale the wall up to the balcony. It was bedlam one afternoon I was there. Uncle Sammy, the whole thing is appalling. It really is. What on earth made you buy a cinema in the first place . . . and of all places the Pantheon?'

'Because I fancied myself in showbusiness. That's how.'

She laughed. 'Showbusiness! The Pantheon! Goodness, Sammy, there's more showbusiness goes on at the Rechabites on their lantern-slide nights.'

'Oh don't mock me, Star. I know I was deluding myself about the showbusiness bit.'

'But you must have known, Sammy . . . you must. You of all people must have known what they would be up to being left in charge like they were.'

'Of course I knew, Star. I knew but I didn't want to be told. The ostrich with its head stuck in the sand. That's been me. And it's had to be that way. Star, take a seat. You need an explanation and what I've to tell you is a long and not very pleasant story.'

Star was surprised at her uncle's sudden change of mood. Before he had been either casual or vague when she had pressed him about his business and events of the past. Now he looked deadly serious. It was the first time she had seen him look so earnest.

'Like I said, Star, I didn't want to know what was going on in the business. In the past, when I was actively running things myself I knew everything. I was right at the front. I dealt with the money. I dealt with the goods. I dealt with the people, except for the ones handled by a couple of guys who helped me. That was when I was running the house-letting business. Two of them helped me . . . one of them was Claney. That's right, your old friend at the Nevis Bar. He was one of my agents. My rent collector, if you like.'

'The landlord's man?' The words obviously angered him and Star wished she hadn't made the comment. 'I'm sorry, Uncle Sammy . . . I was a bit quick there.'

'You were. This story is bad enough for me to tell . . . and I do have a conscience about such things. Anyway, my two agents . . . rent collectors . . . landlord's men . . . what have you . . . started their own wee enterprise when they were collecting the money. It was a chance they saw and took it. I didn't blame them. It's the way, isn't it? You're a mug if you don't do it . . . and they don't like mugs about the Gorbals. Well, as I said, Claney and his mate pushed it a bit much when they were collecting the rents. I won't go into all the details of the story, but it ended up with there being three murders. Aye, Star, three of them.'

Star gasped.

'Aye, like I told you. It's a bit of a story. A long, long story but I'm just giving you the outline of it. There were the murders, as I said. And there was more than murder. My wife Peggy died because of it. A long, agonising death she had. Like she was being tortured to death. And it was all because of this one man. He was called Holden. Steve Holden, but he never got the Steve bit. It was always Snakey. And it was Snakey Holden who killed your father, Jamesie.

'After that he became one of those no good, low-life fly men. A small-time confidence trickster making just enough money to live from one drink to the next. He also ended up as one of our tenants in the houses we ran in Caledonia Road, just opposite the cemetery. That's where he got involved with Claney and my other agent, Rab Blair. Unknown to me they were charging more rent than they should have. The houses were in a state and I said eventually that they were to stop collecting from them. But they didn't. Somehow he got to know that I was the owner of the houses and everything went wrong from there. It was the name Nelson that blinded him, Star. It was like a curse to him. For after he killed Jamesie, he himself became the number one hard man in the district. And every other hard man in the Gorbals was after him, for whoever got him would then be the number one. See these Wild West pictures . . . the Jesse James stuff and that. It's exactly the same situation as that. Might sound far-fetched but it's a fact. It's all about men . . . the wild men: the men that don't know any better and the only way they can show what they are in life is by being top dog of one kind or another. One lot use six-shooters, another lot knives and razors. Funnily enough, no one ever tried to take on your dad on their own. For everyone just accepted that Jamesie was king . . . man-to-man no one could touch him. And the Holden one knew he could only do it when he got a gang together. But not for a contest . . . for an execution. I'm sorry to have to go into these details, Star, but you had better know the whole background.

'After they did that to Jamesie and he was no more, Holden, as I said, became the number one. But he didn't realise what he had taken on. No one challenged your dad single-handed, but they did Holden. And within a year he was scarred and beaten something terrible. He didn't last long as number one.

'It ended up with him leaving his wife and family, becoming an alcoholic and spending the rest of his days living on his wits and making money in all sorts of nasty ways. He became one of those vicious pests which we've no shortage of in the Gorbals. That's how he hated the name Nelson for he blamed Jamesie for everything that happened to him, and when he discovered that I was running the houses and that there were still people of the Nelson family around, he set out for revenge. The worst part for us was when he started menacing us here in Pollokshields. The worry of it drove Peggy frantic. It got that bad she had a nervous breakdown from which she never recovered. She went stark, staring mad. It was horrible. I never knew people could sink the way Peggy did. I never want to know that again.'

Star was shaking her head. 'I never realised any of this . . . oh my God, poor Uncle Sammy. What a time you've had. And you said there were murders . . . three of them. It's all so unbelievable.'

'Aye, I know. That's what I often think myself. Sometimes I feel it was all a bad dream. A nightmare that never was. But that's just wishful thinking on my part. For it really all did happen . . . and it happened to me. And what worries me is, what part of it happened because of me and because of Jamesie? Was it Jamesie's ways and then my ways that made it all happen? Authors of our own misfortune . . . is that the saying, Star? Were we the authors of it all? Aye, Star, that's what haunts me. But you had better hear the rest.

'As well as Claney and Rab, I had an old Irish fellow, Mickie Doyle, helping me. Holden found out that Mickie was connected with me over the houses. And he murdered the old soul. Did it in his very own house.

'He was a lovely old fellow as well. Wouldn't have hurt a fly. A Guinness and a wee sing-song and old Mickie was in his own wee heaven. Then this brute Holden got him. God, he never deserved that. It was some time after that when Holden got Rab. He knew he was the rent man and followed him home one night before waylaying him near where he stayed in Adelphi Street. It was one of the worst murders they had known for years. Terrible. Really terrible, so it was. And Rab. What a beautiful guy he was. Smashing wife and family and everything. One of the best drinking pals I ever had. Well, that was Rab. The police never made any arrests. There wasn't a clue. Nothing for them to go on. But we knew . . . Claney and I. We found out independent of each other. And also unknown to each other we set out to get Holden. That was when another discovery was made . . . that Holden's next victim was . . .'

Sammy paused to take a deep breath. 'This next bit will come as a bit of a shock for you. The discovery was that his next victim was you. Aye, you, Star.

'He had seen you in the street and someone had said to him you were the daughter of Jamesie. He was out to do us all, Star, but when he discovered the daughter of the very man that he blamed for everything, you went right to the top of the list.'

Star couldn't be shocked any more now and at that relevation she merely stared at her uncle in the same disbelief she had felt when he set out to tell her the dramatic story that had linked their lives.

'But we got Holden first. It will never pass my lips how he was got or who got him and please, never ask me. But he was got. And done. The police never found out who killed him. Nor were they really that interested for they detested him. And that's why that secret must always stay with me. After that we were left in peace . . . but it was too late for my Peggy. She was too far gone by then and the fact that he had been disposed of and that there would be no further threat to our lives didn't make the slightest difference.

'That's why I had to change, Star. I had vowed to Peggy that it would only be the straight and narrow path for me in the future. But apart from that promise, I *had* to change my ways. I never consciously did anything wrong, Star. I kept telling myself and Peggy that all my life. But nevertheless, what life I did lead had something to do with everything that happened . . . two innocent men murdered, the murderer himself then being done, and my poor, dear Peggy. If only I had stuck at being an ordinary worker, the man at the hardware counter in Myer's Store. I'd probably still be there and we'd be living in the room-and-kitchen we had in Carfin Street. If only . . . So you see, I had to change, for there *was* a connection between my life as it was and those terrible events. That's why when I invested my money in the pub and the picture house, I didn't want to know what was going on. As long as I got what they said was the profit I was happy. If they were at the fiddle, then so be it. It had nothing to do with me. And obviously knowing the kind of people they were, I knew they would be at it. But then everyone else is. It's the way . . . isn't it? So there you have it, Star. Now you know why the pub and the Pantheon were run the way they were. When I got you involved in the business, I merely expected it would be a good outlet for you and that you would sharpen things up a bit with all your college training and that. Get them to make a bit more profit. Sort out all the books. That kind of thing. I never thought for a minute you would find out what you did about them and the way they ran the places. But then I didn't know at that time you were the determined kind of person you are. There's a lot of your father Jamesie in you, Star. And I mean all the best bits.'

Star smiled fondly when he said that. She had sat in rapt attention, almost trancelike, as he had related the long and grim story to her. When he was finished there was a long silence between them, Sammy sitting with his eyes staring down, his mind a flood of memories of those years. Star gazed at him fondly with all the love of a daughter for a father.

'Oh dear, my dear Uncle Sammy, I never realised any of this. Never.'

Sammy stayed silent for about another minute, his eyes unblinking. Then he took a long sigh . . . 'Aye, Star, it's a load off my chest telling you about it. I felt so bad that you never knew. I've been dying to tell you for ages.'

'I'm so glad you have told me everything, uncle. There were so many question marks in my mind about you, the pub, the picture house . . . everything. There are none now.'

He paused again, then smiled. 'Right then. Now that's over, back to the Pantheon. What shall we do about it? Sort them out like you did at the pub or put a new team in?'

'I've got some other ideas. How much did you pay for the cinema?'

'About eight thousand.'

'Well, at least it was not a bad investment.'

'How do you mean?'

'Well, it's worth double that now.'

'Sixteen thousand quid for the Pantheon! How do you figure that out?'

'Well, I've had talks with the J.B. Group. They're on a big expansion drive at the moment as are some of the others and they're snapping up little cinemas all over the place. Good business sense, actually. The more they have the cheaper they can show their films. Also, if the J.B. Group are to survive in Scotland and compete against the likes of Rank and Gaumont they'll need more houses in their chain.'

'Gees, Star, you haven't been sitting still. How did you manage to get talking to them?'

'Quite easy. I merely telephoned J.B. himself and he invited me to meet him with his group manager Lawrence Stokes. They were quite surprised when I told them the Pantheon might be for sale. They told me that they had already approached your Mr Compton about seeing you and he had told them that there was no possibility of you considering a sale. Anyway, I asked what they were likely to offer and they indicated it would be in excess of fourteen thousand.'

Sammy whistled in astonishment. 'Fourteen's not bad, Star. Did you say we'd be interested?'

'Oh yes . . . but not at fourteen. They were obviously keen so I thought I would play them along a bit.'

'What did you say?'

'I said I was your junior partner and not empowered to make any decisions in the matter and that if they were still interested they should keep in touch. And sure enough, the very next day Stokes, the group manager man, phoned to ask if you had made any decision. I told him you were having talks with Gaumont. He asked if I had any more details and I merely said that as far as I knew Gaumont had been speaking to you in terms of a figure in excess of sixteen. That's when I knew I had him. He asked if there was any way I could get in touch with you quickly to persuade you to make no decision until you heard from them again. He said he was going off to have a meeting with J.B. and the board of the group and would be in touch soon. Then this came this morning.' She produced a telegram envelope from her handbag and handed it to Sammy.

He read the contents aloud. 'Seventeen thousand if acceptance by 3 p.m. today. Stokes. J.B. Group.'

'It's one o'clock, Uncle Sammy. Do you want to phone them?'

'Star, I can hardly believe what I'm hearing. Seventeen thousand smackers for the wee Pantheon? And you doing all the business to get the deal? Flabbergasted . . . that's the word. I'm bloody well flabbergasted. You're a right wee genius, Star.'

'Less of the wee. I'm five foot seven.'

'Aye and full of ideas like they Frenchmen with the sharp knives in their restaurants. So what do we do next?'

'Accept, of course. And with the money we can borrow more

and we'll invest it in a much more profitable fashion, like some new lounge bars. And I've got some other ideas we could employ in the drinks trade.'

'I'll go along with that, Star. In fact, I'll go along with anything you suggest now. I never knew you had it in you. I never knew this would be so much fun. What an idea that was about saying I was talking to the Gaumont group. What a whopper!'

'Uncle Sammy, I don't tell whoppers. There actually were negotiations with Gaumont. I met them and they were interested, they said, and had already made an assessment of it with a view to making an offer.'

'And did they make an offer?'

'Yes . . . between thirteen and fourteen would be their limit, they said.'

Sammy beamed. 'And you told J.B. sixteen. You don't miss a trick.'

'That's business, uncle. Not missing tricks. And using sharp knives, of course.'

8

Leaving Lahore

In accordance with Rasool's instructions, Javaid went to the bank on that second day of *Shawwal*, the first day of the Muslim month beginning with the new moon of the evening before. The manager, Mr Khaled, said he had been expecting him. He handed him a long envelope.

'I have never had a letter before,' said Javaid handing the envelope back to the manager who slit it open and showed him three pieces of paper.

'This one,' he said, holding up a buff-coloured ticket. 'That is for your train journey to Karachi. This other one, the bigger one, that is for your passage from Karachi to England on the ship SS *Stratheden*. It sails for Glasgow on the fifth day of this month which means you will have to get the train to the south either tomorrow or the day after. The ship sails with the tide at seven o'clock in the evening of the fifth day of the new month. It's a P & O ship returning from Australia so you will have an excellent voyage. This third piece of paper is a note from your friend which says you must bring your birth certificate to prove you were born in India. You need no other documents to enter the Mother Country. And there is an address which you must not lose. It is where to find your friend.' He pointed to it as he read it out. 'Rasool Hanif Jehan, 155 Abbotsford Place, Gorbals, Glasgow, one up, right. Best wishes to you, my friend. May Allah be with you.'

BOOK II

9

The Gorbals Gathering

The Gorbals. 1953. The war had come and gone leaving a Glasgow that had been neglected and decayed. An industrial revolution had come and it was to go, too, stamping its own blight typified by tall factory chimneys that once belched and were now becoming a petrified forest, like accusing fingers pointing to the heavens. And there had been landlords, the absent and the present, who had compounded the neglect and the decay and the degeneration that became a rottenness.

Much still survived in the Gorbals and in Glasgow from the ways of the twenties and the thirties and even earlier days. There were cobbled roads and there were trace boys with colossal Clydesdales harnessed to aid struggling carthorses climb steep city streets. There was a river that lived with big ships that came from India and the Indies, the Americas and Australasia, and smaller ones that went to Ireland and our own islands and ones they called puffers, minikin merchantmen with caricature captains and character crewmen. There were street entertainers, ultimate descendants of the wandering minstrels who fiddled and sang and played jews' harps and melodions, and artists who canvassed Highland cottages and unreal sunsets on pavement slabs where other men with mates with caps for pennies did Houdini routines with fearful straitjackets or performed Samson feats like having quarry stones sledgehammered on their bare chests as they lay prone on chilled pavements. There were stage legends like Tommy Morgan playing his Big Beanie act at the Pavilion and incomparables like Gigli and Frank Sinatra who would come, one to a splendid concert hall, the other to a celebrated theatre.

The Gorbals of 1953 was of a Glasgow that still had an old-fashioned bustle and which in so many ways reminded them of the vibrant style of life which they had known in their own towns and cities. They were strangers in a strange land, but there was an empathy between these newcomers with the brown unfamiliar faces and the community among whom they had come to live; there was an identification between them, a bond forged by the struggle which marked both their lives.

They started to appear in the Gorbals in the early 1950s, although they could speak about some early pioneers who had been there before the war; before the First World War even, like the bold wanderer Noor Mohammad Tanda, who they said had come to Scotland in 1875, followed by Atta Mohammad Ashrif, who arrived early in the century, and thereafter an occasional one or two. They came from the land that the British had united and called India, but they were Muslims and after Independence and Partition in 1947 they were known as Pakistanis. In 1953 there were 500 Pakistanis and Indians in the West of Scotland. About that same time there was a count of pedlars' licences and it showed that 271 had been issued to what the official report described as 'coloured men'.

The Gorbals was well used to its migrants. They had come from the Highlands when their beloved clan chiefs decided they preferred sheep to people for the simple reason they were more profitable. So the clanspeople were ordered from their lands, many of them coming to the Gorbals. They came in even bigger numbers from Ireland when the potato failed them and later when they bickered and warred, one about their Irish Problem, the other about their English Problem, both of them forgetting about a nation's very own problems. And they came too from Italy: the people of Ciociaria in the early part of the nineteenth century, itinerant musicians and beggars who were to become ice-cream salesmen and fish and chip cooks, followed in 1860 by other Italians – the Barghigiani from Tuscany, in pursuit of their trade as pedlars of plaster statuettes and with passports which bore the unique injunction: 'We invite the civil and military authorities of the Duchy, and pray the friendly powers, to allow the bearer to pass freely and to give him assistance in case of need and offer complete reciprocity in conformity with local rights and customs.' And they came too from the Baltic States, like the Irish, victims of famine and political strife, together with the Jewish people from all the countries of Eastern Europe, bullied and burned from their homes merely because they were of a race which did not please those among whom they had lived.

And now, from Lahore and Lyallpur, Multan and Mirpur, Gujranwala and Gujrat, a new collection of victims seeking what all those others had sought when they had come to the Gorbals . . . a better way of life.

The Gorbals, such as it was in varying ages, was the measuring stick of just how bad had been the previous conditions of the migrants who came to it. Gorbals life had always been the hard life. Its birthpangs had been harrowing – a dumping ground for the lepers and other incurables from the burgeoning fishing village that had grown to become a town on the opposite bank of the River Clyde and which they called Glasgow. For a while the merchant people lived in fine terraces in the Gorbals but the industrial revolution and its wake brought an end to that residency and thereafter foundry and factory lived cheek by jowl with human and horse, the one as crowded in tenement as the other in stable.

In the early 1950s there were plans and the Gorbals, said the men who ordered the plans, was to be no more. It was to be redeveloped, announced the town council, which in Glasgow they call the Corporation. But the old Gorbals was to take a long time to despatch. Its death gargle was to be the occasional rumble of an inhabited tenement building collapsing of its own accord through the wanton negligence of venal landlords. And there were all the other symptoms which signify the demise of an urban community – abandonment of pride, social indiscipline, vandalism, crime and more.

Yet such had been the poverty from which they had come, even one of the less salubrious streets like Nicholson Stret, which was to become the Gorbals home for many of the new migrants, was many steps up the social ladder for them. And if you had lived, like Javaid, up the alleyway of the narrowest of streets, past the yoghurt maker, the hookah merchant and the butcher with the skinned goats' heads, then Nicholson Street could mean a great leap up that social ladder. You had also achieved your first target in your new life as a migrant.

They used to meet in the house at 27 Oxford Street. One street back from the waterfront, Oxford Street was a typical Gorbals thoroughfare. There had been no zoning when they had built and developed the Gorbals and most streets were still a mixture of houses, commerce and industry, just as they had been in the early nineteenth century. Oxford Street had a police station, a clutch of tenements owned by a property syndicate, one of whom gave an address in Melbourne, Australia; Jeanie Hill's the confectioner, with conversation lozenges and rhubarb rock; Gilfeather's the draper and Benton's the newsagent, and the arresting camphor pungency of firelighters and neat rows of wood kindlers they called 'sticks'; Elston's the warehousemen nearby a mantles' shop, a coppersmith's, a plumber's shop, a dentist and a spirit dealer; Lithgow the printer's and its clacking machines and Allan and Gilmour the bacon curer's whose smoke fumes could rouse appetites from one end of the street to the other; a Maypole Dairy with marble slab counters that had bulk butter and big cheeses they sliced with wire cutters; the Workman's Synagogue, where devout men prayed on a Saturday Sabbath, and a branch of the Rangers Football Club Supporters' Association, where devoted men spoke their Saturday shibboleths. Number 27 was just an ordinary close, as they called a tenement house entrance. There was a house owned by the Merchant Navy Welfare Board where they had picture shows of Indian films for the Lascar seamen whose ships were in the port, another house with a family called Martin, one with a family called Ashton and another for the Jamait Ittihad ul Muslimin, a united fellowship of Muslims. In the house of the Jamiat was their *zawiyah*, the name they gave to a little one-roomed mosque. The room contained no furniture, except a slender nimbar, a lectern pulpit. Nor were there any pictures on the walls. The soft pine flooring was covered with a variety of scatter rugs with prayer mats which pointed significantly to the south-east, the direction of Mecca, their spiritual home.

Only a small handful would be there for the daily prayers, but there would be more on a Friday, the Muslim Sabbath, especially for the nightfall *isha*, the last of the five prayers. And afterwards they would stay to talk together, just as they would have done in their little villages and markets and other places where the men would gather and speak together at home in Pakistan. They would talk about their jobs in their new country, the problems they were encountering, titbits about news of home from letters, what new supplies of the food they liked that Sadiq's had in stock. '*Ham watan*,' one would say, 'have you heard they got a new supply of tinned okra in this week?' 'And you can now get fresh halal meat,' said another, and that was important to them for their holy Koran book said that the meat they ate had to be halal, which meant that it was killed according to the laws of their book, and that a Muslim butcher would invoke the *takbir*, the repeating of 'God Is Great' three times, on the unstunned animal as it was slaughtered. They would speak too about their relationship with the people of the land among whom they had come to stay.

Javaid had been in the Gorbals for about six months and, on the advice of his friend Rasool, had 'gone with the case'. Rasool had done that when he arrived for, although he was acting as an agent for a variety of Pakistani companies, the goods were to take time to arrive by sea. He had already sold all the first orders which he had brought from Pakistan and had confirmed to himself that there would be a sound financial future as an agent once the flow of goods had been established. Caught in a time gap between the first goods arriving before taking second orders he had, like so many before him, 'gone with the case'.

Sharif, one of their countrymen, had a wholesale warehouse from which the men they knew as 'Johnny Pedlars' would obtain their merchandise – varied knitwear and other small clothing items. They could go to Sharif as soon as they arrived and get themselves a case, for he also supplied another vital commodity – credit.

'Going with the case,' Rasool had told Javaid, 'is the best way to get to know the people and make yourself good money at the same time. You will make more than working for someone else . . . and anyway, we Punjabi like our independence, do we not? The first thing it helps you with is the language. There was me, Javaid, with one of my degrees from university in English. And a good degree at that. And do you know I had trouble in understanding them when I came. The first man I met when I went out with the case was from a place called Aberdeen. Do you know, I thought he was from a different country! I got him to speak very slowly and I began to understand him a bit. He asked me what I was doing and I told him that I was selling in order to get to know the people and the language better. He seemed a nice man so I said to him, "Friend, with the accent you have, I think it should be you that's going with the case." Well, he understood all right . . . then I sold him a couple of cardigans and made half my profit for the day. Do you know, Javaid, with some little money I had and the rest I have made since coming, I have been able to buy the house in Abbotsford Place. These used to be the best houses in the Gorbals, you know.'

'Yes, I remember when I first arrived how impressed I was with their wide entrances and the big sweeping staircase at the back of the building. Not like the ones down in Nicholson Street. Why do the *gora* (the white people) call our street the Burma Road, Rasool?'

'That was the famous road they used during the war to take supplies from India to Burma. It's just a place they associate with India and Indians . . . and us.'

With Rasool's advice, Javaid had established 'runs' for selling the clothing he bought wholesale from Ashrif's. Rasool had been a good teacher about life on the road as a door-to-door salesman. 'The first thing you must do,' he said, 'is sell your stuff away from Glasgow. There are too many shops here in competition . . . and also there are enough of our *ham watan* (countrymen) already selling in the suburbs. Get out into the country. They don't have so many shops and there are lots of little villages and communities where you can make money, even though you will have bus fares to pay. I got a map when I came and established all my runs in Lanarkshire.'

He went over the map with Javaid and suggested some runs he could make. 'There's some little towns in Ayrshire . . . they're not too far away. See, there's Hurlford, Galston, Newmilns, Greenholm and Darvel. They're all close to each other and with lots of houses and good bus services. You could spend two days, maybe three, going from one to the other. You could spend two or three days in all the towns past Paisley in Renfrewshire – Johnstone, Howwood, Houston, Milliken Park, Kilbarchan and down to Beith . . . look, Javaid, lots and lots of villages there. You could spend two weeks there alone. Then you go back to Galston, Newmilns and Darvel again. And after that you go back

to the other ones in Renfrewshire. You see, that's business,
Javaid. You build up customers. Get them to trust you. Give
them good prices. And get orders from them . . . that's
important. Always get more orders. And you can give them
credit too . . . charge them a penny in the shilling for that. And
be regular. Get them to know when to expect you. They like
that. If they can rely on you like that, they will even get a neighbour in to see your goods. They're good people in these little
country places, Javaid. They've had hard lives too. But they're
cheerful and hospitable and they like what they call a good
"crack". That's one of their words in the country, Javaid. It
means a good gossip. You know, they like to tell you about
their families and the children. And don't be afraid to speak
to the womenfolk. You'll find that strange at first, but it's
quite acceptable. In fact, Javaid, you'll find that in most of
the houses the men don't bother. They tell you to speak to
their wives and they even leave it up to them to pay and everything. And, no bargaining, Javaid. You tell them the price and
they accept it.'

'My goodness, Rasool. They must have many strange ways. It
is going to take me a long time to get used to these kind of
customs.'

'You'll learn quickly, Javaid. I know their ways are very, very
strange at times, especially the ways of their women. But they are
easy to get used to. You'll adapt quickly.'

Javaid started on his great adventure as a door-to-door salesman that week when he set out with a case so loaded with
knitwear and shirts, gloves, ties and handkerchiefs, it was a
struggle to carry. He got one of the first buses down to Ayrshire
in the morning and got one of the last ones back at night. To save
money, he walked from the bus terminal at Waterloo Street back
to his little house which he shared with some of the other new
arrivals in Nicholson Street in the Gorbals. It was nearly
midnight when he counted his money, deducting the bus fares
from the profit. It wasn't difficult to count. All he had made was
sixpence. But he remembered Rasool's advice to be patient until
he learned their ways and the language and the way they used
that language. He worked six days a week, observing the
Christian Sabbath not only because his pedlar's licence prohi-

bited Sunday selling, but his friends had advised that it would be 'unwise'.

The highlight of the week was the Friday night visit to the meetings of the Muslim Fellowship at 27 Oxford Street. As well as catching up on all the gossip about themselves and about home, they could solve many of their problems from the advice they could get from others who had been in Scotland much longer. There was always a regular group who would be there on their Friday Sabbath evening. There was Iftikhaar, the bus conductor, Haakim and Ali, both pedlars, Taariq the watch repairer and market trader, a man they said was a magician with faulty clockwork, and Umar, a driver on what was known as 'the red buses', the ones which did services to the country areas outside the city. They had many good talks together about the good old days in Pakistan. Like all exiles living the 'little death' of exile itself, the days in their homeland, no matter how hard and poor and trying they had been, were always remembered with fondness and affection; bad times dissolved in the memory; the good times were always there.

'You know what I miss?' said Ali, one of the pedlars. '*Burfi*. Our very own *burfi*. No one can make sweetmeats like we can. My favourite was *badam ki burfi*, the almond sweetmeat. My mother used to make big trays of it, soaking the almonds overnight so that they all puffed up till they were twice the size, sometimes even bigger. Then my sister would grind them till they were a paste and then they would mix that with dissolved sugar and some *ghee* and spread it out and leave it for another night until it had set and we would all wait anxiously for it to be ready. Oh, the taste of it when it was just newly made! Nothing like it here.'

His friend Haakim had sweet memories too. 'What about *aam wali*? You never get mango ice cream here. And why can't we get *gulab jamun*? Surely they could make them here. They are just milk balls made in a syrup. We used to get them at the *namat kadah* shop in the bazaar. What a taste! Oh, how I could go for some just now.'

Taariq, the market trader, said he was surprised they didn't have restaurant stalls at the markets. 'All they have are the people who sell mussels and those little shells they pick with a pin and those smelly stalls that sell the pies. Have you seen the *ghee* jump out when they bite into them?'

'They don't use *ghee* in those pies, Taariq,' said Umar. 'That is animal grease.'

'When I saw how bad their food was, I was going to open a cooked chicken stall,' went on Taariq. 'Do you know the ones in that little street just off the Dil Mohammad back home? Well I thought they would have liked that here . . . pick your own chicken live from a cage, then we cut its throat, skin it and prepare it right in front of them and serve it cooked with beautiful herbs and spices and all within fifteen minutes. But Sam, the man who owns the markets, just laughed at me when I asked for one of his stalls to do this. He said I would "get the jail". Then he explained there were all these officials and you should have heard the list of them . . . health regulation inspectors, cruelty to animal inspectors, council bye-law inspectors and even the police. And there were others. Why should all those people stop me killing chickens that the people have chosen to eat? What could be more fresh than that? Better than those terrible pies. All they have here are dead chickens. You should see a chicken live before you eat it and see how healthy or how unhealthy it is. Well, I wouldn't buy one of their dead chickens. Anyway, they are not halal chickens.'

The ways and customs of their new country were a never-ending source of talk among them and they had many laughs together about some of the situations in which they had found themselves during the first days and weeks after their arrival.

'I didn't know Scotland was a different country from England when I came,' said Umar. 'I used to tell people "I love your England" and I used to get some very funny looks from them and loud remarks too.'

'I told all my friends in Lahore I was going to Glasgow in England and no one said anything about Scotland,' said Javaid. 'I even had my friend Rasool's address written out on this sheet of paper so that I would get here all right and it said Gorbals, Glasgow, England, and when I showed it to a man at the Euston railway station in London he got very angry with me. He even grabbed the paper from my hand and scored out the England word and wrote Scotland in its place. I didn't understand what the word meant, then a kind lady explained it to me on the train. It was the first I knew!'

'I had a door slammed in my face the very first day I went out with the case,' said Ali, one of the pedlars. 'It was my first customer and I had practised what to say: "Good morning, lady. I am happy to be in your England. I have some wonderful English clothes to sell to you." It took me a whole weekend to get the words right. I didn't understand what the lady said at the door, but she was very angry . . . you know that angry way they can get . . . and the door closed with a very loud bang. I was really puzzled for a while.'

'Maybe you can tell me,' said Javaid. 'Why is it that you must say everything is small? You know, this word "wee". They say it about everything. I get very confused when I'm selling. One woman said to me that she would like to see my wee jumpers. My goodness, you should have seen the size of her . . . like one of those wrestlers in the Old City, the ones who drink milk and yoghurt all day to make themselves bigger and stronger. Anyway, I thought she might want a small cardigan for someone else in the house and I went all through my case to pick out the smallest one and you should have seen the look I got when I handed it to her. She said, "Do you think I am Jane . . ." something; I didn't catch the other name she said.'

'Russell,' said Iftikhaar, the bus conductor.

'That's right. That's the name,' said Javaid. 'How did you know?' And some of the ones who had been in the country for a longer time smiled knowingly.

Undeterred, Javaid continued. 'This same woman asked me if I would like a wee cup of tea. And what do I get . . . this big mug. You should have seen it! Big as the washing can we take with us to the toilet. Then she said her husband preferred his tea in a wee bowl and she shows me this big bowl.'

'Maybe she has a wee husband who is over six feet,' joked one of the men.

'I don't know. He wasn't there. Although I was sure he must be in the house somewhere for I didn't know that a woman would be allowed to talk to another man without her husband being there. Her daughter was there and they asked me if I wanted a "wee piece". Piece of what, I asked, and they thought I was joking and laughed. Then they gave me this big sandwich of bread and jam. I didn't like it very much but ate it just in case I offended them. All the time I was still terrified that the husband would appear and catch me in the house talking to the two women.'

'Some of them carry big razors,' teased Iftikhaar. 'You would have had your throat slit, ear to ear.'

'He's joking with you,' said Ali, an older man. 'It is their way here. They don't mind you talking to their wives and daughters. I too found it very strange at first, though.'

'I know,' said Javaid. 'Rasool, my friend – you know the agent who lives in Abbotsford Place? – well, he told me all about their women when I came. Rasool is very wise and has read lots of books. He explained to me all about the *gora* attitude to women. But when you have been used all your life never to have the eyes of another woman meet yours, except those of your own household, and then all of a sudden you are allowed to look at strange women and strange women are allowed to look at you without a veil and without the *doputta* to hide the shape of their breasts, then it is very frightening. Very, very frightening.'

Taariq said he too had been frightened by the women when he first arrived. 'Like Javaid I found it odd that you could look into their eyes and that they could look at yours . . . but I was frightened of them because they reminded me of men. Those coarse voices, and smoking cigarettes in public! Have you watched them nipping the cigarette? You watch them. They do it exactly like the men. They stop, flick off the burning tip with their thumbnail, then stamp and twist their foot on the hot end on the ground. Why do they do this? The street cannot go on fire.'

'But they don't put the cigarette end behind their ear like the men,' said one of them.

'No . . . that bit is different. They put them in their coat pocket or I have seen others put them in their purse. And tell me, why don't they like children? Have you heard the way they talk to them? I have watched them in Argyle Street on a Saturday afternoon. I walk along there when I go to my stall at the Barrows markets and you can hear them screaming at their children and smacking them in front of all the crowd and no one seems to mind. They are very fearful some of these women . . . and so big and muscular too.'

'That's not muscles,' came the voice of Haakim, one of the pedlars. 'That's fat. They eat bad food. Cook everything with the white stuff they call lard or suet.'

'It's their *ghee*,' said one.

'No it's not,' said Haakim. 'It's all animal grease. I asked a butcher at the market about it. The lard is the rendered fat of the pig and if you are a good Muslim, never ask them for a fried egg for they fry it in this pig fat and that is *haram* food, food that is against the laws of our Koran.

'The other stuff is suet. That is the fat they take from around the kidneys of the sheep and other animals. We use it to make candles in Pakistan. They cook with it here. That is why they all smell like they do.'

'So that's the smell,' said Javaid. 'I wondered about that.'

'Yes, they cook everything with it in their frying pans. The smell of it sticks to everything, especially if they use the same stuff several times and if you put that smell together with that tobacco they use in their cigarettes you get the terrible stink that's everywhere. You need a strong stomach for it.'

'Just like our sewers,' said someone.

'That's different. That is what we are used to. Anyway, an open sewer is a wholesome smell. It is the stuff of new life in the fields. But this animal grease smell! Ugh! It is the smell of evil.'

Javaid returned to the subject of the women again. 'Those ones you were talking about, Taariq: the very rough ones. Are they from a particular tribe or caste?'

Two of the men laughed loudly, one saying, 'They are like the *Harijan* caste of the Hindu people, Javaid . . . the Untouchables.'

'Don't you listen to them,' said Ali. 'They do not have tribes or castes here.'

Umar, the driver of the red buses, said he disagreed. 'They don't call them tribes or castes but they have these different classes which make them look like they are different tribes. I have been here for three years now and when you have been a conductor and then a driver on the buses you get to know them fairly well. The women you talk about, Taariq, are all from the poorer classes. They live in the old houses, just like ours in Nicholson Street, or else in places they call "the schemes", those big areas their town council built for them. They have had the hard life, these people. That is why they look the way they do and act the way they do.'

'But we have ten times the poverty in Pakistan that they do here,' argued Taariq.

'I know, but we are mainly from the country and we are close to the soil and we have sunshine all the time and the food we eat is all fresh and natural food and our womenfolk know all about the great flavourings for the food and all the best ways to cook it and from when they are little girls they are taught to look after the men. Here it is different. They are not close to their soil or their food and the young girl is not trained to look after the man. I can tell the poor have the very hard life here because on the routes I drive I go to areas and it is like a different country from here in the Gorbals. One of my runs is to the town called Ayr and most of the way there it is very different people you see. They are exactly like the Hindu's *Vaishyas*, the caste of the business people. They speak different to the poor caste. They are usually gentle and polite. They are even a different shape from the poor. They probably eat different food and you don't get that same smell from them either.'

Taariq, the watch repairer, said he had read about the different classes in the newspapers. 'It is true, there is this class system here and it is just like the Hindu and their castes. There's the upper class. Sometimes I think they call them Lords and Sirs and Ladies and Duchesses. They're like the Hindu *Brahmin*. Then there's the middle class. That's the *Vaishyas*, the ones that Umar sees when he's driving his bus to the town called Ayr. Then they have their working class, that's like the *Sudras*, the Hindu servant class. And, of course, there's the poor class, the *Harijans*. So they are just like the Hindu as far as I can see.'

'And do they have to wait until they die like the Hindu before moving up to another class?' asked Javaid.

'No, that is the one big difference between them and the Hindu,' answered Taariq. 'They tell you that they can move from class to class if they wish, but I don't think they do. I don't think their upper class would want to marry a man from the poor class.'

'But that's like us Muslim people too,' said Umar. 'Our parents choose a wife for us and it is always someone they know and who knows their family as well as all their friends, so therefore they choose someone they think is appropriate. But I have noticed here that when people go out of their caste . . .'

'It's a class they call it, Umar,' interrupted Taariq.

'That's right. When they move out of their class they always seem to talk about it. They are often writing in the newspapers about the miner's son or the labourer's son who becomes a rich man or the big boss of a company or a prominent person of one kind or another who began life as a humble working man. So you see they seem not to be ashamed if they come from a lower caste, I mean class, and move on to another one.'

'What class are we in?' Javaid asked with a smile.

'*Harijans* . . . Untouchables,' joked one of the men and they laughed.

They stopped suddenly when Iftikhaar said that sometimes he thought that the *gora* people did think of them as Untouchables. 'Do none of you get the feeling that the *gora* resent us being here? I do. And I ask is it because they think we will take their work or is it because we are a darker colour than they are?'

'You are a bit sensitive, are you not?' said Taariq. 'I have never found that all the time I've worked at the markets. They joke with me sometimes. I didn't understand it at first. They kept saying, "Some tan you've got, Taariq. . . Are you just back from Ostend, Taariq?" But it is just their humour. I don't think they feel bad about us.'

'I'm not taking anyone's work,' said Javaid. 'You don't see any *gora* going round with the case. It is just us Pakistanis and some Indian Hindus and Sikhs. One customer told me she preferred me to the Sikhs . . . she did not call them that. The ones with the turbans, she said. They were dour, she said, and didn't smile like we did.'

'You should be on the buses at night, like I am,' said Iftikhaar. 'Friday night's the worst. They often call me black bastard on a Friday night.'

'But that's because they are all drunk on the Friday night,' said Taariq. 'If you were a *gora* like them they would call you a Catholic bastard or a Protestant bastard. That is what they call each other every Friday night. It is the night for it.'

'How,' asked Javaid, 'can they tell a Catholic bastard from a Protestant bastard. We can tell a Hindu from a Muslim because of the way we dress in our country. But how do they know here? They all seem to dress the same.'

'They have ways,' said Taariq. 'Some do it by shaking hands with each other. I've been told that some of the Protestant ones have a secret code when they shake hands and it lets them recognise each other. But there's other ways and I don't really understand them. But they seem to know just the same.'

'They often ask me on the Friday night if I am a Catholic or a Protestant,' Ikftikhaar said, 'And when I say I'm Muslim they just grunt. It's like they're disappointed. And do you know? They never call me a Muslim bastard. I wonder why that is?'

Taariq had his view. 'I don't think they understand what Muslim is. They know about Protestants and Catholics and Jews but not about us Muslims and Hindus.'

'They always call Jews bastards. Both the Protestants and the Catholics do that,' said Umar. 'Why is that?'

'I've heard some of the old ones in the Gorbals say it's because they came and took their jobs years ago but I don't believe that. I think they don't like them because they've got money now, yet they were poor when they came. You hear them say it about their own people too, however. Rich bastards, they say. I don't think they like the rich too much.'

'When I came at first,' said Javaid, 'I thought everyone must be rich for there was no one sleeping in the streets like you see at home. And I saw very few beggars. Everyone lives in a house so they must be prosperous, I thought. But after a week or two I began to see them in a different way. Like Umar was saying, there is a poor class and they have a hard life. But why are there so many when it is such a rich country . . . many many times richer than our Pakistan?'

Rasool had joined them when Javaid had been speaking and after they welcomed him he took up the point about the poor.

'It's the alcohol and the way they live that makes them poor,' he explained. 'You take our men who are driving their buses and working as conductors on them. They all have the same wages as the Glasgow men but look how much better off our people are. Most of them are buying their own houses, which is something they could never do driving a bus in Lahore or Rawalpindi. Yet hardly any of the Scottish men doing the same jobs on the buses are buying their houses. There are two reasons for this . . . because we don't drink the alcohol and because of the different attitude we have to borrowing money. Take the alcohol first. Do you know how much their whisky costs them? I've been studying their ways and have discovered quite a lot. A bottle of their whisky costs them one pound and fifteen shillings. Their average wage is eight pounds a week, but after you pay the tax and the stamp it's about seven pounds and ten shillings. So a bottle of their whisky is costing them almost a quarter of their wages. Now if they are buying their house, the price of that bottle of whisky would be the same as the weekly cost of paying back a loan, and that's even including the rates tax.'

'But surely there are some who don't drink as much as a bottle of whisky a week. Why don't they buy their houses?' came a question.

'Because of the other reason I mentioned. Their different attitude to money. Now if you or I want to borrow money, we just ask each other as a matter of course. It's the expected way of us, is it not?'

The men nodded in agreement.

'Our Islamic law prohibits us from charging interest so when you do loan someone money, that person is not only obliged to pay you that money back, but he is in your favour: he must help you in some kind of way because of the help you gave him. Now that's something we all understand because we grew up with that way of life. But it is not the way of the people here. Anyone who asks another for money, unless they are very, very close relatives or friends, is suspected in some sort of way. They would only ask if they were in a bad debt or some kind of trouble. They would never ask someone for a loan to use as the deposit for a house or to buy a business. Asking for a loan is like losing face to them. They speak badly of people who ask for loans, so do not ask any of them or else they will speak unkindly of you and of us. They called such people "tappers" and it is not a good thing to be known as one of them. That is why so many of them stay in houses that are owned by others and pay landlords instead and why they live in those other houses, the ones they call Corporation houses.'

'But I have seen moneylenders advertising in the newspapers,' said one of the pedlars.

'They are usurers. They charge more in interest than the actual loan. You could never get a house with their money.'

Taariq had his ideas too why the local people could never save money. 'Have you seen them if they have something to celebrate? The whole world must know about it. So they have what they call "a night out". It's always "a night out" with them. They go to the fish and chip shop, the ones that have a sitting-in place. Then after that they go to the pub and spend the whole night there or else they go to the pub first and the restaurant afterwards. You hear them talking about it at the market. "Spent a whole week's wages last night," they tell you. And the more they spend, the better the night out is to them. We like celebrating too, when we have our wives and families with us, that is. But we always have it in the house and the wives prepare for it for days, making all sorts of special meats and delicacies. But it doesn't cost much money . . . maybe a day's wages at the most. And we can have a banquet for that. Ah, I can think of the one before I left . . . that was *dal aur phali ka salan, masoor ki dal methi ke sath* and *shahi murgh badaami*. Oh, that royal chicken in almond sauce! I can taste it now.'

'Enough,' said Haakim. 'No more talking about the food we miss.'

Umar changed the subject for them. 'Did I tell you about my friend Imraan . . . you know, the one who was with me earlier in the evening at the *isha* prayer? Well, Imraan is a very devout Muslim. He's also a bus driver. Works out of the Larkfield depot, which is handy for the men from the Gorbals. Well, he carries a compass and his prayer mat in the bus with him and when he gets to the terminus and it is near a prayer time, he gets out and checks his compass to get the direction of the south-east then spreads his mat on the road in front of the bus and does his duty to Allah, which is very splendid of him.

'Well he was telling me tonight that when he was doing the

asar prayer this afternoon he heard this bell ringing wildly just as he was finishing. It was an ambulance wagon. Someone had seen him from a nearby house and thought he had taken ill and there were two ambulancemen trying to carry him away! They told him that the call had said the driver of the bus had collapsed in front of it with an epileptic fit.'

When the men finished laughing, Umar continued. 'Imraan is a bit of a character, you know. Before I went to the red buses I was his conductor lots of times. Know what he does sometimes? If he has an empty bus and knows there are no inspectors about, he takes the bus up all the side streets and watches all the little corner shops to see how much business they are doing. He says he is saving all his wages to buy a shop one day and is making a study of them. I've seen him driving his bus for miles like that and you should see the looks we get when he drives it up all those streets that have never seen a bus before. Once they caught him and he just said he had got lost and he wasn't reported.'

They laughed at that as well. 'But he is a very fine man is our Imraan,' said Umar. 'Do you know his great ambition? Well, it is to learn the entire Koran off by heart. He says he has tried but no matter how much he reads it he can only remember about half of it. That itself is an amazing feat for there are as many words, if not more, in our Koran as there are in the Christians' Bible. Imraan has now asked his cousin in Multan to find him a wife. He says he wants to have a son who will learn all the Koran by heart and to become an Imam. That's his great ambition now, which is why he drives big double-deck buses up and down the side streets looking for a business. He wants to make lots of money, he says, to give his son a fine education . . . and he hasn't even got a wife yet.'

Just at that the Imam of the little *zawiyah* mosque, a small man who lived in a flat on the top floor of the tenement, spoke up. 'I was listening to your story about Imraan and some of the things you were saying about the people of the host community. I think there is a good lesson for all of us in the way of Imraan. He has the Koran to show him the way and it should be the guide for all of us. There are many temptations for us here. It seems to me that Satan is very easy to find in this country. What *ham watan*

Rasool says about their ways is quite right. It is in the Koran. On wine and gambling it says "in them there is great sin and some profit for men; but the sin is greater than the profit". Good words to remember, my friends.'

'Goodness, look at the time,' said Iftikhaar. 'Ten o'clock . . . and I'm on the early shift in the morning. I have to be at the garage at five o'clock.'

The other men spoke too about the need to be home and to bed for their own early rises. And another evening at their Jamiat Ittihad ul Muslimin, their United Fellowship of Muslims, was over.

10

Together Again

Javaid sounded excited when he phoned Rasool at his home one Friday evening in 1956. 'Are you coming to the Jamiat Ittihad meeting tonight, Rasool?' He replied that he probably would not be there as he had just returned from a long business trip to the north of England canvassing for new customers for his import agency.

'You must be very busy,' said Javaid. 'You have not been with us for a few Friday nights now. But you must come tonight, Rasool. You must. I think you will find a most pleasant surprise.'

'What . . . has someone discovered a tandoor or something?'

'Even better than that, Rasool. Try to be there before the last prayer.'

'I did plan to have an early night, Javaid.'

'Please, Rasool. As a favour to me.'

'How can one refuse a friend? I'll be there.'

Some little street urchins, crowds of whom were always at play or at mischief, even long after it was dark, saw Rasool get out of his big black Wolseley. They were cautious at first for it was the same model that the police patrol units used. But as soon as they saw the dark face there was an excited rush towards him. 'Gonnie watch your car, mister,' which sounded an altruistic gesture but in fact was beginner brigandry and meant that a refusal to pay over some coins would result in scored paintwork or flat tyres or both. Also, the front wings of the Wolseley were the best chute slide this side of the Smith Street or Richmond swing parks. Rasool handed three of them a sixpence each. The car would be safe.

There were about two dozen men gathered in the lobby adjoining the prayer room engaged in the usual gossip while others were in the area which had been the kitchen and were going through the process of the ritual ablution of the Muslim before prayer, the wash which rid them of any unclean thoughts, beginning, as the custom has it, with the hands, then the mouth and nose and the face, then the arms, the right one first, then the left, always starting from the elbow, then wetting the head by stroking the hair with wet hands, and finally the feet, again the right first, the left last. On completion they were ready for their precious moments of spiritual union with their God, their Allah, the Allah they said was the Lord of the Worlds, the Merciful, the Mercy-giving. There was no other god apart from Allah.

One of the men loudly announced Rasool's arrival as he came through the door of the fellowship house and Javaid with another man rushed forward to meet him. Rasool didn't look at the other man at first, merely greeting Javaid by warmly holding his hand. 'Look,' said Javaid, 'do you not recognise our friend?'

There were animated shouts between the two men as they excitedly greeted one another, repeating the name of the other over and over.

'Rasool!'

'Maqbul!'

'I can't believe my eyes.'

'After all those years.'

Rasool poured out a host of questions. 'When did you arrive? From where have you come? What are you doing? How did you find us here in Glasgow?'

'There's about half an hour's talking in just one question,' said Javaid, as the two men continued to greet each other warmly, their arms grasping each other's shoulders then shaking hands over again.

'I've been in England for six years now,' replied Maqbul. 'It was 1950 when I came. Our little farm near Gujrat could not produce enough to support us and the family put all of their money together to give me my fare to come here. I've a cousin in Birmingham. I worked in an engineering factory there and the money was good, lots of overtime and everything. But they said there was better work at Coventry in the car factory so I went there about four years ago. The money was even better there. But the work was terrible. I was on the assembly line. That is no job for a man from the land who likes his independence. I used to go to the Jamiat Ittihad in Coventry and some of our *ham watan* there said that I should go right to the north of England to

Glasgow where they heard it was much better for us. One of them had a cousin in Glasgow and he said he would help me.'

Rasool and Javaid were smiling. 'You had better not tell the people here that you are in the north of England, or you won't find it a better place,' said Javaid. 'You are now in the country they call Scotland.'

Maqbul gave an understanding smile. 'You mean it's like the difference between the Punjab and Sind or Baluchistan?'

'Something like that,' answered Rasool.

'I must remember. Anyway, I came to this address in Nicholson Street to the cousin of my friend . . . and does he not live in the very same tenement property as Javaid? My friend is on the third floor, Javaid on the second. And last Friday when I came here to the Jamiat we met.'

'Incredible. Absolutely incredible,' smiled Rasool. 'The three of us . . . together again. I never thought that would ever happen. Allah must have willed it.'

The men's spirited conversation was interrupted by the call to the *isha* prayer and they filed into the carpeted *zawiyah*, the prayer room, leaving their shoes with the others in a long file in the lobby. Javaid whispered on the way, 'We have a meal prepared at the house, Rasool. We can do lots and lots of talking after the *isha*.'

The houses in Nicholson Street, soot-blackened tenements like the other parts of the Gorbals, had a smell that began at the common entry, the close, a smell of their own decay, of rotten plaster and sodden wood, of mildewed wallpaper and blocked drains. The smell only varied in degree according to the state of the decomposure of the building. Some had a smell which was even worse than the tenement in which Javaid and his friends stayed, although not many. But not even that could overpower the aroma of the meal which had been prepared for their reunion that night. And at each pace up the two flights of the worn, knife-edged steps of the common stair, the heavy pungency of spices and sauces and meats got increasingly stronger, every nuance of it flooding them with memories of their own . . . a street kebab stall; a roadside curry seller; a favourite restaurant; their own mothers and sisters at work in their kitchens at home; a particular meal with particular friends.

'Just like home, eh?' said Javaid, adding, 'It even looks like the Old City here, except for the streets. They are so wide.'

There was a woman stirring the contents of one of the pots huddled round the four gas rings of the stove in the corner of the kitchen which was also used as a dining room. She was wearing the traditional clothes of a Pakistani woman, the *shalwar qamiz* tunic with trousers gathered tightly at the ankle, all of the garment loosely fitting lest a prying eye should detect a rounded buttock, a shapely breast.

She adjusted her chiffon *doputta* scarf, putting an end of it veil-like over her head and avoiding any eye contact with the strangers in the house. 'This is the wife of my friend Mohammad Fayyaz with whom I stay,' said Maqbul. 'She has cooked some of the food and Javaid and myself did the rest. We have a feast all ready, Rasool. Look, we even have the finest *paratha* and *nan* which Mrs Fayyaz has baked for us.'

There were lots of dishes, said Javaid, which they wanted to have but couldn't obtain the ingredients for. On others they had improvised, he said as he listed the menu.

'Mrs Fayyaz has made special samosas, the kind which they make in the little village near Sharqpur from where she comes. Wait till you taste the pastry of them, Rasool. And Maqbul prepared some *nargisi* kebab this morning.'

'The secret,' said Maqbul, 'is the right proportion of cinnamon and cardamom with *channa dal* . . . which I bought in Sadiq's shop, and after that you must make sure the eggs are boiled very very hard before wrapping the meat round them.'

'And there are two meats,' said Javaid, 'one with cauliflowers, yes the real *gosht aur phoolgobi ka salan*, and another with onions, the genuine *do-piaza* with twice the weight of onions as meat. And our friend Mohammad says he is the finest sweetmaker in the Gorbals and has prepared *gajjar ka halva*. This is a good sweet to have here, is it not? They have always got good carrots in the fruitshops with which to make it and if you get the little ones it tastes so much better.'

They spoke eagerly as they ate. 'You look so prosperous, Rasool,' said Maqbul. 'But then I remember you went to Aitchison's. All Aitchison's boys have a good destiny, do they not?'

'I never met one who had to work like me in the streets of the Old City,' said Javaid.

'Yes, what you say is true,' answered Rasool. 'But that only applies in Pakistan. They don't know about Aitchison's here.'

'Yes, Rasool, but a school leaves a mark on a pupil. I noticed your English ways that very first day you joined us on the march.'

'Of course it has helped me. Knowing the language as well as I did when I came here was a great benefit to me, especially when I had to speak with the sales directors and other executives of the big companies on whom I call.'

'Are they buying your goods,' Maqbul wanted to know.

'Yes. I have found lots of markets. My next step now is to get a little office somewhere with a secretary and a store with a manager to be able to build up a good supply of my imports so that customers will not have to wait so long for deliveries.'

'You will do well, Rasool.'

'And yourself, Maqbul. What will you do?'

Javaid answered first. 'I know what Rasool will advise you, Maqbul. Go with the case. It is the way to get to know the people of the country.'

Rasool laughed loudly. 'Well, it is. I did it. And made enough money too in order to buy my first house here, the one in Abbotsford Place. That's in the Gorbals too,' he explained to Maqbul. 'They were fine houses, although like the others they too are deteriorating. I saved £500 from the case to be able to buy it. That was all of my money, though, and I had nothing left with which to buy furniture. But you are better with a house that you own and no furniture than owning a lot of furniture and having no house. I got the furniture after a while. Then after two years I was able to save more money, sold the house in Abbotsford Place for £750 and put it all into a deposit for the house in which I live now in Pollokshields.'

'Rasool lives in a mogul's palace now,' smiled Javaid. 'I have been to his house. But tell me, Rasool. Why don't you have a staff working for you there? In Lahore you would have at least five people to help you with a house like that.'

Before Javaid got his answer, Maqbul told them that he had an uncle who was a servant in a house. 'He was my Uncle Arshad and he was a bearer to a British army captain in the cantonment at Sialkot. Do you know how many servants he had? Eleven altogether. There was my uncle, who acted as major domo, an *ayah* as personal servant to the captain's lady, a *khidmatgar* to look after the living rooms of the bungalow, a cook and a cook's helper because cook refused to prepare vegetables or wash dishes, a sweeper who emptied the toilets, a boy to look after the dogs because the sweeper refused to do that because it was not on his list of duties when hired, a *bhisti* to carry water from the well and to heat it for baths but who wouldn't carry water for the gardener because it was not on his duty list, and because the gardener didn't have it on his list either he had to have a water carrier, and lastly an old man as *chowkidar* to guard the bungalow at night. And the officer who had the house was only a captain. There were lots of them.'

'Oh, I know what it is like at home,' said Rasool. 'When my family were alive we too used to have lots of servants like that. But it's difficult to prevent, isn't it? You open your house to one member of a family and the next thing you know you have all the others as well as some friends on your staff. But we cannot have servants here. They cost too much money.'

'You should have kept the house in Abbotsford Place,' said Javaid, 'and did what the others are doing with them, dividing them up into rooms and making lots of money. What they do is put a gas stove in every room and let it out as a house. Lots of the poor *gora* people are living in them and the landlords are making fortunes out of them. I think some of our *ham watan* are doing that and making themselves very rich.'

'They should be careful,' cautioned Rasool. 'I have already read a story in the newspapers about one of ours who is doing this and it said he had cut off his tenants' electric and gas supply because they had refused to pay the higher rent he demanded from them. The people here do not like the landlord. They have a different attitude to them from what we do in Pakistan. The landlord can be a very hated man here and we should not be associated with them or at least the ones who are behaving like this. The host community have been good to us. And anyway our Koran tells us we should not exploit people. We must be compassionate to others.'

'Yes, but you know, Rasool,' Javaid answered, 'there are lots of Muslims who pray much more than I do and who never miss any of the five prayers on a Friday but when it comes to money they are different people.'

Rasool asked Maqbul if he would go back to Pakistan. 'When I first came here, all the men said they would go back when they had saved enough money, which was why they hadn't sent for their wives and children. Now they are starting to say they may settle here and already some of the women are beginning to come here.'

'I was going to go back when I lived and worked in Birmingham and Coventry. But I may not now. I have repaid my debt to my family as well as having sent them more money. I have an older brother and it's his responsibility to look after my parents, so therefore they will be all right. I have asked him to look for a wife for me and when he gets the right one I will have her sent here. Then I will be happier to stay here. But I will not work in the factory again. No more assembly lines for me. I am not so *bonga*.'

'But there are lots of them do it . . . they cannot all be foolish like you say.'

'Their minds have been taken away from them, Rasool. I would rather push the plough than do that again.'

'So what will you do?'

'I may go with the case like Javaid. He is doing well with it. But first I want to look at other opportunities. Is there a bazaar here?'

'Yes,' said Javaid. 'They call it The Barrows. I am not going with the case tomorrow so I can take you.'

The Barrows of Glasgow is an age-old institution, a Crewe junction of character and patter men, spielers and dealers, hawkers and gawkers, fly men and con men with traders selling the full range of goods that would handsomely furnish any tenement house, vitals like linoleum straight from Kirkcaldy 'that fresh it was still warm when we unloaded it off the lorry this morning missus'; dishes of delf they say is china as they toss them in the air with music-hall flair to attract the customers; carpets and rugs said to be surplus orders from the Royal yacht that they built on the Clyde; yesterday bikes, rusted and twisted that 'a wee clean would make a great present for the boy's birthday'; curtain material that was better than anything you could buy in the big stores up town and which they weren't selling at half price but for you, missus, quarter the price: men who sold the bits and pieces that could make unworkable wirelesses, cameras, motor bikes, gramophones and watches workable again; strange-looking dark men with elixirs and oils and potions, one drop, swallow or rub of which would cure corns and warts, coughs, bronchitis, asthma, insomnia, stomach disorders and baldness; other dark men they called the Lascars, high-stepping and sockless with curly hair and frightened eyes carrying off loads of sewing machines and hats, jackets and shoes to sell when they had sailed back to their hometowns of Bombay and Mangalore, Pondicherry and Madras; strolling vendors with pockets stuffed with shoelaces and razor blades, pencils and batteries; and others who whispered as you passed with the word they were straight from the Ayr races where the top trainer himself had given them the names of three horses which would be winners next week and they were written inside this envelope 'yours for two bob, mac'; decrepit caravans which had outlived their holiday use at Seamill and Barassie and were now 'Joe's' and 'Archie's' and selling tea in mugs the size of paint pots and chips in bags they called pokes and bread rolls with greasy lorn sausage that was *haute cuisine* on a cold Saturday; and shops that wafted out the vinegary smell of boiled whelks and mussels and bree and giant fleshy things called clabby doos.

The Barrows were great.

'The nearest I've seen to the Anarkali . . . you know, our big bazaar in Lahore?' said Javaid when he walked round the various stalls of The Barrows that afternoon.

'We have one like it in Gujrat too,' Maqbul replied. 'And there's also one in Gujranwala to which I used to travel. But we have more food stalls at ours . . . eh, Javaid!'

Food or not, Maqbul liked what he saw. 'You know,' he said, 'I don't think there is any need for me to go with the case. You have to go looking for customers when you do that. Look at this. All the customers come here, all looking for something to buy.'

They're all right here, Javaid, in the one place. I think I can make money here.'

'But it's only for two days of the week, Maqbul.'

'There's bound to be other barrows markets in other towns. I could travel to them on the other days. Perhaps. First I must decide what I shall sell. I must make a study.'

Maqbul made his study. He returned to The Barrows on the Sunday and the rest of the week he wandered the main shopping streets of the city, the ones where he found the same kind of people he saw as customers at The Barrows, places like Argyle Street and High Street, Gallowgate and Trongate, and the long London Road. He went back to The Barrows yet again for the two days of the following weekend. One night in the week after that he revealed his plans to Javaid.

'Have you noticed,' he asked, 'what almost every man wears?'

'Shoes,' replied Javaid.

'That's everybody, Javaid. I mean every man. Well, nearly every man. Anyway, I will tell you. A hat.'

'A hat?'

'Yes . . . a hat. A *topi*.'

'You mean a *topi* that's flat like a *paratha*?'

'Yes, that kind of hat.'

'Well, they don't call that a hat, Maqbul. They call that a cap. But the Scottish man calls it a bunnet.'

'Then I've discovered they have no bunnet stall at The Barrows. I have been round all the shops and the cheapest I have seen is ten shillings and sixpence going up to fourteen shillings and sixpence and some very special ones at sixteen shillings. If I can get a good supply I could sell them cheaper at The Barrows. A seven-and-sixpence bunnet would sell well, don't you think, Javaid? The three-half-crown bunnet. That would be good, eh?'

'It could. But where would you buy them, Maqbul?'

'I've already fixed that. First of all I went round all the shops that sell the hats and bunnets and got to know all the prices. Some of the salesmen were very friendly and told me where they bought theirs from. There's a big factory makes them in Dundee. They say this is far away. But others come from Bridgeton and that's in Glasgow.'

'That's right. It's where the Protestant people live.'

'I was there and I did not see any different people, Javaid.'

'That's right. They don't look different. But they say that's where they live. When I came here at first I was warned by a Protestant man that if I had anything coloured green in my case and tried to sell it there they would chase me for my life.'

'They don't like green?'

'It's the Catholic colour.'

'And do they not like them . . . the Catholics?'

'That's right. They are the great enemy, the Protestant man told me.'

'Are there more Protestants than Catholics?'

'Yes . . . it is a Protestant country.'

'Then I had better sell fewer green ones.'

'Did you go to the factory when you went to Bridgeton?'

'Yes. And I've been to see them at The Barrows and my stall will be ready for this Saturday.'

Maqbul had been busy that week. He had first of all gone to inquire about renting a stall at The Barrows. He found the offices in a building at the rear of the site. They were in an old brick building at the entrance of which there was a sliding window with the word printed on a piece of cardboard, 'Office'. After he had knocked on the window twice, the face of a little man appeared. The butt of a cigarette was attached to his lower lip in such a fashion that when he opened his mouth and spoke it remained firmly fixed in place.

'Aye, what do you want?' he said brusquely, annoyed at having to repeat himself because Maqbul hadn't understood his 'whitja-wahnt'.

'I want to speak to the boss,' he had replied.

The face at the window gave a slight snigger. 'The boss, no less. Don't you know the boss is a millionaire?' he said in that disdainful and offhand fashion. What he really meant was: 'Who are you, ordinary man, to have the impertinence to ask for my boss who is rich?'

'I want to see your boss because I want a stall.'

'I telt ye,' he said. 'The boss is a millionaire.'

Maqbul stayed his ground, unimpressed. 'Then tell him Maqbul who is going to be a millionaire wants to see him.'

'Mac who?'

'You tell him Maqbul Hasan has come to see him.'

The sliding window snapped shut. About five minutes later a middle-aged man appeared wearing slippers and a shirt without a tie.

'Aye . . . Mr Mac is it?'

'Maqbul Hasan.'

'What can I do for you, Mr Bull?'

'I have this idea,' Maqbul replied. Then he outlined the plan he had told Javaid about of getting a stall which specialised in goods which none of the other stalls sold.

'Aye, sounds a good idea,' said the man. 'I might be able to help. There's two or three stalls, but there's always a list of traders wanting them, like.'

'But I want a particular one.'

He was surprised at that. 'So you know what I've got then?'

'There was one empty last week. A good long stall. It's at the corner near the stall that sells the tea and hot food.'

'Aye, near Joe's pie stall. Know the one you mean. That's a dear barrow that one. In a good position. Fiver a week it'll cost you. Plus two bob for every light bulb and there's five of them. So that's another pound for lights plus your fiver. Six pounds for the two days.'

'I'll give you five weeks' advance rent if you give it to me for six weeks.'

'You're not on, Mr Bull. I'll take a month's advance rent for a month's use of it. Youse boys bargain. Us boys don't. And six pounds is the price.'

'Can I come and work on it tomorrow, then?'

'What work . . . there's no trading tomorrow.'

'I want to decorate it. Make it nice with bright paint.'

'Aye, do your own thing, Mr Bull. What's your initial again?'

'Maqbul.'

'Aye, that's right. Jimmy! Give Mr Mac Bull here a receipt for his month's advance rent.'

He turned at that to shake Maqbul's hand. 'All the best to you, Mac.'

Javaid had been late when he had returned from his Renfrewshire run that night and they had stayed up talking till the early hours of the morning.

'You see, they wait for me at some of the houses to which I go. Every fortnight, like I was tonight, I call at this house in Johnstone and, do you know, they won't start their tea till I arrive?'

'But surely they can pour a cup of tea at any time.'

'No, you don't understand, Maqbul. Tea is dinner. And dinner is the main meal but sometimes it's at lunch time.'

'You mean lunch can be dinner and dinner can be tea.'

'That is right, Maqbul. They have funny ways these Scottish people. But they are good people. As I said, they wait for me every second Monday at this house. It's always sliced lamb with cabbage and turnip and a big pot of potatoes which they put on the table and you help yourself and they have Scotch broth soup before it. They give me a telling off if I'm late just like they would one of the family. When it's wet they take my coat to hang up and dry. They even want me to come to the daughter's wedding. But no more of that. You must tell me all about your stall.'

He told Javaid the story of going to the office of The Barrows and about meeting the man they said was a millionaire boss and how he had been friendly and had rented him a stall.

'I have been painting it all day . . . all the bright colours, you know. The ones we like, purple and pink. They don't like colours here, Javaid. Everything is either brown or green. Why is that?'

He didn't wait for an answer. 'Then I went to the bunnet factory in Bridgeton and asked for the boss there. It was like at The Barrows, Javaid. Bosses are very hard to meet. But I am a persistent man. If you have had to plough a hectare field with a sick or a lazy buffalo, then you have got to have persistence. They said he was not available. So I told them I would be back the next day, which I was, but this time I had a business card printed and gave it to the woman at the reception office. I think they are like us and the Indian people for the business card seemed to impress them and the boss man came to talk to me. He laughed at first when I told him what I wanted, saying that they only dealt in big orders, ones for thousands of pounds and that it was only all the best shops in which their goods were sold.

'I asked him what happened to their seconds . . . you know, ones that are maybe not made properly. He said they would never leave the factory with their label on them. I then said, "What about my label?" He seemed interested then and asked if I would maybe want out-of-date stock. I asked him to explain this and he said that many of the patterns went out of fashion and sometimes they had stocks of these and he thought I might get them for a special price. "With my label on them?" I asked. He said he would make inquiries. When he returned he said he could let me have £500 worth with my label on them and when I did my calculations this worked out I was getting each cap for five shillings. So I said we were in business.'

'Five hundred pounds, Maqbul! How can you get £500?'

'Easy. After we had made a deal I asked him if he would give me credit.'

'And he agreed?'

'That's right. He said that anyone who had the nerve I had deserved to get credit.'

'And this label you will have in your bunnets, Maqbul. What does it say?'

'The same as my business card,' he replied, handing one to Javaid who read the big lettering first.

'Mac Bunnets – Scotland's best'. And in smaller print beneath, 'Proprietor, Mr Mac Bull of The Barrows'.

'Who is Mac Bull?'

'Me, Javaid. Maqbul. Mac Bull. It is easier for them to say. Besides, it makes me sound like one of them for there are lots of Macs here, are there not?'

Javaid grinned. 'I think you'll do well, Mr Mac Bull.'

11

Prosperous Days

The three men, Rasool, Javaid and Maqbul, like hundreds of their fellow countrymen during the late fifties, became firmly established and part of the West of Scotland way of life. And they all prospered, some more than others, much more than they would have had they stayed at home. The fortunes they had come to find were there for the taking, even though to some that simply meant a good roof over their heads, a steady income and not having to worry how they would be able to scrape up enough to feed themselves and any other mouths which depended on them.

It was said that they were greedy for work. Maybe that was right for many of them were getting the chance to see and feel and appreciate equitable sums of money in exchange for their labour and skill. If you were enterprising and brave enough to take on a new country, then you gave of your best in that new land and reaped the rewards.

They had a facile sense of humour that readily blended with the sharp and observant Glasgow wit. They were quick to learn the language, even quicker to adapt to the Glasgow *patois*. Work as conductors and drivers on the public transport was a favourite occupation. There was lots of overtime on the buses and even if they worked double shifts as often as they could, they would be merely approximating the kind of hours they had worked in Pakistan or India. Working hours like that often brought them wages which were twice those of other local workers and that was many times more than they had ever earned in their lives for a week's work.

They preferred to work as conductors rather than drivers. Drivers had a bigger basic wage but because of transport driving regulations which stipulated compulsory rest breaks, they couldn't work as much overtime. A conductor could work a double shift. A driver couldn't. And many of them were more than happy to work double shifts for their six-day working week as well as work the day the transport men called their 'red' day, their official day off and for which their labour drew double-time rates. 'Red' days were good days.

As young men learning about life in the Sub-Continent, they had been indoctrinated with the same ground rules as young men in the older civilisations of Europe about the use of money – if and when they ever got any, that is. The two cardinal rules had always been to invest in bricks and mortar, and gold. The latter was impractical in Britain, so they concentrated on the former. Get your own house quickly, they were told by those who had arrived before them and who themselves had either done just that or were in the process of doing so.

It was easy on the buses to save the £100 deposit that would secure a loan to buy a house, albeit it a humble single room or a room-and-kitchen in the Gorbals or, better still, over the railway tracks and a rung up the property league ladder in the suburb of Govanhill. And when that house was being paid up with their earnings, they would look for another one, the profit from the first helping them on their way. From their single-ends, the little one-roomed houses where you slept, cooked, dined and performed your daily ablutions all in the one tiny apartment, they moved on to room-and-kitchens, the room being bedroom, the kitchen everything else. And after a while that would get them enough to move on to a two-bedroom-and-kitchen flat and on yet again to a pinnacle of local luxury, a two-bedroom-and-kitchen-and-lavatory. Having your very own lavatory inside your own house instead of using the shared one on the stairhead was real luxury in the Gorbals.

Going with the case suited Javaid's way of life. He enjoyed the company of the friendly customers he encountered on his two regular trips to the little working towns in Ayrshire and Renfrewshire. And he in turn became firmly established as one of the most well-known characters in the areas of the two counties which he toured with his case of varied clothing goods.

They knew him as Davie the Paki, Davie being their way of saying David, David their way of saying Javaid. They hadn't heard a name like that before and quickly decided that as the last syllable sounded familiar, then David it must be. Year after year he returned to the same houses. He went to their weddings and often their christenings and was the man who was invited more than any other in the two counties to be with them for the 'first foot' celebrations of Hogmanay, for the custom had it that it should be a dark man that crossed your threshold for the first time in the new year and who better than their Davie? But Scottish merriment and the ways of a Muslim were incompatible and he always declined. However, he was there at most other occasions of their normal lives, awarded the same kind of respect they would give to the local doctor or minister. When the young members of a family started their own homes, Davie the Paki would be the first who would be given their address so that they too could have him as their door-to-door man. They trusted him just as he trusted them. If they wanted credit, he gave it to them and it was always repaid. Relying on turnover more than mark-up for his earnings, he was able to keep his profit to a minimum and give them prices for the vital clothing that no shop could match. If he didn't have their size or colour of shirt or cardigan or lumber jacket the details would be meticulously entered into his notebook and the sought-after object would be there in the case on the next run their way.

Davie never failed them with their orders. Nor did he ever fail to remind them that it was the man of the house's birthday next month and that maybe they would like to order a shirt for him. Details like that were in the notebook too. And there was always a reminder that the school would be restarting after the summer holidays and that now was the time to get orders in for school jumpers and socks. That too, they knew, saved them precious shillings from the prices they would have paid for them in Kilmarnock or Paisley. In the early weeks of December when the first of the tinsel started to appear, Davie would be telling them that the early orders would get the best of the goods for their Christmas-present time.

Such was his success after four years on the road that he no longer had to knock on doors to find potential customers. His regular customers were such that he could rely on them. And his reputation was such that they in turn would bring him other customers. He often found a group of wives waiting for him at one house. 'Having a hens' party, hen?' he would joke with the woman of the house. The hens' parties were good business for Davie and he knew it.

The hours were long, the case was heavy and the weather could be vile. But he was always there, even when the big red Leylands had to follow the snowploughs over the treacherous and desolate Fenwick moor on the Ayrshire run; even when it rained as though one monsoon season was following another – and it could often do that. Despite the snow and the rainstorms and the days when it would be so bitterly cold his hands would be numbed useless, Javaid always remembered his life in the Old City of Lahore when he never knew what the next day might bring . . . if anything.

At least in the wind and the wet, there was always a tomorrow that would be a secure tomorrow, as would the day after that and the one after that. Beyond that there would be even more prosperous days. He was convinced of that, especially when after his fifth year with the case he turned up one week for the start of his regular run in a little Morris Minor van which he proudly pointed out to the customers. '£25 deposit and £2 a week and do you like the way I've got my name written on it?' He had done the signwriting himself, the bold letters proclaiming 'Davie's for Clothing. Wholesale and Retail'.

It was the word 'wholesale' that was most important to him. He explained that to his customers. 'You see that means I'll be dealing from now on with the manufacturers and selling to the shops as well as to my customers. I won't need to go to Ashrif or the other wholesalers in Glasgow for my goods. I'll be dealing direct and you'll get a better selection.' They liked the sound of that. It also meant that there would be more profit for Javaid with his being able to cut out the middle man. But first he had to persuade the manufacturers that he was a big enough fish for them to deal with. It wasn't to be so easy. Writing the name 'wholesale' on the side of his van was one thing. Making it a fact was another.

It was Maqbul who had advised him on going direct to the factories or the mills to buy his goods. But it was to take six months after buying his little van before he eventually persuaded one manufacturer that he would be a reliable customer.

He had called regularly during that time to the many knitwear factories in Ayrshire. Most had refused to even speak to him. But he had expected that. Rasool had told him that it was not the way of small Scottish salesmen like them to go knocking on the door of the factories. The manufacturers had agents who dispensed their goods to the wholesalers.

'At the same time, that is where we have an advantage,' Rasool had said. 'We do not have the constraints of the Scottish businessman and the way he does his trading. We are a part of their community but in matters like this we can practise the customs of our homeland. We have the culture of the entrepreneur and we must use it to the best of our ability.'

That ability was put to its full use as Javaid toured the factories. One after another refused to even speak to the one-man entrepreneur who was determined to become a success in the clothing trade. At each refusal he was always optimistic enough to believe that it would be the next factory where he would get a deal.

At Stewarton, the little mill town near Kilmarnock, the optimism looked as though it would pay off. A haughty-looking woman in her mid-fifties had a headmistress scorn in her voice as she chided him. 'You know, we never speak to travellers or others who call without an appointment. I mean to say, we are one of the biggest knitwear manufacturers in the county. We're very busy, you know. And we usually ask for references before we even speak to a new customer.'

Javaid was unperturbed. He had got past the reception desk and was speaking to the company sales director, Miss Marjory Morton. He had called at the same factory three times before but didn't mention that. On Maqbul's advice he had had business cards printed and Miss Morton held one in her hand. The big print read, 'Davie's for Clothing', just like it said on the side of his Morris Minor. Beneath in smaller print were the words, 'Wholesale and retail specialists in knitwear and cottons throughout the West of Scotland'. And in the bottom right-hand corner – 'Managing Director, Mr J. Khan, 27, Nicholson Street, Gorbals, Glasgow'.

'Well, we don't often have managing directors actually calling on us,' said Miss Morton.

'We're just a small company,' Javaid smiled.

'How small?'

'Very small. But very well known.'

'How well known?'

'Missus,' said Javaid in an accent that was more Galston than Gorbals, 'you can ask them from one end of the Irvine Valley to the other or from Paisley down to Beith about Davie's Clothing. There's nobody more well known.'

'And your company premises. Nicholson Street, is that right?'

'Aye, that's right. That's my company headquarters.'

'The minimum order we would even consider would be 300 dozen.'

Unflinchingly, Javaid smiled and nodded in approval with not a hint of the problem he would have in storing such an order. But he knew by the way she was talking that not only did he have one foot in the door now, both feet were now there and the awesome Miss Morton, he was convinced, would make him a deal.

'You see, we have two agents who handle all we can make. They're based in England and make a fortune from us in commission. And all of our goods only go to the best of shops . . . House of Fraser, Selfridge's, Harrods, places like that. Davie's Clothing is hardly our market. I mean, what would the stores' buyers think if they discovered we were dealing with . . .' she paused searching for an appropriate term . . . 'with, eh, a little company from the Glasgow Gorbals?'

He felt one of his feet going out of the door again. But she is still talking, he thought to himself. Why? There must be something she wants to tell me or else she wouldn't be giving me so much time. They don't like giving you their time, some of these people. Maybe there really is something in the wind.

'And besides,' she went on, 'much of our produce is made exclusively to order. Some ladies, you know, do like to think that if they buy fashionwear in Harrods, they're not likely to find it being worn by ladies who got it elsewhere.'

'This Harrods, miss. Where is it?'

Her eyes widened in amazement. 'Goodness gracious,' she exlaimed. 'Harrods. *The* Harrods. My dear man, Harrods is in London. It's the finest store in Great Britain.'

'But my customers are in Lochwinnoch and Darvel. They're

not likely to be meeting the wives that buy the stuff in London, are they?'

The point wasn't taken.

'What I was going to say, Mr Khan . . . We do occasionally have a surplus order in stock. And as a matter of fact I know there's one at this very moment. It's a beautiful line of cardigans. Three hundred dozen. They were made for one of the stores down south but it would be indiscreet for me to say which one. There's an agent coming to see me tomorrow about new orders and I know they could be away with him.'

'They could be away with me today,' he quickly replied.

Both feet were firmly back in the door.

The little van had never been so loaded, the cartons of cardigans squeezed into every inch of space, including the passenger seat. Others were tied to the roof rack.

Maqbul was at home that night when he arrived at the tenement houses where they lived, number 27 Nicholson Street, the same address that was listed as the headquarters of 'Davie's for Clothing'. With the help of Mr and Mrs Fayyaz, the two men carried the boxes up to company headquarters, the room-and-kitchen house in which Javaid stayed with the couple. They piled the boxes into the little bedroom of the house where Javaid slept, stacking them floor to ceiling, and when they were finished there was only room enough for the door to open about eighteen inches, leaving a narrow corridor of space to the bed.

Afterwards they had a meal in the kitchen which doubled as a bedroom for the Fayyazes. 'Do you know,' said Javaid, 'that's my biggest ever business deal. Three hundred dozen . . . I still can't believe it. And I've got them for fourteen shillings and sixpence each. I'll be able to add a shilling on to that for profit which will make me a total of £180. One hundred and eighty pounds. I normally have to work for weeks to get that. It's more money than I've ever made in my life.'

'They must have cost you an awful lot of money to buy,' said the man of the house.

'That's right. The invoice is for two thousand six hundred and ten pounds.'

The man shook his head in disbelief. 'Where did you get that kind of money?'

'He would get credit,' came in Maqbul.

'That's right,' said Javaid. 'As soon as the sales director at the factory said I could have an order, I asked straight away for credit. It was a woman I was dealing with. I think she liked me for she didn't even hesitate when I asked.'

'How long did you get?' asked Maqbul.

'Three months.'

'You're right. She must have liked you.'

Javaid was back in Stewarton six weeks later to call at the same factory again. The week before he had sent them a banker's draft for the cost of his first order. He had sold every one of the cardigans in just over three weeks, enrolling for himself a string of shops in the southern suburbs of Glasgow as customers of his new wholesale agency and telling them that he could get plenty more good-quality produce just like the cardigans. He had also kept back a supply for his door-to-door customers who eagerly snapped them up. Davie the Clothier now really was a wholesaler as well as a retailer.

Miss Morton was slightly better disposed towards Javaid on his second call and was quick to tell him about a surplus order of lumber jackets. 'Absolutely top end of the market stuff,' she said, which was true. 'And absolutely the height of fashion' – which wasn't true. The fact was that they were surplus from a previous year's order which had been sold at a fifty per cent mark-up because they were of a fashion range which had to be moved quickly. One batch hadn't gone quick enough and because of the height-of-fashion angle the agents didn't want them any more. But what might be out of fashion on the London scene could be *haute couture* in the southern suburbs of Glasgow and the absolute ultimate in Lochwinnoch or Darvel.

'I had half promised them to another long-standing customer . . . but you did meet your bill very quickly, Mr Khan,' she said. 'But you'll have to take them all. I can't let them go in small lots.'

'How many?'

'It's a 600-dozen order.'

Javied tried to hide his glee at getting such an order while at the same time wondering how he could possibly accommodate twice the amount of goods that he had last taken home.

'That should be no problem to a company like mine,' he replied cheerfully. 'We're getting more and more customers so I won't have them for long. But I'll only take half of them today and return tomorrow for the other half. We have a little transport problem at the moment with the company. You know how it is! Usual credit terms?'

'That'll be all right, Mr Khan. You're a customer of standing now.'

Maqbul and the other couple helped him once again to carry the boxes of lumber jackets up to the bedroom. Then Javaid broke the news to Maqbul that he would require to use his bedroom also to store his goods.

'You've got a problem, then,' said Maqbul. 'I've got a big order coming as well. Ties and scarves as well as bunnets.'

'Ties and scarves?' queried Javaid. 'You're the bunnet man, Maqbul.'

'Yes, but I'm going to be more than that from now. I've got another stall at The Barrows and I'm adding them to my range. The man at the factory in Bridgeton with whom I deal for my bunnets told me about his friend at a mill in Paisley when I said I wanted to do more goods. So I went to see him and I got a big order from him. So I'm going wholesale too . . . just like you, Javaid.'

'Then we've got a problem?'

'What do you mean . . .we?'

'Well, you're wholesale in scarves, ties and bunnets. I've got knitwear and will soon be getting shirts as well. Why don't we team together? We could get our own store and supply more and more shops with a real variety of clothing. With my van I could still do my rounds in the country and you could keep on your stalls at The Barrows.'

Maqbul was silent for a few seconds. 'Why didn't I think of that sooner?' he then replied. 'You people from the Old City . . . I must say you've got enterprise.'

'We had to have enterprise, Maqbul, or else we didn't live. Do you know there was one trader I knew and he thought up this idea to get a living? We called him the dirty rupees man. He traded clean rupee notes for dirty ones. He would give you 99

clean notes for 100 dirty ones. Then he would have them
laundered and sell them again, 99 for 100. But he made a living
from his one-rupee-at-a-time profit. And there was another who,
like the rupees man, had no possessions or skills. What he did
was to go about the city looking for a suitable hole in the
pavement. One just over a foot across would do him. Then he
would fill it with charcoal which he would burn and into which
he would roast spiced sweetcorn to sell. You see, he couldn't
even afford a little stove like the other roast sweetcorn vendors so
he just went about from one hole in the pavement to another. It
was from people like that and many, many others that I learned
about enterprise, Maqbul. There's always a way to earn money,
especially here where they don't have to go around trading old
currency or looking for holes in the pavement.'

'No, the *gora* are not like that, Javaid. Are they? All they want
is a boss to work for. They don't seem to want to be independent
like you and me.'

'Oh, that's just their ways.'

'What shall we call our business then?' inquired Maqbul
enthusiastically.

'M and D Supplies sounds good to me.'

'You mean M and J . . . Maqbul and Javaid.'

'You're forgetting, Maqbul. We're Mac and Davie.'

Maqbul laughed loudly. 'Aye, Davie,' he said still laughing, 'I
did forget. I often forget we're not in Pakistan any more.'

The following day they went in search of a store. They didn't
have to look far and found premises less than a hundred yards
from their weekly Jamiat fellowship house in Oxford Street. It
was a former spirit dealer's and consisted of a small office, a
telephone, two filing cabinets and three big store rooms. M & D
had found a home.

A year later, the partners were on the move again. The success
of M & D was beyond even their optimism. Freed of wartime
and post-war restrictions, there was a boom in the clothing trade
and M & D were riding high on it.

'This time we'll buy a property,' insisted Javaid. 'No more lost
money with a rented place.'

Their new headquarters were in Bridge Street, one of the
commercial hubs of the Gorbals. The building had formerly been

a busy department store and offered them three floors of storage space with offices and other facilities. It cost them £8,000 but there was no problem in securing a loan from their bank, not every local manager having such a highly successful company on his books. They had the front of the building flamboyantly decorated with the parent name of the company, M & D Supplies. A brass plaque at the main entrance also displayed the name as being their registered office and beneath the names of their subsidiary companies – M & D Fashions, M & D Mantles, Mac's Caps Ltd and Daviewear Knits Ltd.

Both of the men had moved away from the Gorbals, Javaid to an expansive semi-detached villa in Maxwell Drive, Pollokshields, and Maqbul to a similar residence in Newlands, a prosperous suburb on the south of the city.

Rasool was proud of the achievement of his two friends, he himself having further prospered over the years. The leather goods he had imported from Pakistan had met with tremendous success and he now had a team of salesmen working for him throughout Britain to secure new orders while he made extensive tours of Europe, establishing offices in Lille and Ghent. The name Russell was to stick with him which was why he had called his company Russell Imports, and then eventually Russell Imports and Exports.

The three had become something of a legend in their own community in Glasgow. While most had thrived and blossomed in so many ways, few had done so well as the three. When they met for gossips at the halal butchers or the Jamiat, newcomers would be told over and over again the stories of Javaid, the boy from the Old City who could neither read or write when he arrived, Maqbul, the poor farmer's son from Gujrat who had spent his early days behind a buffalo and a crude plough, and Rasool, the rich man's son who, following the agonies of Partition, had been left with nothing except a brilliant education and native enterprise and was now a very rich man with one of the best houses in Pollokshields, and for the men who did the double shifts on the buses as well as work their 'red' days, the three men were an inspiration and a lesson that they were, indeed, as they had been so often told, in the land of plenty.

While their language and dress and manners and ways had

become that of the born Briton, and in the case of Maqbul and Javaid, the born Glaswegian, their beliefs were still those of Islam. The outer man was of the West; the inner man of the East. They subscribed to the five pillars of their religion, that of belief, of prayer, of fasting during the holy month, of giving to the poor and of the pilgrimage to their Holy Land, only Rasool having so far accomplished that latter object.

When Maqbul became the first of the three to marry, it was to be the Islamic way. He had asked his elder brother in Gujrat to arrange a suitable woman to be his bride and in due course the beautiful Meera, ten years younger than he was, had arrived. They had exchanged photographs prior to that, as well as letters, and Javaid had joked with him about her picture. 'You know they pay special fees to the photographers who specialise in making ugly women beautiful? Others send the pictures of their younger sister, you know,' he had said. But Meera had been everything that her photograph had conveyed.

The women displayed the real distinction between East and West. When the men came, they had the freedom to work in public places, as with the bus and Underground crews. They could wear Western dress and, with the exception of taking alcohol, could participate in most of the customs and ways of their new homeland. But not so the women.

The women of Islam have a much more special place in their society than the female Protestant or Catholic or Jew. For centuries the cultures of the East and the West have chosen different routes in their attitude towards the female. The gap is now such that there can be great difficulty in one trying to comprehend the ways of the other. Who of the West can understand why a woman can have her marriage partner chosen for her? Why must she dress herself so that all the attributes that are normally considered those of beauty and sexual appeal must be permanently hidden from all, except those of her own household? Who can comprehend that a woman must never leave her own home or invite anyone to it without the permission of her husband and that when she does, her face must be covered and her eyes are only for sight and must never meet the eyes of another man? Who can agree with a society that confined its wives to a near-Carmelite social order, forever garbed like technicolour nuns? Who can reason that adultery is no mere social sin but a punishable crime of the state to be equated with the same kind of loathing as the rapist? Who can appreciate that the woman divorced is a woman shamed and must for the rest of her life live out that shame?

The Eastern mind can understand all of those things. The Western mind cannot.

Likewise, who of the East can understand the way of life where the sex object dominates? Who of the East can accept a pattern of life where there is such a flagrant fixation on sex? How can it be reasoned that a civilised society emphasises so much on the female that flaunts, the male that taunts? What is to be made of a culture that seems besotted with beauty and the breast? How can it be explained that the sexual drive should be the ruling force of dress, of the media, of commerce, of music? Why is it that sexual inequality is based on biological inferiority?

The Western mind can understand all of those things. The Eastern mind cannot.

Meera went to stay with the Fayyaz family, Javaid's old friends, in Nicholson Street when she arrived. They acted as her local parents and together with some of the other women of the community she went through all the various pre-marriage rites and customs of their society in Pakistan. She had brought with her the various coloured clothes which it is ordained be worn during these ceremonies, including the mustard dress to be used throughout the first week of confinement with her adoptive parents during which she must not speak with outsiders of the house.

She had to stay there too when Mr and Mrs Fayyaz paid the prescribed visit to the house of Maqbul, followed by a return visit to the Fayyazes' house the next day by a couple who took the role of Maqbul's mother and father. They touched her hands symbolically with the henna which gives the visit its name, the *Mehndi*. When the visits were over some women then gathered at the Fayyaz home to perform the long and tedious rite of decorating the bride's hands and feet with henna. She wore yellow clothing for this and the process took so long, because of the elaborate and intricate patterns to be woven on her skin with the henna, that she had to be fed throughout the day, unable to feed herself less she smudge the dark red dye.

The pre-marital customs went into a second week during which a priest visited both bride and groom to ascertain if each really wished to marry the other. The groom then paid his respects to the home of the bride and after that she attended a reception at his house accompanied by all her friends. Rasool and Javaid were there and they joked among themselves about which one of them would be next to marry. Rasool pointed at Javaid and assured everyone that he would be the next to take a bride.

'I'm already married . . . to my business,' pleaded Rasool, then added for emphasis, 'And what's more, we love each other very much.'

'But a Muslim can take a second wife,' said Maqbul.

'That is true . . . but only if he can afford the second wife and not neglect his first. I would really hate to neglect my first.'

The smiles and jokes hid a moment of private grief for Rasool as he remembered his own marriage and the happy year they had spent together before that tragic day when she and their baby had died in childbirth. It had been one of the happiest years of his life, and despite what he said about loving his work, he envied Maqbul and his bride.

BOOK III

12

Friendly Advice

She had only occasionally returned to the 'girls' coffee morning which they held weekly in the houses of nearby neighbours in the best part of Pollokshields, where the houses were the grandest – four to the acre, sometimes just three, now and then two, and the very best having a football pitch of their own as the measurement of a back garden. All, of course, were designed by the very best of Victorian architects, Clifford and Rowan and Turnbull, and the one they called 'Greek' Thomson; men who created beauty from stone and mortar with love and devotion, just as Delacroix or Gainsborough or Rubens did with oil and canvas. But Star had made a point of keeping in regular contact, sometimes by telephone, other times with visits, to Janice Kyle's house in nearby St Andrew's Drive. She had liked Janice from that first meeting at her 'coffee' and the feeling was mutual. Janice, worldly and urbane, was everything Star's mother Isa hadn't been. She felt a comfort just being in her presence: she was someone who was rational and wise and in whose counsel she could trust. Star could never have confided in her mother, she could with Janice. She could never have explained to Isa about the complexities of business life or the intricacies of her Uncle Sammy's character or the shortcomings of her own love life. She could speak about all of these things with the utmost of confidence to Janice.

'Your uncle seems a fascinating man in many ways,' said Janice that afternoon in her house when the two of them had one of their regular meetings over a coffee, Janice proudly flourishing the glass jug of steaming black liquid before her. 'Like it? It's my new cona pot. Percolators are finished, darling. They stain and give the coffee an acidy flavour. So the salesman said anyway when I bought this at Wylie and Lochhead's. Your Uncle Sammy . . . yes. What an amazing story. Absolutely amazing.'

Star had been telling her about the man called Holden and the

129

drama of the murders, although she judiciously censored the part about Sammy's refusal to go into detail about Holden's own death.

'And imagine him running his business all those years and not being really involved. I assume, Star, that you reassured him that his ways weren't actually the cause of what had happened.'

'Well, not really. I mean, I suppose in a way they were responsible for what happened. Just like he said, had he not done some of the things he did, then he would never have come into contact with this terrible man Holden.'

'That's only true in a sense, Star. But one is what one is. You are what you are. Every single thing or action you take in life affects someone, somewhere. The only remedy to not influencing others in life is to be locked away in a room the moment you are born. And even that would affect someone . . . the parents who brought you into the world for a start. There is no escape from being a part of the life of others, and of others being a part of your own life. Of course, one can change one's lifestyle and by doing so you can affect others in a different way. But then who's to say that different way would be a better way or the right way? Jesus had a good effect on those with whom he came into contact, apart from the Romans that is. But look at the effect some of his followers have on each other. Catholics and Protestants and all that nonsense. So while one can set out to be a good influence in life, that good can so easily be perverted. I don't think your uncle should blame himself for what happened. He didn't create it. He was merely a cog in the wheel of life, part of a pattern into which Holden and all the others fitted. Your uncle is certainly a more complex person than I think he even realises himself. But fascinating just the same. I think even Mr Freud would have a few comments to make about him.'

'I wonder what he would have to say about all those I've encountered who are on the make in one way or another. All those schemes they've devised, the effort they go to . . . for what? A penny here, a penny there. It's so cheapskate. So petty. Is that the way we are? Us Glasgow people? Us Scots? How often do you hear them say they can get you such and such, but don't ask any questions where it came from? Or else they'll wink that it fell off the back of a lorry. Cheating and pilfering . . .it's all so acceptable. It's the normal way of life for them.'

'Oh, I do know what you mean. I've even heard hubby Harold speak about similar things going on among the chaps at the golf club.' She paused at that to take up a mocking West End accent. 'And at Whitecraigs of all places!'

They laughed together then Janice said, 'But, seriously, I do know what you are getting at. I just wonder if it's in our character or is it in the character of people of a certain class? It's difficult to talk about class without being accused of snobbery, but let's face it, whether we like it or not our little country is as riddled with it as anywhere. And if anyone has a need to try and wangle themselves that little bit extra, it's surely the working class. I don't fiddle anyone because I don't need to. But I remember Harold telling me about his experiences in Paris where he used to work in the summer vacation when he was at university. He had a job as a waiter and he said that in lots of restaurants they wouldn't let them work with their shirt sleeves rolled down in case they hid stolen money in the cuffs. And the patron of the premises or his closest relative always sat at the till. Perhaps what you feel about us or certain sections of us is in fact the same the world over?'

'Maybe you're right, Janice. I know I can be quite critical about us at times but I think one of our problems is that we're far too uncritical of ourselves. We delude ourselves that we're great . . . great like we used to be. And we were great . . . weren't we? All those incredible explorers and scientists and doctors and inventors and evangelists all coming from this little country. I bet they didn't come from a society whose minds were concentrated on the next deceit that would make them a couple of pennies.'

'Yes, maybe you have a point, Star. Maybe you do.'

It was Star who changed the subject. 'How are all the coffee morning crowd?' explaining before she could get an answer that she would have been to more than the occasional one herself had it not been for the pressure of their expanding business.

'The girls don't change all that much,' said Janice. 'You know, they've all got the usual problems. Jane can't make up her mind whether to go on a Mediterranean cruise or take a villa at Cannes for the summer holidays. Shirley's husband wants to make their attic into a snooker suite but she says she would rather make it into a self-contained flat for grandma. Imagine sticking granny in the attic? I ask you! And Sandra is in a dilemma whether to go for fox, lynx or mink for her new coat. Oh dear, we girls in the 'Shields do have some terrible problems.'

After a good laugh together, Janice continued with all the latest gossip. 'Do you know about the new neighbour round the corner in Nithsdale Road? Remember there was a coloured family there? Well, they're away. Gone back to India or Pakistan or wherever. The house has been bought by another Asian family. The girls think it's a family, that is, but they say it is only a man that has been spotted so far. Sandra seems to know something about him for he's had dealings with her husband Daniel. He's an importer of some kind. They call him Mr Russell. I didn't know they had our names . . . did you? Anyway, according to Sandra who's met him, he's a bit of a smasher, as they say. But you know Sandra! Can't take her eyes off the men. Speaking about men, Star, what about yourself? No one calling for tea these days?'

'No . . . no one, Janice. Doesn't seem to worry me either. Maybe it might if I had more time on my hands. But the business is the greatest thing that's ever happened to me. I'm the happiest I've been since the time during the war when I lived in the country. I stayed at a farm and used to work at all sorts of things and it gave me a great sense of satisfaction. After that there seemed to be a great void in my life until Uncle Sammy came on the scene and changed everything. Maybe running a chain of lounge bars doesn't seem much of a challenge, but believe me it is. I'm helping them with the designs of some of the places now. They need the old female touch, you know. You should see the garishness of some of the others. And their colour schemes! Maybe my work has become a love substitute.'

'Be careful about that, my dear. That happened to my lovely Aunt Ellie. She got involved in the family business. Beautiful girl she was. Then one day, as she told us herself, she wakened up and realised she was fifty . . . and never had a lover. Bit late trying to look for one at that age. Men are not without their problems . . . God, I know that with my Harold at times. But then, there can be bigger problems when women are without men. So don't you be like my old aunt, Star. There are other things in life than work.'

132

13

A Holy Policeman

Superintendent Tom Graham of the Central Division Criminal Investigation Department looked more like the man from the Prudential than the police. His soft hat had once had a shape but was now a part of him, as was the shabby and unbuttoned gaberdine raincoat with its redundant belt flapping in the wind and the shallow-bowled pipe which had become as much a fixture to his face as was his nose or chin or ears. Without them he could walk past his best friends unrecognised. He had a gaunt and pallid face and his frail body was such that it was a standing joke at the Central Police Headquarters that a good feed would have killed him. But they didn't make many other jokes about Graham. For there were none more dedicated, few more competent in all of Glasgow's constabulary than was Graham as a detective.

Tom Graham was about goodness as he saw it and that was the way the Church of Scotland saw it. Goodness was about the Sabbath and the Ten Commandments and being a good Protestant, and the emphasis of that word was in the protest. It was about those who had protested and still protested about the ways of that other church, the one of Rome.

He loved his work which he carried out with a passion and zeal that only a man with a cause could do, his cause being that he saw himself not so much as a detective of the City of Glasgow, but as a policeman of the Kingdom of God. When he had been a uniformed man he took as much delight in arresting Sunday street footballers or illicit Sabbath pub drinkers as he would some serious weekday felon. He never openly showed any prejudice towards non-Protestants, but those few senior policemen who were really close to him had noted over the years his interest in inquiring which school a suspect had attended and the way his eyebrows would arch if they were after someone called Michael or Brian or Patrick.

With some other top-ranking detectives, Superintendent Graham had been summoned for a conference with the Chief Constable. All of them had been actively engaged for the past year in gathering evidence about the tallymen, the illegal moneylenders who were operating extensively in the south side of the city. Such practices had begun in the Gorbals, just like cholera and the waves of poxes that area had known. There had been various tallymen who operated the evil trade in the years before the war and older ones could tell you they were doing it prior to the war before that as well. But this time it was different. In the past it had never been highly organised, merely a few individuals, each of them vicious and ruthless men who would willingly maim or murder to enforce their collection of debts with extortionate interest. Now there was a whole network of them masterminded with an efficiency that was rare for the Glasgow criminal.

No matter what cases they had been working on, everything, said the Chief Constable, had to take second place to rooting out the tallymen. His crime graphs had been soaring because of them and he was being sorely pressed by the Corporation's Police Committee, one of whom had been particularly caustic in his aspersions about the efficiency not only of the Chief Constable but of his entire detective force. He had hammered home that point to the senior men before him.

'I know you've never done it before, but get out there and into the pubs and make speeches and appeal to them for their help. There must be dozens of witnesses who have either seen, heard or been victims of the louts who are running this racket. I'm told it's Riley and his mob who are behind it. Yet there's not one statement, not one witness, and as a result we've got the worst crime wave we've known in the city since the war. I'm telling you, each and every one of you, questions are being asked in high places about us and our methods. For God's sake, get out there and get these people.'

'For God's sake!' 'For God's sake!' Tom Graham kept repeating the words to himself. They didn't have to say 'For God's sake' to him. Everything he did was for the sake of God. But if the Chief Constable was also feeling that this cause really was for the sake of God! Well . . . so be it.

Usually-when Tom Graham went into a public house looking for information he would have a quiet drink by himself, Mackeson's sweet stout, nothing else, and such was his insignificance he could stand alone listening to various conversations, no one ever paying attention to him: the invisible man with a glass of black stout. This time, however, on the instruction of his Chief and in the name of God, Graham was going public.

Accompanied by another detective he began a tour of some of the heartland Gorbals pubs, pubs with names that ranged from the ordinary, like Jackson's, Morrison's, Munro's and Watt's, to the extraordinary, like The Bible Class, The Why Not, The Hole in the Wall and the Glue Pot. There were over a hundred of them, but Graham and his colleague concentrated on the ones about which they had received information on the presence of the tallymen.

When they went into the first of these pubs, the detective accompanying Graham had a few words with the manager before the Superintendent took a chair, placed it in the middle of the bar and stood on it, much to the surprise of the drinkers. A mutter of reaction went round, with the usual witticisms . . . 'Some bam's gonnie gie us a song' . . . 'Bet he's a Holy Joe telling us Christ didnae drink'. . . 'Ah think he's gonnie stand us a' a drink' . . .

'Can I have your attention, please!' And in an instant the pub silenced.

Graham liked that. There was almost a gospeller feel about getting such immediate and devout attention. 'My name is Tom Graham. Superintendent Tom Graham of the Central Division CID. And I need your help. We know that a vicious gang of tallymen are operating in this area. We know they've been operating in this and several other pubs in the Gorbals. We know who some of them are and the kind of terrible tactics they've been up to. I know too that some of you here will know all about them. That some of you will have seen them in operation. That some of you may have friends who have had dealings with them. That some of you yourselves may have recourse to use their services. And it's those of you who have information such as this that we want. Just in case some of you don't know the methods of these tallymen, let me spell it out to you. They're charging four shillings in the pound interest rates. If you miss a payment it goes up to eight shillings in the pound. Miss it again and it's up to twelve shillings . . . for your one borrowed pound. And if you miss any more after that, then we'll be picking up what's left of you from some back close or lane. I don't need to tell you that's why Harry Hudson was found murdered on the pavement outside his house in Kidston Street. Everyone knew he was in debt to them and couldn't pay them back. And how do you account for all these robberies and muggings that are going on? That's being done by people desperate for the money to repay these gangsters. I'm telling you, they're the worst bunch of neds that's ever operated in the Gorbals. And that's saying something. Unless we weed them out now there'll be a lot more of you getting involved with them. But we must, I repeat must, have witnesses. That's why I'm making this appeal to you. Obviously I'm not expecting anyone to come forward here and now. But you can get me anytime on the 999 emergency phone system. Just ask the operator for the police. Then ask for me. Tom Graham. Superintendent Tom Graham of the Central CID.'

The silence of the staring faces continued for a few seconds after he got down from the chair to join the other policeman. It was the wisecrackers who were first to begin the rumble of conversation . . .'He'd have got pennies thrown at him if he was at the Empire' . . . 'A thought he was gonnie gie us *The Sash*' . . . 'There was me thinking that tallymen was Gizzi and a' that mob that sells ice cream and that.' Soon the laughter and the banter made it the normal Glasgow pub again. But there were those who remained alone and silent long afterwards, staring at the umbilical drinks which sustained their lives. There were always men like that in Glasgow pubs.

Tom Graham looked at the other detective and shook his head as they left the pub. 'Have you ever in all your life seen such a bunch of woodenheads? What a right lot of gangrels. Not a bit of emotion, not a glimmer of response . . . not even a glint in an eye from one of them. I knew that's what we would get. But still, that's what the Chief wants us to do so we'd better get on to the next pub.'

Sonny Riley laughed out loud that night when they told him in the Old Judge bar about the activities of the various senior policemen around the pubs. The Old Judge in Lawmoor Street was as decrepit as the tenement under which it squatted. An ugly brown water stain surrounded an area of what had once been ornate plaster but had been flushed away with the continuous coursing of water which had seeped down over the years from the top of the building through the little houses on the three floors above, making a similar mess in each of them.

Sonny Riley had become a part of the living folklore of the Gorbals of the fifties. Every generation had them. To understand Riley, you had to understand the Gorbals. The Gorbals was about many things. It was about goodness and heart where you could still leave the key in your door and your house would be safe. It was about neighbours who cared for neighbours and a helping hand never far away. It was of character and of characters. It was a showcase of the human spirit in glorious triumph over adversity. Adversity! The Gorbals was about adversity all right, the City Council itself confessing that on the dawn of the sixties in the heart of the suburb 63 per cent of the houses were unfit for sanitary or structural reasons. And 99 per cent of the houses were of the lowest structural category, that category being just one higher than the stage where they fell down. They knew about adversity all right.

The Gorbals was about a lot of good people. It was also about a few bad people – about men like Sonny Riley. Sonny too was about the human spirit in adversity, but in his case it was what happens to that spirit when it doesn't triumph, when it crumples and degenerates to a state where the only morality is immorality: where badness is goodness, where evil is virtue. Sonny was a corrupt version of the old Gorbals hard man, the warrior of the streets who with fist and foot and knife and razor lived a life of confrontation with other similar hard men demonstrating the only way they knew that they were king. Their battles were among themselves, and the respect they had in the community was for what they did in those duels. Their names and their deeds became legends that were spoken of through the generations.

Jamesie Nelson had been one back in the twenties and they still spoke about him. Sonny Riley, in his twisted way, thought he was one. But what Jamesie Nelson was, Sonny Riley wasn't.

137

The character of Riley had been forged in a single-roomed house in Camden Street, not far from the Old Judge pub, and where he had been born just before the war. Life had been a struggle for survival from infancy, as it was for so many others. The house had been shared with six other children, a hapless mother and a moronic stepfather who had only two expressions in life, hatred and violence, varying only in degree according to the amount of drink he had consumed. That same unfathomable hatred coupled with his unpredictable violence had made Sonny the most feared man in the neighbourhood.

Only the hard men had feared Nelson and his like, for it was only them that had anything to fear from what he might do. But everyone feared Riley, for no one was safe from what he might do. He used to laugh as a teenager when he robbed old women or beat stooped men to the ground for their coppers. Once, just to demonstrate the terror he possessed, he ran the length of three blocks of busy Crown Street near where he lived slashing at everyone in sight with a pair of open razors. The ultimate in bravado and defiance to him were the ones who would occasionally run on to the football pitch at the Ibrox or Parkhead stadiums and gesture to the opposing fans that they would single-handed take them all on, all 30,000 of them. He had performed his own version of that in the Gorbals when he went to an area dominated by a rival gang, stood in the middle of the road and challenged them all to come and get him. They did. And that accounted for some of the scars his still boyish face displayed. It was said that he only did such things because of his enormous consumption of beer and amphetamine pills, the current method of what to many was escape from the inescapable.

It was Sonny Riley who had organised the Gorbals tallymen, a simple form of applied intelligence in which the equation was that intimidation and violence equalled money. There was nothing complicated about their system: they were uncomplicated men. They made it known there was money always readily available for the borrowing. You need give them no guarantee, nor name them any guarantor. You were the guarantee. You were the guarantor. And the collateral? That was your fear. For they always made it publicly known that when someone was found in a tenement back court or in one of the tracery of quiet lanes behind busy streets with a face that would never look the same again, it was because his collateral had expired: he was an unfortunate who had confused the extendable with the expendable.

The rules were simple: twenty per cent per week or, in more simple terms, which they preferred, four bob in the pound, doubling up every week. So the bottle of fortified wine for which you craved and cost the pound you didn't have could be got immediately with a loan. And you paid them back one pound and four shillings the following week or one pound and eight shillings if you waited till the week after that.

Riley now never handled any of the actual loan money, neither giving it out nor collecting it back. He had started the racket in the Old Judge public house, the demand making him realise the potential. Thereafter it went from pub to pub, a corrupt contagion that emanated from the diseased mind of one man. But it could only be operated in a particular pub with his approval and, of course, provided they paid him a stipulated amount based on what he reckoned the pub to be worth as a loan centre. He had put his fear on franchise and no one was to step out of line. Two did by extending the sanctioned operation they had in one pub into a nearby pub without informing him. Riley himself led a team against them, all of them armed with heavy joiners' hammers. The police found the two beaten victims on the street later that night, one of them dying from his wounds a day later, the other, his legs so badly smashed he was never able to walk again. The attack had taken place outside the busy pub at the 9.30 closing time and had been witnessed by dozens of men. No one came forward with information about the attack. Another who had tried a one-man operation on his own had to have his hands prised from the bar of the Bundoran public house to which they had been tortuously affixed with six-inch nails. The man told the police that he didn't recognise any of his assailants.

The whole crime pattern of the Gorbals changed drastically as a result of Riley and the tallymen. Desperate to repay their loans, customers resorted to violence themselves. Keys were no longer left in door locks or house doors left open as burglaries, petty thieving, assault and robbery figures soared. It was as though a pestilence had descended upon them: the Gorbals was in its dying days and one man was making that death an agony.

The police toured the bars of the Gorbals and the other neighbouring districts for nearly three weeks in their unique attempt to try to win the vital information that would pin the man they already knew to be the originator of the corrupt trade that had affected so many lives. There were the usual number of anonymous calls, all of which named Riley. More important, there were two calls from witnesses who said they would not only name Riley but testify against him, provided they were given some kind of protection and helped to leave Scotland afterwards. One wanted to go back to his home in Ireland, the other chose to be in London. Promises were given.

Tom Graham's eyebrows went into that familiar arch when he went over Riley's criminal record for the first time. As always, he had noted the school . . . St John's Boy's School, Portugal Street, Gorbals, which was part of one of the three Roman Catholic parishes of the area. His record was more than impressive. It started at the age of eleven when he was sent to an Approved School for stabbing a youth in a gang fight, then there were further terms for more acts of violence, Barlinnie at eighteen for a murder charge that had been reduced by varying stages to one of being part of a disorderly affray, another murder charge which again had been reduced to serious assault, whereupon Graham shook his head and cursed a legal system which he and many of his police officer colleagues said was designed in favour of the villain and not the victim. That last reduced murder charge had got him two years. There was another eighteen months for an assault and robbery and a three-year sentence for yet another gang fight assault, that period being served at the Alcatraz of Scottish prisons, Peterhead, a lonely and forbidden outpost in the north-east of Scotland. So Sonny had made it to the highest university of Scottish penitentiaries.

Graham had hurried through the file at first quickly noting the school then running his eyes over the long list of previous convictions. Then he went over it for a second time in order to digest it more thoroughly, memorising each word as he read it over to himself.

Steven Riley or Holden. Alias 'Sonny'. Born 5/9/34. Father Steven Holden. Stepfather Francis Gerard Riley. Mother Bernadette Riley or Holden née Docherty. The eyebrows arched again. Then he looked at the pictures accompanying the file, expecting the usual stare, the customary tight and menacing lips. They were told not to smile, but somehow Riley had managed to defy them and get his cocky grin in the picture. Handsome bugger, thought Graham. Not the usual-looking ned. But then do they have to be?

When they received the information that Riley had made his headquarters in the Old Judge bar, Graham had four plainclothes policemen posted there, working in teams of two. They had to take very special care over their disguises as strangers in bars like the Old Judge were forever noted, often suspected, always resented. A bar was a place of familiar faces so that it took on a pattern, each lunchtime and evening session having its own personality make-up. The real regulars could quickly run their eyes around the room and without the help of a clock or calendar, tell the day of the week, and whether it was afternoon or evening by the particular assembly that would be there. The Old Judge was that kind of pub.

The first two of the plainclothes men turned up as itinerant Irish labourers, of which there was never any shortage in the area. They looked the part too with their muddied clothing and down-at-the-heel Wellington boots, the kind that looked slept in. And they even had the name of a local Irish labourer who drank there and for whom they asked, knowing he had just been sent to Barlinnie for three months for brawling and not paying a previous fine. The other two arrived in a Gas Board van, one with his battered bag of heavy fitter's tools which he expertly thumped to the floor in that gas man's fashion, a sort of wordless proclamation which meant, 'I'm here. What's your problem?'

'I'll gie the bastards a fright,' laughed Riley when one of his men whispered that the Gas Board men weren't what they were made out to be. 'Get a load of their plates,' Riley had said. 'Imagine coming in here like that with their coppers' boots on.' He got up at that, snatched the cap of one of the men who had been sitting with them and walked over to the two men, nonchalantly drinking pints of beer at the bar.

'I'm collecting for the police widows and orphans fund, boys,' he said, holding the upturned cap out to the two plainclothes men. At that he laughed loudly into their faces then turned round to look over his shoulder at the group he had just left, all of them intently observing the incident and loudly guffawing at the antics of their leader. When he turned round again to the two men, the smile had vanished, replaced with a menacing leer, a frighteningly insane-like stare in which his whole face seemed to have changed from its youthful insolence to a hideous mask of hate. 'I don't like fuckin' busies drinking in my pub. The next two that try it will have fuckin' orphans and widows. Now fuck off.'

Graham was furious when he heard about the incident and immediately ordered the other two undercover men from the premises. They protested to him that their disguise had worked but reported no exchange of money from Riley to borrowers, although they had seen lots of envelopes being passed to him by various men who came to the pub.

It was the day after the incident with the two policemen that Riley's uncle, Freddie Holden, came into the bar. He would come occasionally to visit his nephew, knowing such a mission would mean a good drink as well as a 'bung' of money, thrust into the palm of his hand, to which he always muttered a refusal but always kept.

Freddie Holden was one of the army of single men that are part of the Glasgow street scene, invariably feckless individuals who have been incompetent with their lives, incompatible with wives until being cast out on their own, destined for a sad and sorry demise. They live in a variety of establishments which cater for them, some called hotels, but having little similarity with what that word usually means, others in lodging houses, all of which are grandly described as model lodging houses and are mainly Dickensian dormitories, some board partitioned into 6 x 6 feet chambers called bedrooms where a mattress and a hook on the wall suffice for the lonely man's needs. Freddie was reduced to being one of the 'modellers' as they were known, although from time to time he would find himself a shared room in one of the old tenements.

Riley had a soft spot for his Uncle Freddie, being as he was the only living member of the older generation of his family, about which he knew so little; but that softness never went as far as conferring him with the avuncular title. 'Still in the Portugal Street doss house, Freddie?' he inquired after setting him up with a whisky and a pint of beer chaser.

Freddie relished the drink with open glee, licking the froth from his nicotine-stained lips with a 'Christ, that was great' after downing the first long draught. 'Naw. Been away from there for over a month. The thieving and the fighting was something terrible. Aw they Irish navvies, so it was. One lot from Monaghan, the other lot from Donegal and you know what happens when they two get together . . . You've never seen anything like it. As for the thieving. I had to end up sleeping with my clothes on or else they would have been knocked.'

'So where are you now?'

'Up at the top end of Abbotsford Place. But it's just as bad. Ah don't mean for fighting and thieving. It's rooms. Run by one of they Indian Johnnies, or what is it they call them now . . . Pakis? Fly bastards, so they are. This one works on the buses and he runs a shop, and in his spare time has bought a pile of old houses and lets them out as rooms. Making a fortune so he is, especially from the ones he has in the big old tenements. There's four of us in my room giving him two pounds each a week wi' the electric on top of that. And when it rains it runs right down two of the walls. Stinks to high doh with the damp and the drains. He gets three to four pounds off others for a room wi' a gas stove. That's supposed to include their light and if they get behind with their rent he doesn't pay the electric folk so they come and cut them off. Half of them are living up there wi' candles for lights. Like the bloody Middle Ages so it is.'

'He's not one of they Singh brothers, is he?'

'Naw. They call him Ifty. Shifty fuckin' Ifty. Doesnae even gie you a rent book so you've just got to take his word for it whether you're due rent or no'. I'm telling you, son, you cannae keep up wi' they darkies. Come here wi' nothing and end up owning the place so they do. Like the Jews so they are. Even look like them some of them.'

'How do you pay the rent? I mean, has he an office some-where?'

'Naw. He comes round with a bag man. He's one as well. Paki, like. You'd think they were taking bets for the Ayr races to look at them. And a' the rents get shoved in the bag. He'll take more in a night than a' his houses put thegether are worth. Sure did you no' read about him? They had one of they reporter fellahs from the Sunday papers chasing him up because he had cut off some families' electric and they did a big write-up in the papers about him.'

'When does he collect his rent then?'

'Thursdays. Always on a Thursday. The day we get our Assistance money. He spends most of the night going about a' the streets up at the top end of the district, Cumberland Street, Apsley Street, Abbotsford Place and a' round there. Christ, I fair enjoyed that pint, son. You do your old uncle well.'

The police kept up the pressure on trying to pin Riley. The speeches in the pubs slowly paid off, another witness coming forward about Riley and several more volunteering information about the others involved in the talleymen racket. But other complaints were also coming in about the Riley operation, it having taken a sinister new development in the form of the forcing of shopkeepers and public house owners into paying protection money. Graham reintroduced the undercover men, this time personally supervising their disguises, although keeping them away from the Old Judge. He would be looking after that one himself, he said.

14

Meeting a Friend

Star and her Uncle Sammy would often sit in the magnificent lounge of their Pollokshields home and discuss together the ups and downs of that week's trading in their growing number of lounge bars.

'What puzzles me is this notion you have for licensed grocers, Star,' he said to her one Sunday evening in the early autumn. 'You won't make more of a profit from them than your lounge bars which are doing us right well, thanks to your enterprise.'

'Uncle, don't you realise, the real drinks war hasn't actually started? The trade gets away with murder here with the mark-up they charge the customer . . . you know that. Eighteen per cent profit on a bottle of whisky. Twenty-seven and a half per cent on a bottle of sherry. I ask you! No wonder the trade loves the Government's Resale Price Maintenance regulations which stop them from cutting the price. It's a damned scandal. Government is not supposed to be about things like that. They keep telling us we're a free country but the only thing as far as I can see that's free is speech. Give them their Hyde Park Corner and that as a sop to keep them happy and thinking they're free then you can slap on as many other regulations and rules and laws as you like. That's what Government policy appears to be. Tory and Labour. I think it's all a big confidence trick.'

'But that's seven licensed grocers you've got now. That could have been seven more lounge bars you could have bought.'

'Hardly. Costs more to get a pub and convert it and build up the business into a good lounge. But that's not the point, uncle. I'm thinking ahead. The licensed grocers will do us all right in the meantime, but once they change the resale laws, and they're talking more and more about it, then we'll be ready. You've heard of Ted Heath?'

'Aye, the band leader.'

'Oh, don't be funny. Ted Heath. That young-looking one who

145

is the Secretary of State for Trade. Well, he's talking about introducing a Bill into the House of Commons to abolish the regulations. I know governments can be all talk, but they say he's serious about this one. You know, there's others with the same idea as me. Well, at least one other I know of, that is. The last three licensed grocers I went after all were snapped up, even before they were advertised, which has me wondering. I got the newspapers early on the Wednesday morning, the day that they carry the businesses for sale advertisements, and as soon as the agents' offices opened I was on the phone to make inquiries only to learn they had already been sold. Ronnie, our lawyer, checked on them for me and each of them had been bought by a firm called Russell Enterprises. Mean anything to you?'

'Never heard of them.'

'Neither have I. Whoever they are, they're moving really fast. Would love to know their secret.'

'So you think then that when they change these laws you'll be able to cut the price of whisky and that to what you like?'

'Of course you will. The trade would love it if no one did, though. Lose an eighteen or a twenty-seven per cent mark-up! You must be kidding. Not them. I told you, they're greedy. Greedy and complacent. And the poor punter is the one that suffers. What they need is a bit of good old-fashioned competition. And I'm telling you, I'll give it to them once they change these laws. Maybe even before it.'

'And do you think this Russell company has the same idea?'

'Well, I can't be sure, but I have my suspicions. Whoever they are they're providing as much a nuisance to me as that little Pakistani shop which has opened up near our place in Shettleston Road. Did I tell you about the butter war we're having? No, I remember, I didn't. It was those dreadful tallymen we spoke all about last Sunday. Well, Andy, the manager in the shop, took a halfpenny off the price of butter, just like he does other goods from time to time, and painted a big sign to that effect in the front window of the shop. This was about three weeks ago. Next thing you know, the little Pakistani put an even bigger sign up undercutting Andy's butter by a penny. And, right enough, it did a trick for him. They started flocking to him from one end of the road to the other, and you know the length of Shettleston

Road. And, what's worse, our takings dropped drastically. So Andy cut his price once more and immediately thereafter so did the Pakistani. The next thing you know, they're right down to cost price and then the Pakistani went below cost price.

'Rightly or wrongly, Andy went a penny below that, making his tuppence below cost price. So the Pakistani puts an even bigger sign up – "Cheapest Butter in Scotland". We just can't afford to sell butter at a loss, even although you do get some extra custom for other things. The big puzzle, though, is that Andy says he is selling twice as much butter as before, and presumably so is the Pakistani. Where is it all going? So, there it is. My big challenge for the week. Solve the problem, then find a solution to the great Shettleston Road butter war.'

'You know, these Pakis . . . they're all Johnny Pedlars. They're like the Lascars that used to come off the big merchantmen at Govan docks and walk all the way to The Barrows. Do you remember them, Star? Bunch of characters they were. Used to walk like they were stepping on hot coals. They said that was them practising for fire walking. You used to see them going back along Argyle Street with half The Barrows loaded on their backs . . . sewing machines and waistcoats and hats. Aye, they used to wear all the hats stacked up on one another on their heads. Funnier looking than Big Beanie in the pantomime. And they used to buy up washing boards as well. Imagine going home to the wife and telling her you had brought her home an old second-hand washing board from the other side of the world! That's the kind of people you're up against that's selling the butter.'

'Oh, Sammy, you're an old rascal getting. The Lascar seamen have no connection with the people we have here from Pakistan and India. They're from a completely different area.'

'Well, I never was good at geography, Star. But you know what I mean? They're all darkies.'

'Sammy . . . you know that word makes me angry.'

'What . . . darkie?'

'It's an insulting word.'

'Aw, c'mon Star. You know me. I don't mean it like that. You make me sound like they big cops over in Alabama that's giving all they black folk a hard time. Did you see them on the telly the other night? Thumping hell out of them, so they were, wi' these big sticks all because they wanted to ride in the section of the bus they keep for the white ones. Terrible so it was. I'm not like that, Star.'

'Oh, I know. But it begins with little things like that. Maybe it's just a sore point with me, but I just abhor any kind of prejudice and my God we've enough of it here with the Protestants and the Catholics.'

Andy Anderson, who was in charge of their Shettleston Road licensed grocers, had been the manager when they had bought it over and had been retained by them together with the other members of the staff. Andy was a grocer of the old school who spoke fondly about the good old days when the grocer was an artisan and not a shop assistant, and of how he could cut a pound dollop of butter to the nearest ounce from the big bulk mound on the shelf and slap it into a neat yellow bar with the ribbed paddles they called butter hands, and put the wire through a red Cheddar that had a flavour which vanished with the war, and of how his shop had been full of bulk goods all hessian sacked, with customers walking between rows of them, oatmeal and oatflakes, butter beans and haricot beans and marrowfat peas and macaroni and soap flakes and tea that came in tinfoil-lined chests that made a cuppa with a flavour that had gone the same way as the red cheese.

'Mistress Nelson,' as he always called Star no matter how many times she reminded him it was Miss, 'Mistress Nelson, I've been in this trade since Nineteen and Nineteen, the year after the Armistice, and I've never known anything like it. It's this man Mohammed something they call him. Now he's put his butter down to fourpence below cost. You just don't do that in the trade. It will ruin us all. I'm selling twice as much butter as before and every pound that leaves the shop is costing me threepence. How can I be selling so much when he must be selling even more? Has everyone gone butter mad or something?'

'Yes, it is difficult to understand, Mr Anderson. Is it your same customers that's buying the butter or is it new people that's coming into the shop?'

'The same customers, really, although a lot of women seem to be sending their wee boys in to buy three and four pounds at a time. Nothing else, mind you. Just the butter. It's like the war, when people used to hoard things. There would be rumours that matches or shoelaces or razor blades were going to be scarce and next thing you know everyone is buying them up and because of that they really went scarce. That's just what it's like with the butter. Got me blooming well baffled, Mistress Nelson.'

'It's Miss . . .'

'Aye, Mistress, I keep forgetting. But we can't cut the butter any more. Can we?'

'Would you mind if I served alongside the rest of the staff today just to see things for myself?'

'Please do. Anything that might help.'

She had only been working behind the counter for about an hour when she heard a boy of about thirteen asking one of the assistants for three pounds of butter.

'Three pounds?' queried the assistant.

'Aye, it's for my mammy.'

Star slipped off her white shop coat at that and quickly left the shop, heading in the direction of the Pakistani licensed grocers. There were some customers already in the shop and she deliberately lingered behind them. It wasn't long before she guessed what was happening. The little boy who had been buying the butter came into the shop with it, walked behind the counter and deposited the six half-pound packs of butter and some change on a shelf. Something was said between him and the man whom she took to be Mohammed and the boy then left the shop again.

When it came to Star's turn to be served, she leaned over the counter and in a quiet voice said, 'Mr Mohammed?'

'Yes.'

'Can I see you? It's private.'

They walked to the side of the counter where Star produced a folded card from her handbag then put it quickly away again before he had time to read it and said 'Corporation. Sanitary Department. Are you the owner of this shop?'

A look of mild shock came over the man's face.

'We haven't done anything wrong, Missus,' he said.

'I'm not saying you have. All I merely asked was are you the owner of the shop or are you the manager?'

'I'm the manager. I work for Mr Jehan.'

'Jehan?'

'That's right. His company is called Russell Enterprises.'

'Oh yes. I've heard of them. He's got other stores like this.'

'That's right, Missus.'

'And did he tell you to buy the butter from the other grocer's up the street?'

'No. That just happened. It's no' against the law, Missus. But I told Mr Jehan about it. And my shop is clean, Missus. You can inspect it for yourself.'

'No. Not just now. It's the butter I'm concerned about. I mean, it is a highly unorthodox method of buying goods. Anything could happen to it on the way from one shop to the next, especially with little grubby boys transporting it like they do. I'm afraid I'll have to make some kind of report. I'm sure someone in the Corporation will have something to say about it.'

'Look, Missus. Nae reports. I'll stop buying the butter from the other shop. That's a promise.'

'Well, in view of that I could delay the report. I'll just make a note of it for myself and check back later to see that everything is normal.'

'It will be, Missus. But nae report.'

'By the way, what did your Mr Jehan say when you told him about your method of buying the butter?'

'He just laughed.'

Sammy laughed too when she told him that night how she had stopped the butter war in an instant. 'And to think,' she said, 'we were losing threepence every time we sold a pound of butter and Mohammed was selling it cheaper but only losing a penny a pound because he was buying from us. And at night time when we closed, he was putting his butter up to the normal price. So he was ending up making a profit . . . out of *our* butter. I suppose you've got to admire his initiative . . . but really, a bit cheeky.'

'What did I tell you, Star!'

'Now don't you dare say it. No colour prejudice in this house.'

'But I told you what they're like.'

'Oh, I know what they're like all right. Damn fine traders, actually. All Mr Mohammed was doing was some old-fashioned business dealing. I know it wasn't exactly our ways and that, but

150

it's the kind of enterprise this country needs, you know . . . the trader who gives a service like staying open later at night. Who else do you know who stays open after five o'clock at night?'

'The Italians.'

'There. You see. You've hit the nail on the head. Another group of migrants who came here and showed us something. Where would we be without them? You know what Glasgow is like after five o'clock at night. Dead. Absolutely dead, except for the Italian cafés. Now we've got Pakistanis opening their little grocery shops late at night and giving people a service. And look at the customers they're getting. People can hardly believe that they can go out at night and actually buy a loaf of bread or a pint of milk . . .'

'Or a pound of your butter.'

'That was an exception, Sammy.'

'By the way, you didn't tell me exactly what you said to the Paki. Did you just say . . . Corporation?'

'No. I said I was from the Sanitary Department, which gave him a bit of a fright.'

'And did he not ask for a card or something?'

'Yes. I showed him one.'

'What?'

'My driving licence!'

Sammy roared with laughter. 'You're getting good, Star.'

'Anyway, the butter war has done some good. It has made my mind up about the drinks situation. I'm going to have the price of whisky cut in all of our shops. It was in the *Telegraph* today that Heath is pushing ahead with the Bill to repeal Resale Price Maintenance and I reckon that if a small trader like ourselves cuts the prices now, no one would bother taking us to court. It would be all rather pointless, especially with the legislation coming forward. And I checked with Bill McLaughlin, you know, the United Distillers' man, and he reckons his firm would make no complaint. If there's no complaint, there's no case. And if United don't take action, I don't see anyone else doing it.'

'What about your Mr Mohammed and his boss's shops?'

'What about them?'

'Well, they're not going to stand by and let you get away with beating them at cut-price whisky.'

'Fair enough. I've thought about that and have my contingency plans made when and if the situation arises.'

'And what price will you be charging for the whisky?'

'Well, we'll start with a couple of shillings off. And if need be I'll bring it down to thirty-five shillings.'

Sammy whistled. 'Thirty-five bob. You're mad.'

'I'll sell twice as much, if not more, and be up on profit. You wait and see.'

He didn't have long to wait. The cut-price whisky was a sensation. Having the importance it does in Scottish life, Star's idea made front-page news. A rash of other shops quickly followed suit, including the Jehan stores. Star monitored those in direct competition with her shops, like the one in Shettleston Road. In each case, their price was lower, usually by about sixpence. Her contingency plans were quickly put into operation. Using a group of staff, including some of the Steel family, Star rotated them round the Jehan shops buying the whisky, six bottles at a time. The butter war had come to whisky. This time Star was winning.

The Russell Enterprise shops had concentrated on cutting their whisky, but only slightly reducing the prices of other drink. Sammy and Star's shops, which they called Sammar Licensed Grocers, vigorously cut all of their drink prices. Then, suddenly, the Russell stores called off their undercutting of the Sammar whisky price. With all their drink prices down, the crowds flocked to Star's shops.

'The figures speak for themselves,' she explained to Sammy at the end of the first month of the price war. 'The turnover of everything in the Shettleston Road shop was £750 a week, of which £110 was at the off-licence drink counter. At the end of the first week the drink turnover alone was £250. Then I put an advertisement in the newspapers and the drinks turnover shot up to £500 by the end of the second week. In the third week it went to £750, the same as the entire shop's turnover just three weeks before. And there's still three weeks left to Christmas. So, I've got shopfitters in working nightshift changing the scope of the Shettleston Road and some of the other shops. The groceries will be cut down to a small corner, the rest all shelves of drink. And if it works out we'll do the same to the rest of the shops. What am I saying . . . if it works out? Uncle Sammy, we've hit our biggest ever goldmine. And we've caught Russell Enterprises and the others all napping. Did I tell you that Russell's didn't even retaliate when we undercut his whisky price. He was our only immediate threat and it looks like he doesn't want to take us on. Which really surprises me. He had the same opportunity to do it as us. I wonder why he didn't take it? Maybe he's got other plans. Oh, I nearly forgot. We've been asked to Sandra's for pre-Christmas drinks this Saturday. Do you have a clean suit?'

'Who's Sandra?'

'Sandra Ryan. She's one of the local coffee morning girls. Lives in Nithsdale Road. I thought you knew of her.'

'Do you know I've lived nearly twenty years in the 'Shields and never put my foot over another door.'

'Well, Sammy, you've no one to blame but yourself for that.'

'And what's this about a clean suit? All my suits are clean.'

'There's clean and clean, Sammy. I mean freshly cleaned. What about putting that nice grey one into Pullar's for a freshen up?'

'God, Star, you're worse than a wife.'

There was a full turnout of the 'girls' that evening for Sandra's little party and Star enjoyed meeting the various husbands, making mental notes of how, like clothes, some suited them, others didn't; how some would demonstrate that they were in charge of their house, while others had it revealed they were not. Sammy had tried to feign tiredness in order not to go, but Star had anticipated that. As it turned out, he found himself in good company and when Star saw him obviously hitting off a good relationship with Janice's husband Harold, she left him to meet some of the other guests.

It was Sandra who stopped her in her tracks.

'Star Nelson . . . I haven't seen you for months. All we seem to do these days is blether on the phone to each other. Delighted you were able to make it. Daniel my husband is dying to meet you and so is someone else. I think Daniel wants to thank you personally for bringing down the price of whisky.'

They walked together to the far end of the room where three men were having a lively conversation. One of them had looked round as they approached and she returned the long stare and smile he gave her. He was a tall man with a Mediterranean face and a dark complexion which in the first instant she thought might be that of a Greek or southern Italian. After Sandra had introduced Star to her Daniel and the other man, she then turned to the man who had been looking at Star. 'And this is our dear neighbour Russell . . . well, that's what we all call him. What is your other name again?'

'Rasool. Rasool Jehan.'

'Jehan . . .' exclaimed Star.

'That's right . . . you look surprised.'

'Not the same Jehan of Russell Enterprises? Russell, of course, now I get it. It is you . . . isn't it?'

'Yes, it's me all right. You mean . . . me, Russell of Russell Enterprises?'

'That's right.'

'Yes, the very same person. And you're Star Nelson of Star Lounge Bars and Sammar Licensed Grocers.'

'How did you know all that?'

'Oh, I make it a point to know certain things.'

'Right, then. Now that I've got you right there in front of me . . . how were you able to buy those shops that were up for sale before the advertisements even appeared in the newspapers?'

He threw his head back in loud laughter at that, his dark skin highlighting his gleaming teeth.

Smiling, and not waiting for an answer, Star asked him if that's how loud he had laughed when he heard about Mr Mohammed's butter war.

Sandra interjected at that.

'I take it you two seem to know of each other . . . I'm away. I'll leave you to your questions.'

'Yes, I did find the butter war amusing. Actually, Mohammed blames your manager for putting the notice in his window. He took that as a challenge of some kind and it just went on from there. But I didn't know about the little boys buying your butter until after he had been doing it for a while.'

'And the shops? How on earth did you get to know so quickly they were for sale?'

'Well, I'll tell you but I wouldn't tell anyone else. You see, my business philosophy is that you must always get to the origin of things. My main business is in leather goods. I came here to sell them. I could easily have got them from an agent or a wholesaler. But what I did before leaving Pakistan was to buy in bulk from the factories which made them. And I bought such large quantities that I was able to secure the absolute lowest prices and could also insist that I got nothing but the very best quality. I sell direct to the shops so therefore I can get the wholesaler's mark-up. I don't have to use agents so I can save there as well. When I started out to buy some grocer shops I was beaten on a couple of offers after having spent money on valuations and that sort of thing. So, I found out the agency who places the advertisements with the newspapers and persuaded a fellow who works for them to let me see them in advance. After that it was easy. I merely went to the vendor and made an offer that had to be accepted by three o'clock that afternoon. People like quick clean offers like that and in each case I got them. Simple as that.'

'Sharp knives, I would say.'

'Sharp knives?'

'Oh . . . just a family joke I share with Uncle Sammy. Just something that sums up a clever operation like that.'

Star looked up at Rasool's handsome face and smiled. 'You know, I still can't believe that I've caught up with Mr Russell Enterprises himself. I often wondered about them . . . who they were and everything. And little knowing that the man himself lived just around the corner from me. Janice, my friend, mentioned you once but said you were in import or export or something.'

'That's right. I have an import and export agency . . . for my leather goods, you know. But it runs like clockwork now so I decided one day that I would diversify a little and put some money into getting a little chain of food shops going.'

'I note you went for ones with liquor licences.'

'Yes, like yourself.'

'*Touché*. But I thought drink was against the religion of Indian people?'

'Really, I'm a Pakistani. But like all Pakistanis of my age I was born in what used to be called India. It's us Pakistanis who are very much against drink. You see, we are from an Islamic country and alcohol is against the code of our bible, the Koran.'

'I take it then that you are not a strict Muslim?'

'Actually, I am. But religions can be interpreted in so many ways. Some of my friends read the Koran one way, others another way. I have countrymen who say it is wrong for those who are grocers to even sell things like bacon or sausages or suet and lard and hamburgers. The reason is that some of these are from the pig, a prohibited animal for Muslims, and others are products of animals not killed in the Muslim fashion. They are what we call *haram* . . . forbidden.'

'You mean, like the Jews with non-kosher food?'

'Just the same.'

'But what kind of grocer's shop could you have here if you didn't sell bacon or sausages? You wouldn't last a week.'

'But I say to my friends we are in another country and it is all right for us to deal in the same goods as the people deal with here. And I have that same attitude about alcohol. It is an acceptable and perfectly legal commodity here, so why shouldn't we trade in it? At the same time I don't believe in being flagrant about it. That is why I had second thoughts about becoming really involved in the whisky war. I was quite willing to do the same as you and change my shops over to alcohol only. I even had a bigger team than you ready to buy that whisky back off you which you were buying from me.'

Star put her hand to her mouth to hide her astonishment. 'How on earth did you know about that?'

'Oh, I knew someone would do a butter war with the whisky. Then I had some of your people followed.'

'Why did you go to that trouble when you had changed your mind about being involved in the price cutting?'

'Well, I was of two minds for a while. But then the half of my conscience which was saying "no" took the upper hand and I instructed all my managers to concentrate on the food side of things . . . which they did.'

'So you like your conscience to be squared?'

'Very much.'

'That's like my Uncle Sammy. That's him over there . . . I live with him in his house. That's the one at the corner of Nithsdale Road.'

'I know . . . Sammar. The same name as your grocery company.'

'Oh, so you know it?'

'Yes, I've seen you several times when I've been driving past. The last time you were speaking to Janice Kyle . . . I do business with her husband Harold. I was going to stop in order to get an introduction. I'm sorry now I didn't.'

Star looked down momentarily as she felt her cheeks flush, then turned quickly to hide her emotions, looking again in the direction of her uncle. 'Look at him. He seems to be the centre of attraction with that group of men. He can be a bit of a character at times. Wonder if he's telling them what he did during the war.'

'Was he a soldier then?'

'No . . . my dear uncle was never a soldier. Not that he didn't want to be. He was 4F . . . you know, medically unfit. They said he had bronchitis and flat feet. Look at him. Smokes like a chimney and fit as a fiddle. Never had a day's illness in his life. Actually I don't know the full story of what he did during the war. He's told me bits about it. Did a lot of trading in various things and made a deal of money. Not in armaments or anything like that. Just plain old-fashioned trading over in the Gorbals where he was born.'

'He would make a good *ham watan* for me then?'

'I beg your pardon!'

'*Ham watan* . . . fellow countryman.'

'He certainly would. Some of the tricks he used to get up to . . . Goodness, the way I said that! Sounds bad, doesn't it? Like saying the Pakistanis are up to all sorts of tricks.'

'It's all right. I know what you meant. You obviously get on well with your uncle.'

'Sammy is like a father to me.'

'Did I hear you two talking about me there?'

Sammy had joined them and she introduced him to Rasool, telling Sammy that he preferred to be called Russell and that he was the man behind Russell Enterprise shops.

'I know,' he said. 'One of the men over there was telling me all about you.'

'I hope he didn't tell you too much.'

'Oh, just enough.'

'You seemed to be getting on well with the men, Sammy,' said Star.

'Aye. You wouldn't believe it, but I know two of their fathers. I went to school with one of them and the other has a pub in the Gorbals. See the one I went to school with! Well, if you'll pardon the expression, Russell, but he never had an arse in his trousers.'

'Sammy!' said Star.

'But neither he did. And that's his boy over there. One of the top surgeons in the Victoria! Just goes to show you, doesn't it? You two seem to have had plenty to talk about yourselves. I was watching you from over there.'

'See what I mean, Russell? You never know what my uncle is going to say.'

Just at that point Sammy turned to answer one of the other men who was suggesting they meet the following Friday at the nearby Clydesdale Cricket Club for a drink. 'I'm a member so will sign you in,' said the man.

Rasool leaned towards Star while Sammy was speaking with the other man. 'Would you care to have dinner with me sometime? Next Saturday perhaps?'

She didn't hesitate in her reply. 'Why, I'd love to.'

'Saturday is the only day I have free as I'll be away most of the week and on Friday we have our fellowship meeting which I must attend as we have a few problems in the community.'

'Saturday it is then.'

'I'll phone you.'

15

Letting the Side Down

Their problems were usually more family affairs than anything else and they would discuss them at their Jamiat Ittihad fellowship nights after prayers.

One had been in trouble with the police for beating his wife. He wasn't present but another man said he and his wife would try to help the couple. There was a discussion on the merits and demerits of various areas of the city, a consensus being that the old tenements which formed a section of the Pollokshields were among the best places for families to live as the houses were reasonably priced, but more important than anything it was a 'dry' area with no public houses. That was attractive as wives and children were beginning to join the men to settle in Glasgow and it was important they should have a drink-free environment. Then they discussed the plight of two families who needed financial assistance because the husbands were in hospital, and there was the case of a deserted wife who needed advice on how to get help for her young family.

'And what's to be done about Iftikhaar?' two of the men asked at the end of the meeting. 'There have been more complaints about him than any other person in the entire community.'

'He's gone mad about money,' said another. 'He's working on the buses. Every day a double shift. He owns a big shop and he has all those houses which he is letting out. It's the houses that all the complaints are about.'

'They say he has become a Rachman,' a man said.

'What is that?' asked someone.

Another answered it was a swearword: 'Just like *haraami* or *chootiya*.'

Some of them laughed at that then one of them corrected. 'Rachman was a London slum landlord who used to extort money from his tenants. It is a very bad name to be called.'

One of the traders who worked at The Barrows said his

customers had been speaking about Iftikhaar, especially since the story appeared about him in the Sunday newspaper. 'Did you read it? It was nearly a whole page. And pictures too. So everyone could see he was one of ours. Do you know, I've never had an insult from a customer till that story appeared – except from the drunks that is, but you expect that from them. Now it's good people saying things to me like "How many houses do you have, Abdul?" and "You Pakis are all the same." And we're getting all this because of one man.'

'Did anyone ask him to come to the Jamiat tonight?' asked Javaid.

'I did,' said the one they called Haakim. 'All he did was laugh at me, saying he was too busy.'

Rasool frowned at the discussion. 'This is very bad news for us,' he said. 'So far we have had a good name with the host community. They say we are honest and hard working. I have heard them say some unkind things about other nationalities who are here but never us. One man should not be allowed to make difficulties for the rest of us. He must be spoken to. Where is the best place to find him?'

'He stays in Govanhill, but you will never get him at his house. He only sleeps there,' volunteered one.

A bus conductor in uniform said that he worked out of Larkfield Garage but you would have to know the precise time to be there to catch him. 'You can often see him in his shop on a Sunday. A family work it for him. It's in Crown Street and he calls it "Bestprice".'

'The best place of all,' said Taariq, the watch repairer, 'is when he collects his rents. The man who runs his shop goes out with him. Every Thursday night without fail. It's the day the tenants collect their Assistance money. You can see him go from close to close with the other man who carries a bag for the rent money. They do it between five and eight o'clock. He always tries to finish then before the worst of the drunks appear.'

'Where are these houses?' asked Maqbul.

'Roundabout where Rasool used to stay at the top of Abbotsford Place. The big houses, you know?'

'Then we must send a deputation to talk with him,' said Rasool.

'You should be leader of it,' said Taariq.

'I intend to be there to speak to him,' replied Rasool.

'And I'll be there too,' said Javaid.

'And me,' added Maqbul.

'The three wise men,' someone laughed.

'That's right,' replied Maqbul. 'The three wise men of the East.'

Rasool told Star the story about Iftikhaar the following night, the Saturday of their first evening together. He had taken her to the Gay Gordon Club in Exchange Square, the nearest Glasgow had to a nightclub and one of the few oases of sophistication in the city.

'I feel very responsible for people like him in our community,' he said. 'We have had a good name so far. The standard of behaviour has been good, no one being involved in fights or assaults or anything like that. And then there is this big story about Iftikhaar and his houses. I don't know him well. I just remember him coming to our fellowship meetings when I first arrived. I suppose in a way it is kind of understandable what he is doing. Like many of the men he never had money before, nor had he the opportunity to make money. Then he finds himself in another country where there are so many opportunities and like someone finding a treasure chest he wants to plunge both his hands into it and pull out as much as he can . . . all at the one time, regardless of who might get hurt. But it would be terrible if we all did that. However, Star, I didn't ask you out for the evening to bore you all about our wayward fellow countrymen.'

'What was that expression you used again?'

'Which one was that?'

'About fellow countrymen.'

'Oh . . . *ham watan*.'

'That's it.'

'It's an Urdu expression, Urdu being our language . . . the language of the camps. We had so many armies pass our way over the centuries – Persians, Arabs and others – and our language is made up from many words of theirs. Your own name, Star. That is not common here. In fact, I have not heard it here before.'

'It was an idea of my father's. He was Sammy's brother. Maybe he had a romantic streak or something – anyway the first

161

time he saw me in hospital he said I was his little Star and that's what the name was to be.'

'A man of taste obviously.'

'Russell . . . I was about five hours old when he said it. I wouldn't look much of a star.'

'It's quite a usual Muslim name. There are several names for Star. There's Najma, Najam and Sitaara, each qualifying a different kind of star.'

'Don't like the sound of the first two. Sitaara's all right though. Now tell me about yourself, Russell. What made you come to Britain? I mean why Britain and not another country?'

'Well, if you come from India or Pakistan you already know British people and their customs and everything. If I had gone to France or Italy or some place like that it would have been very strange for me, although I did study French as part of my degree from university. Coming here is almost like coming to our second home. We do feel at home here . . . despite the weather. And we trust British people. Some of us even have a saying – roughly translated it means that you should not trust another Muslim but you can an Englishman and a Christian. Ah, the band is here. Shall we dance?'

They danced closely together and when they left the small dance floor of the restaurant to return to the table their hands lingered longingly as did their eyes when they sat down.

'You know, I still can't believe it,' said Star. 'Of all the people who has to take me on my first date for . . . well, I won't say just how long, it has to be you, Mr Russell Enterprises.'

'It's no surprise to Mr Russell Enterprises.'

'What do you mean?'

'Well, I knew he would be sitting here one Saturday night looking into the wonderful eyes of the woman he had admired for so long.'

'Oh do tell me more.'

'Ah . . . that would be me giving away secrets.'

'Don't tease me, Russell. I'd love to hear.'

'No recriminations?'

'None.'

'No telling I told?'

'Swear to goodness.'

162

'Well, when Daniel – you know, Sandra's husband – mentioned they were having their evening and invited me, I asked if you would be there. He said he didn't know who Sandra had invited. So I asked him to find out. The following week he told me that Sandra had given her personal guarantee that you would be there and that she would also ensure that we met.'

'Oh, so that was why she made me promise I'd be there. You see I was going away to the country for the weekend. I've some friends down in Dumfriesshire, but she made me cancel the trip and I almost had to sign a sworn statement that I'd be there. She phoned me the night before and phoned again that day just to make sure. You devil, Russell. Touch of the sharp knives there.'

'If you say so.'

It was the Thursday after their first date that Rasool met with his friends Javaid and Maqbul to make their call on Iftikhaar. Rasool parked his new Daimler Conquest in Abbotsford Place near the junction with Cumberland Street and the three men sat in the car to wait on him making an appearance.

'I used to stay over there when I first came,' said Rasool, pointing over to his old house. 'Remember?'

'Remember it as if it was yesterday,' said Javaid. 'You made us a huge pot of *gosht do-piaza* and it was a freezing cold night and the rain had turned to sleet then snow, which I had never seen before, and I had stayed out in the street just to watch it so that I was soaked and chilled to the bone when I got up to your house. And that *gosht* you made . . . I never realised our way of cooking could taste so good. You know, I think because of the cold it tastes even better in Scotland than in Pakistan.'

'The houses were better then than they are now,' said Maqbul.

'Yes, they look in a sorry state now,' said Rasool.

Once they had been the finest houses in the Gorbals, after the palace-fronted town houses of the waterfront Carlton Place. There were main-door flats with projecting porches and Corinthian and Ionic columns and above them were flats of the kind of proportions which afforded a gracious living in the 1830s when they had been built. But now the six-and seven-apartment houses had become fodder for the speculators. Stick an old gas stove in each room plus the occasional sink and your six or seven apartments became six or seven houses. Buy ten of them and that gave you more than sixty houses, and sixty houses meant rents of about £200 a week, or about twenty times the average wage. Apart from the rates tax, it was all-found money for the tenants had to pay their own gas and electric charges. Repairs? There were no repair bills for the landlords. This new breed of them didn't carry out repairs.

'Look how the water flooding down them from the broken pipes has made all the stone crumble,' said Maqbul pointing.

'Yes, and look at the people who are living in them. They're an unfortunate-looking lot,' said Javaid. 'It still puzzles me here, you know, that there are so many poor people, I mean poor-looking people, people in bad-looking shape, yet there are so many opportunities for them.'

'You get the same in America,' said Rasool. 'They have the places they call Skid Row, just like this is now. It's one of the peculiarities of the Western way that so many can make it and yet so many don't.'

'Look,' said Maqbul. 'There's one who is making it.'

It was Iftikhaar accompanied by his bag man. They had come round the corner from Cumberland Street where they had been collecting and were heading for some of the Abbotsford Place houses where he obviously had an interest. The three men quickly left the car and when they caught up with him he was engaged in a fierce argument at the entrance to one of the main-door flats with a man who was obviously a tenant.

When the man saw the three hurrying towards them he shouted and swore at Iftikhaar. 'Is that three of your cronies coming to help you? You're all the same, you Paki bastards. You come here and take our jobs and our houses. Bastards.' The door then slammed shut.

Iftikhaar looked round at the three approaching him but turned away again to knock loudly on the door that had been closed in his face. Then there was the noise of something being smashed inside the house.

'See the kind of people I have to deal with,' he said when the three men came up to him.

'Iftikhaar,' said Rasool, 'why do you do this?'

'Do what?'

'Make money in this sort of fashion?'

'What is wrong with it? They are my houses. I bought them with money for which I worked hard on the buses. What am I doing that is wrong?'

'You are giving your countrymen a bad name. We have been speaking about you at the Jamiat Ittihad and everyone thinks that you are doing wrong.'

'To hell with what you think at the Jamiat Ittihad. Most of them who talk like that are *bonga*. They speak like a *saali*. Jealous as a wife's sister. That's what they are. They're envious of Iftikhaar because they can't make as much money as him.'

'But what about the stories and picture of you in the newspapers?' asked Maqbul.

'They are *haraami* who write that. Bastards. Most of it was lies. The papers didn't tell you about the tenants who won't pay me rents. They would rather drink their whisky than pay for their gas or electricity. That's why most of them sit in their houses at night with candles for light. They don't care as long as they get their drinking. It didn't tell you about that in their newspapers . . . did it?'

'But look at the state of your houses,' said Rasool. 'Are you not ashamed to be connected with places like that?'

'Oh, you should talk, Rasool. The great Rasool Jehan no less. The one who thinks he is our leader in the community . . . and who owns shops that sells them their alcohol. That's *haram* what you do. That's against the Koran. You're a hypocrite, Rasool. I have no time for hypocrites.'

'But I don't give my country or my fellow countrymen a bad name like you do, Iftikhaar. No one writes bad stories about me in the newspapers.'

'Then maybe I should tell the reporters that the people who smash my houses and refuse to pay me rent get their cheap drink in the shop of the noble one, our Rasool.'

'Iftikhaar,' appealed Maqbul. 'You must think of the community. We don't want trouble with the Scottish people. We all want to be prosperous here. No one cares how much money you make. It's the way you make it. We have to live together among the Scottish people and be friendly with them. You are spoiling all this for us. They are saying bad things about us now. Why don't you stop it for the sake of the community?'

'You're another one to talk, Maqbul. What is it they call you
. . . Mac Bull! I think you try to kid them on you are one of them
to make your money. Mac Bull indeed! I don't have to fool the
Scotchmen to make my money. I make it as Iftikhaar Ghani of
Pakistan. And when I make my fortune I'm going back home
and I'm going to have a big house with lots of servants like a rich
man for the rest of my life. Nothing is going to stop me from
achieving that . . . least of all you three and the Jamiat Ittihad
crowd. Now I must go. I've my business to attend to.'

The three men returned to the car and sat in it for a while
watching Iftikhaar and his helper going from house to house
before turning a corner and going out of sight.

'Well, we didn't make much of an impression on him, did we?'
asked Javaid.

'No,' said Rasool. 'None whatsoever. We'll have to try
something else.'

'Like what?' queried Maqbul.

'That will need some thought. I don't have an immediate
answer. But we must try and think of one. We will have to do
something.'

'Are you thinking about violence, Rasool?'

'I was. But I'm not now. I'm not a violent man but I was
beginning to feel that way when I was talking to him there. The
man just doesn't care about his country or his countrymen. He is
a dishonourable man.'

A fortnight later there was another story about Iftikhaar in the
newspapers. This time it wasn't the usual Sunday scandal-type
story. He was in the news because he and his collecting assistant
had been the victims of an assault, the other man getting the
worst of the attack. The incident had followed a discussion about
Iftikhaar and his ways by another group of men. But this time
they had not been his countrymen. They were Sonny Riley and
some of his associates. In the interests of his Uncle Freddie,
Sonny had decreed that three of his men should pay the Gorbals
landlord a visit.

The men were three of Sonny's 'specialists' as he called them,
the ones who had been enforcing his debt-collecting and other
operations, and their instructions were in the tersest of terms,

which was the way they normally were. Like their leader himself, they were no sophisticates, their simple extortion rackets being about the most complicated event in their lives, except perhaps trying to work out a Yankee for the afternoon's racing. The instructions from Riley were that the Iftikhaar one and his man were to be given 'a message'. The indefinite article was important, just as the definite one was when they used that word 'message'. One was clearly defined, exact, explicit. The other wasn't. And what Iftikhaar and his friend were to receive was the other.

They found their prey as they were leaving one of the closes where they had been collecting money in Cumberland Street. The three men stood at the close entrance and pounced without warning as soon as the two men had come down the last of the stairs from the upper floors of the building.

It was all over in a matter of seconds. Both Iftikhaar and his partner were knocked to the ground and the bag wrenched from their grasp. Two of the men then spreadeagled the helper and the third rained blows from a hammer on his hands as Iftikhaar, shocked with horror, looked on from where he lay on the ground.

'So you're Ifty – Shifty Ifty,' said the man who had wielded the hammer, holding it now in front of his face. 'This is just a wee warning, pal. Sonny doesn't like landlords . . . especially fuckin' Paki ones. And if you're back at this game, we'll be back as well.'

The story in the morning papers the following day described the attack as being 'vicious' and 'particularly brutal'. The man helping Iftikhaar had had his hands smashed and most of his fingers broken. There was speculation in one of the papers that it was part of the continuing evil of the tallymen, the robbery having been done to pay off debts. Sonny Riley smiled when he read that.

'Just goes to show you,' he said. 'You cannae believe what you read in the papers. Write a lot of crap, so they do.'

16

The Trial of the Tallymen

The vicious attack on the Pakistani landlord and his bodyguard pushed Superintendent Tom Graham to a new intensity of effort in his pursuit of Riley. Iftikhaar and his man had been shown photographs of some of Riley's accomplices but hadn't been able to identify any of them. Nevertheless, Graham knew the attack had been inspired by the Riley gang. Apart from this assault, there was a growing dossier of evidence against Riley. At least a dozen witnesses had come forward willing to testify against men in various pubs from whom they had borrowed money. They had either paid the debt back at extortionate rates or had been threatened with assault or actually had been assaulted.

After the undercover team had been spotted with their police boots, Graham had taken personal charge of all plainclothes operations. He had ordered a parade at the Central Police HQ of a team that were to be placed in the specific pubs where the tallymen were operating. There were a dozen of them in that first parade, four of them women constables who would take the part of 'girlfriends' out for a drink with their partners. Graham had them lined up in the courtyard behind the police buildings.

'When did you last have a bath, constable?' he asked the first man.

With a surprised look on his face, the young plainclothesman answered, 'Why, this morning, sir.'

'Did you shave this morning?' he said to the next man.

'Yes, sir, I shave every morning after I shower.'

'Is that a clean shirt?' he asked a third.

'Yes, sir. Fresh on this morning.'

Two policewomen were next.

'Is that a new blouse you're wearing?'

'That's correct, sir. It's the first time I've worn it.'

'What about your stockings, policewoman? Any holes in them?'

'No, sir. They're a new pair.'

Another was asked if she had perfume on. 'Smells French to me,' said Graham.

'Correct, sir. A present from my boyfriend.'

After he reached the end of the file he walked to the middle of the quadrangle to address them.

'So you're the undercover squad! Well, I don't know what they taught you at Tulliallan Police College, but whatever it was it wasn't about undercover operations. Do you know what you look like . . . the lot of you? A bunch of cops . . . dressed up like a bunch of cops trying not to look like cops and failing miserably. Do you think any one of you could walk into the Old Judge or the Seaforth or the Moy or The Bible Class or The Devon or any other of the Gorbals pubs and not be spotted? Good God . . . French perfume, clean shirts, Brylcreemed hair, stockings without holes. You're a load of amateurs, that's what you are. But I'll make you look like real undercover people.

'For a start, you'll do plainclothes street duty for a week making observations from outside the pubs and other places to which you'll be assigned. And during that week you will not have a bath or one of your fancy new-fangled showers. You will not change your clothes. You will not shave. You will not put on fresh stockings. You will not use a drop of perfume, French or otherwise. You will not press your trousers or your skirts. You will not comb your hair, let alone put as much as a whiff of hair cream on it. And you'll come back here to this same spot in seven days' time and I want you to smell like you haven't had a bath for a week. I want you to look like you've slept in a house with a maw and a paw and four or five other weans. I want you to look like the only water that's in your house is out of an old spigot that's only got one kind of water, cold water, and it runs into an old chipped enamel sink that's full of last night's tea dishes and your soap's carbolic and it sits in a saucer beside a tin of zebo black leading and an old mug with your father's soap brush and the towel to dry yourself is still soaking from the night before and is foul with the smell of the rotten plaster which it lay up against all that night on the rusty nail it hung from and the only mirror

169

you can see yourself in is your old man's shaving mirror and it's gone funny with the damp as well, just like your clothes have when you put them on, and if you could see yourself properly in the mirror what you would see is a pallid up-a-close face, for that's the way you look when you live up-a-close . . . up a Gorbals close. That's the way you get to look when you live like these poor buggers in their horrible houses. You stink, that's what you do. You stink with the rottenness of the place. And when you parade for me here next week, you'll stink like they stink and you'll look like they do. And then and only then can you go into their pubs and not be noticed for you'll be like them, not like the bunch of toffs that you look like just now. A week from today. Here. Nine o'clock. And sharp.'

Another parade of plainclothes policemen and women were given the same lesson which became the sole topic of conversation with the big mugs of tea and sausage and bacon rolls which seemed to be a basic diet over at the police canteen in St Andrew's Square.

Graham inspected them again the following week when the two squads assembled back at the same spot.

'Well, how do you feel?' he said to one of the policewomen, her hair lank and greasy and falling over one eye.

'Absolutely terrible, sir. I've never felt so filthy in all my life.'

'Good.'

'What about you, constable? When did you last shave?'

'Four days ago.'

'And wash?'

'Just a damp cloth over my face.'

'Aye, and there's a nice hum coming from you. Excellent.'

'What's those white marks on your trousers?' he asked another.

'I've an old uncle lives in the Gorbals so I've moved in with him to get the feel. The white is damp mould. Everything in his wardrobe is that way.'

'Superb.'

Then he turned to address the parade. 'Now you look like undercover people. Sergeant McIntyre has a list of the pubs I want put under surveillance. He also will detail the precise people I want observed. I want you to get near to them, so near conversations can be noted. I want you to see and hear what goes on between them and their customers. Pay close attention to all money transactions. I want all observations entered in your notebooks as soon as you leave the premises. You'll be given a pound a day expenses. In other words drink money. Now you look like them, act like them. The men will drink pints, the women whisky and lemonade or that new Carlsberg beer, Specials they call them. Make sure you spin them out for they'll blow your head off. That's why they drink them. I'll make an assessment of the operation after a week when I want you all back here again . . . and, just in case you forget, I want you in the same clothes. No baths. No showers. And girls . . . remember: no perfume.'

On behalf of Graham, the Lawmoor Street Police Station in the Gorbals had been paying particular attention to the drunks and the breach-of-the-peace street fighters which were the principal category of those arrested at their busiest times, Friday and Saturday nights. He wanted to be told immediately any of the regular drinkers from the Old Judge were arrested. He received the call on a Saturday morning.

'We've got "Boy" Watson in custody,' was the message.

'Is that the old boxer?' Graham asked.

'That's right, sir. Eddie "Boy" Watson. Charged with drunk and disorderly last night.'

'No other charges?'

'No, sir. It was just his customary Friday night. Full to the gunnels then out in the middle of Caledonia Road, stripped to the waist and challenging all and sundry to fight him.'

Such behaviour was a feature of the weekend street scene and it wasn't confined to those who had been the old booth and club pugilists whose wages were hardly even a penny a punch. The drink, they said, revealed the character and if the character revealed the nation then it could be said there was something in the Celtic psyche that had a message for the world. Some thought it was merely that the whisky made them fighting mad. But others saw it in different terms. They made an *apologia* for them. It was the downtrodden race, they said, still smarting from the events of the '45. The Great Defeat had been burned into the soul of the Scot and there it was on a Friday and Saturday night trying to leap out and demonstrate they were no defeated race and were as good as any man. Others read it as The Great Deficiency, the character make-up that couldn't contain an overabundance of aggression and how it was always that aggression that surfaced when the whisky released the *id*. Eddie 'Boy' Watson thought none of these things when his mind was overtaken by the drink. Out there in the middle of Caledonia Road there was a world title to be fought for and there he would stand, legs apart, shirt loosened to the waist, fists clenched and hung low and at five feet four inches shouting, 'Aye you, big man,' to some six-footer. 'C'mon, c'mon, and we'll see how big a man you are.'

'No other charges?' Graham asked the Lawmoor Street man.

'No, sir. Just the usual d. and d.'

'No breach of the peace?'

'We got a call saying there was a man challenging people to fight and when we arrived he was being supported by a lamp post so we picked him up. No breach of the peace, sir.'

'Fine. Bring him over to the Central. I want to speak to him.'

Watson was shocked the next morning when he was told he was 'going up town' to see one of the top brass. The uniformed men joked with him when they escorted him to the 'Black Maria' prisoners' transport van.

'What have you been up to, Eddie? You been doing something you haven't been telling us about?'

'I think youse are having me on. I haven't nicked anything.'

'Oh, you said it, Eddie. Nicked. Got something on your conscience, wee man?'

'Oh, fuck off the lot of you.'

He was led into the office of the Superintendent who told the uniformed men he wanted to speak with Watson on his own.

'Aye, Eddie, this is quite a scrape you've got yourself into. Breach of the peace, disorderly conduct, police assault, serious assault, carrying a concealed weapon, threatening behaviour. Oh, dear. Looks like the Sheriff for you.'

'The Sheriff? Concealed weapon! Serious assault! Jesus Christ. Youse are at it. No' me. No' Eddie Watson.'

'That's what the charge says, then. And it's up to me to pass it to the Fiscal. On the other hand . . .'

'What?'

'On the other hand, I can also tear it up. It can't be torn up when it gets to the Fiscal's Office. But it can here.'

'But I don't carry weapons.'

'Do you remember anything about last night?'

'No. I was broke and was on the mammy. Mammy mine. The wine. They call it Mystic City. I could have been in Eldorado for all I know last night. But don't send us to the Sheriff. I couldn't stand a spell up at the House. I've done a week and ten days and that. But no' a spell. That would kill me. I need to be out and about.'

'Well, as I said . . . on the other hand I could tear it up. You were "Boy" Weston, weren't you?'

'That's right. One of the best flyweights in the Gorbals.'

'You were fighting at the same time as Scotty Deans, Tiger Naughton and Young Donnelly?'

'Aye . . . and Lynch and wee Paddy Docherty. See wee Docherty. You couldnae catch the bugger. He beat Benny. I fought them a'. You're a fan then?'

'That's right. And I would hate to see you away to Barlinnie for a spell. Tell you what I'll do. I'll put this charge sheet in the bucket . . . for a favour.'

Watson looked at him suspiciously. 'Eh . . . you thinking about wanting me to nark?'

'I would never ask that of you, Eddie. Not Eddie "Boy" Watson. But tell me. What do you know about Sonny Riley?'

'He's a wee bastard. Crippled my china Tommy Dunachy. Know what for? The price of a bottle of Lanliq.'

'He's a tallyman, you know?'

'Aye and Santa Claus wears a red gown. Christ, everybody knows that.'

'Well, we're out to do him.'

'But I'm no' narking.'

'I'm not asking you to. But I need your help. I want you to be standing near him when I come into the Old Judge later this week and I want you to recognise me as an old pal.'

'You look too much like a cop.'

'I won't when I come into the Old Judge.'

'What will you be wearing then?'

'Uniform.'

'For Chrissake.'

'The uniform of a lamplighter. And you're my pal.'

'Aye . . . that's good. A lamplighter. They're a' skinny blokes like you. And you say these charges are dropped?'

'Completely. And here's a couple of quid to keep you off the mammy. Mind . . . I want you sober when I come into the pub. So keep on the beer.'

'Don't worry. Last night was enough for me. Must have went insane. Carrying a weapon? Serious assault? Can hardly believe it. Eh . . . by the way, what do I call you when you come into the pub? Superintendent?'

'No. Just call me by my name. But make it Tommy. Tommy Graham.'

The lamplighters were a vital part of the working structure of the Gorbals, just like the midden men, the night squads of workers dressed like miners, with nicky tams and torched helmets and enormous creels to carry the rubbish to their carts, or the gas meter men, one shoulder drooping from the weight of their huge Gladstone coin bags, and them such a frail lot as well, or the coalmen that every house depended on for the weekly deliveries of the universal fuel, or the health inspectors and the penny-a-week industrial insurance men and the water men for the ubiquitous pipe bursts and the factor's men checking for repairs, chasing for arrears. The lamplighters were lonely silent men, always on the move with their long brass and ash carbide lighting sticks to flame the gas mantles that flickered a passing world's glow up the dreary tenement entrances. The Lighting Department of the Corporation, for whom they worked, had them dressed in heavy serge uniforms with silver buttons, but they were men for whom uniforms were never meant and they wore them more like some characters in a farce than members of a force.

Superintendent Graham ensured that his leerie's uniform was as ill-fitting as the next man's and his oversized regulation cap was well supported by his ears. He stood on the edge of the pavement outside the Old Judge dutifully emptying the white carbide powder that mixed with water to manufacture the acetylene gas for the light of the lamp stick. Some children gathered with awestruck faces as the mysterious powder bubbled then frothed furiously in the gutter and he shooed them away telling them they would be burnt. As soon as he walked into the public house they scampered back again with poking fingers and sticks. He stood for a while by the door, gratifyingly noting that he was regarded by all and sundry as just another anonymous lamplighter.

He walked smartly to the bar to order a drink and then ran a quick eye round the room, only the barman giving him a nod, a special nod. Riley, he could see, was in a corner by the door to the gents'. Two men were by the bar near him, one of them Eddie 'Boy' Watson. He nudged him in a friendly manner with his lamp stick when he approached him and Eddie, mindfully, hailed with with 'How'sitgaun, Tommy?' He nodded in the direction of the other man with him that his name was Willie and then told him that Tommy the lamplighter was a keen boxing fan.

'Saw me fight at the booth in Greendyke Street.'

'I used to go there masel',' said the man called Willie. 'That was Tommy Watson's place. Was he related?'

'No. Everybody thought he was and I used to get abused when I won fights for they thought I was his brother or cousin or something. You know what they were like! Gees, they were tougher in the crowd than some of the ones you used to meet in the ring. You would think they were gonnie tear you apart if you didn't give them a good show. Ten rounds for two quid. Liberty so it was. A liberty.'

The Superintendent had made a firm friend. He ordered some drink and the barman gave him the special nod once more. And Sonny Riley and his men never as much as gave him a second look. Everything in the pub was in its place. Riley and his men were in one corner, another group who always met for dominoes was in another, some pensioners were in their normal place, 'Boy' Watson was at the bar where he usually was and the man with him was a lamplighter and nothing else; there was a strange barman, but they were always coming and going; other than that everything was as it should be in the Old Judge.

There were to be more visits by the Superintendent to have talks, always about boxing and the old days, in the vicinity of Sonny Riley.

Iftikhaar didn't waste any time in getting a replacement helper to act as his bag man for his weekly rent collecting. On the Thursday after the attack he was on his rounds again, this time with his new man, one of the *gora*, a local white man. He had asked the people who knew about such things.

'I want a man,' he had said, 'who knows the ways of the streets and the closes and the lanes and the people. Someone who can read such situations before they happen and someone who can handle them when they do.'

Those he asked all mentioned the one name . . . Frankie Burns of the Calton.

Frankie Burns had always stayed aloof from the gangs. He didn't need them. And they kept clear of him. Frankie stood out from the others because of his height. He was six feet tall and men of that size were the exception, not the rule, the tenements and the lifestyle being more conducive to the small than the tall. National Service, with the Scots Guards in Malaya, where he won the Military Medal for bravery, had cut short his career as a promising heavyweight boxer and although he hadn't the kind of face which was about love and understanding, he was considered to be something of a catch as a partner for a date, mainly because of his film-star physical dimensions.

Frankie was a loner which lent an air of mystery to him. He worked as a freelance on a number of jobs, all of which had the emphasis on muscle and might – he was there as a steward at all the big boxing matches as well as at the clubs, as a bouncer in a variety of dancehalls, guarding the bookies at the illegal pitch-and-toss schools. Then, from time to time he would be away from Glasgow, periods which no one ever knew about except those for whom he worked in London. When he returned there was always the new suit and drinks that were paid with fivers and tenners. And now, for a spell, he was to be the Thursday night man for Iftikhaar at £8 a night, more than many made for a week. But it was worth it to Iftikhaar who felt safe in the company of big Frankie.

Exactly a month after the assault and robbery on the Pakistani landlord Superintendent Tom Graham had called a meeting of his senior officers in order to collate all the evidence that had been gathered about the activities of the tallymen. As a result of that conference there was a discussion the following day with the Procurator Fiscal who concurred that there was more than enough evidence with which to arraign the men. No further time was wasted. In the early hours of the following morning there were raids at a variety of addresses in the Gorbals and nearby Oatlands and Govanhill. Sonny Riley and his gang were in police custody. And all over the Gorbals there were house parties and celebrations but without too much of a flourish, for, like the wartime slogans, they remembered that 'careless talk could mean lives'. And just in case Sonny and his confederates were soon back among them they kept quiet about their rejoicing.

It was to be three months before the trial at the circuit High Court in the imposing building of that name in the Saltmarket, an historic site in Glasgow for criminal matters, being adjacent to the old Jail Square where less than a hundred years previously they had held the last public hanging in the city and more than 30,000 had gathered for that most gruesome of galas. The press were to give the trial star billing, endlessly repeating that it was one of the most expensive-ever High Court cases, costing the Crown 'a massive', as they described it, £25,000 to put together.

The daily reports were to make lurid reading. They were used to the normal High Court cases of the feud murderer, the drunken brawl that ended with the plunge of the knife; all conventional and predictable with one set of names merely replacing a previous set linked to a similar series of factors and circumstances. But the tallymen trial was different. This was the organised form of gangsterism about which Glasgow was not. The stuff of fiction had become a reality in the city where realities normally had little romance.

A succession of police witnesses, all from Superintendent Graham's undercover squads, who had nicknamed themselves 'the great unwashed' and 'the unclean team' and 'the sewer brigade', gave evidence against the accused, who were charged with illegal moneylending and, with some exceptions, assault.

Graham had them warned, however, that the secrets of their success as undercover agents was never to be divulged as it would prejudice the safety of future operations of that kind.

The police testified that they had seen and actually heard at close quarters the conversations between the borrowers and the tallymen. They had seen entries being made in notebooks, they had seen money being passed between the various parties. Sometimes there were bundles of notes. Other times it was mere bottles of fortified wine being sold on no-deposit conditions, a pound bottle costing them a minimum of one pound and four shillings in repayments.

The squad who had been posted at another pub told how the tallymen had taken over a gents' toilet and used it as their office for the collection of debts and the giving out of loans. Others had been called to the toilet for what they called 'a talking to' about the increased interest on their loan because of the time they had taken to repay it. Another two had been frogmarched into it in order to be more savagely reminded about their debts, one having his head thrust into a toilet pan which was then flushed. The policewomen too gave corroborating evidence about the exchange of money and conversations about money between the borrowers and the tallymen in various pubs.

There was other evidence from plainclothes teams who had been working outside the pubs and who had followed some of the accused on various occasions and seen them being involved in scuffles with other men. They had seen others being stopped in the street and being held against walls while obviously being given warnings of one sort or another.

Borrowers too were there to give evidence, the two who had been given police protection and the promise of a paid trip, one to London, the other to Ireland, and two others who had not asked for such treatment. And Superintendent Tom Graham was called to give his evidence together with the barman who had regularly given him the nod, he being a sergeant detective whom the bar had agreed to take on their staff rather than have the police licensing squad take a more rigorous look at their premises.

The Superintendent told the court that he had noted on at least twenty occasions men handing Riley envelopes containing money, pre-empting the obvious question of Counsel about how he knew they had contained money by adding that on most of these occasions the money had been taken from the packet and openly counted by the accused. He said he had also heard Riley referring to the fees that were to be paid for certain pubs and talked about the conversation he had noted between Riley and another man as they bargained on what he would have to be paid for extending his operation to a third pub.

'Did you have a drink,' asked the Counsel, 'when you were in the public house listening to all these conversations?'

'I did,' he replied.

'And what did you drink?'

'Beer mainly.'

'You mean sometimes there were other drinks as well . . . like spirits?'

'No, sir. I don't drink spirits. When I said beer mainly I really meant beer all of the time.'

'And how much beer would you drink at a time?'

'Well, it depended. Sometimes my stay in the pub would have to be extended and I would have to drink several pints.'

'Several pints indeed, Mr Graham? What is several pints? Three, four, five, seven, nine . . . pints?'

'Oh no . . . four, perhaps five at the most.'

'Now I'm told, Mr Graham, that you're a man of moderation. Isn't it known in police circles that you rarely drink anything other than a sweet stout? Mackeson's sweet stout to be precise?'

'It is a fact that stout is my normal drink. Whether it is known in police circles, as you say, that it is my drink, I can't answer. That would be hearsay, I suppose.'

'Hearsay or not, wouldn't you agree that a man who is used only to the occasional sweet stout, a Mackeson's, might be what could be termed as "under the weather" drinking four or five pints of beer and that that might affect what he heard or saw in a public bar?'

'Yes, I would agree that would most certainly be the case. And that being so, I took precautions.'

'Precautions?'

'Yes, sir. I had it planned with the barman, Detective Sergeant Wallace. The beer he poured me was five parts lemonade. He used Barr's Irn Bru so that it wouldn't affect the colour. So out of five pints I may have consumed, only one pint was actual beer.'

Even the accused in the dock laughed at that. And there were no more questions from the Counsel about the Superintendent's judgment after drinking his pints of 'beer'.

The trial had gone well for the police. But on the tenth day there was to be a sensation. More experienced ears in proceedings were to take a different view from the police on the outcome of the trial. On the evening of the ninth night of the sitting, the Advocate Depute in charge of the prosecution had a meeting with a senior official of the Crown Office. As a result of this, at the conclusion of evidence the following morning, he stood up to announce to the Judge, Lord Duncan, that he was not moving for sentence. He had taken that decision, he said, because the maximum fine for illegal moneylending was a mere £100 . . . and the men had already been in custody for three months. On the direction of the Judge, the jury found the men not guilty. Thereupon the Advocate Depute announced he was dropping all the other charges against the accused.

The relatives and friends of the men in the dock who had packed the court every day stood and cheered and clapped as Graham and the other policemen shook their heads in dismay while court officials shouted for order and hurriedly cleared the public benches. Another crowd waited on the broad pavement of the Saltmarket outside the court, a crowd that was always to be seen when the High Court was in session, a crowd that invariably represented an aspect of Glasgow life that looked upon the High Court and those who passed through it with the same regard that others might think of an institution where they might receive one of life's honours; their High Court was a place for them to be, a place that they would later talk about with the expertise of the layman, bandying the names of well-known lawyers and Queen's Counsel and judges with the same facility they did the team they supported in the Saturday football. And they cheered the acquitted there too and thumped their backs for the triumph they said was theirs but in fact they had only been bit players in the courtroom drama which had demonstrated to some the meticulousness of proof that was required under Scots law, and proved to others that that same law too often favoured the accused. Superintendent Tom Graham was prominent among those others.

When the police broke up the milling crowd outside the impressive High Court building with its huge Doric portico, one of the biggest in Britain, the freed men turned south to walk the fifty yards to the Albert Bridge that crossed the Clyde where fishing fleets used to berth when Glasgow was young. Then they went across the river and into the dark canyons of the Gorbals tenements and home.

They walked all of the way, like a mob on the move, and you could hear them before you saw them for when they spoke they liked to shout and when they cursed and when they swore, and they did a lot of that, it was that peppering of the four-letter, crude and ugly words that dominated so that it sounded from a distance as if they communicated in oaths; and when they laughed, and they did a lot of that too, it was a demonstration, loud bronchial lungfuls of rollicking shrieks and exultant yells that opened windows a street block away so that the merriment could be witnessed.

They went straight to the Old Judge where there was still another hour and a half left of the lunchtime session which ended at 2.30 with loud bells and even louder yells of 'Time'. It was the biggest crowd the pub had known for years, bigger even than the last Hogmanay celebration.

'Like VE Day, so it is,' said one who had his remark countered with 'More like the night wee Benny came home with the world title' and that was followed by another who said, 'And I was there.' But then there was always someone who said he was there for that; someone who wanted a share, a touch of the one who had really put the Gorbals on the map.

Riley and his men laughed and drank anything served up to them . . . anything except vodka and orange for that had been their sole alcoholic diet for the past three months, passed to them in the shape of fresh oranges syringed with neat vodka until the juice and spirit mixture oozed from the fruit. 'Fuckin' magic they were,' roared one of his adjutants in a laugh-shout that could be heard all over the bar. 'And they daft bastardin' screws couldnae work it out how we were a' fleein' after eating a coupla dozen oranges between us. Aggie McNally from South Portland

Street brought them up to us and she says she could get a bottle of voddy to the dozen oranges.'

They had all come to pay their tribute to Riley in his moment of victory for it meant more to them than anyone. To those not of the Gorbals, the trial had just been another case at the High Court, ten days of sensationalised reading in the tabloid newspapers that would be forgotten with the next High Court case, the one about the sexual indiscretions of a monied West End mistress who conspired to murder her lover. The tallymen and their trial would be history all the sooner. But to those of the Gorbals it was a way of life that had triumphed. A way of life that meant money for some, misery for others. For a few there would be a fortune; for many there would be fear.

The tallymen themselves were more than jubilant for they knew Graham now and all the other senior men who had worked on the case. They knew too about Graham's trick of getting his undercover squads to look grubby and to appear as his version of the typical inhabitant of their district. But there was no disguising the strange face nor was there a substitute for familiarity and from now on no one would be welcome in their pubs unless they were known by them or known to someone who was known by them, but no further down the line than that.

Freddie Holden was there to share his nephew's day and innumerable drinks were thrust in his direction; the mere fact alone that he was Sonny Riley's uncle was worthy of another goldie being pressed into his hands: any friend of the king's was a friend of theirs; any relative was a part of the man himself.

Sonny called him over.

'Was talking to a bloke up at the House, an old lag he was, and he says there was some talk that Nelson who runs they lounge bars had something to do wi' the old man getting done. He says you knew all about it.'

'Were you never told? I thought you knew, Sonny. Aye, the story goes that it was Sammy Nelson who done your Da. Others say it was some of his handlers that done it. Naebody was arrested anyway. But it's no' really Sammy that runs the bars. It's his niece or something. A woman called Star. No' a bad bit of stuff.'

'Is that her you see checking up on them from time to time?'

'Aye . . . might be. I don't go into lounge bars. Cannae get a pint in them.'

One of Sonny's associates shouted over and ended the topic.

'How's yer Paki landlord, Freddie . . . Shifty, isn't it? Bet his bag man cannae unbutton his flies yet,' at which Sonny and the others laughed.

'He's got a new bag man,' answered Freddie, a frothing pint of dark ale in one hand, a tumbler of neat whisky in the other. 'Frankie Burns. Frankie Burns of the Calton.'

'That right?' said Sonny, shrugging his shoulders at the announcement and making no further comment. Burns had that kind of effect on them that knew.

17

Love and Marriage

Star and Rasool were to spend many more evenings together. They did the rounds of what few restaurants the city had in the late fifties, the restaurants themselves being yet another marking point in the social divide: table d'hôte and à la carte establishments were for that minority of the divide who cared little about prices, the remainder, the cafés, being for those who did and if they didn't take a haddock with their chips it would be a pie or else sausages. For them the bread came buttered and the tea strong but tasty. Star and Rasool went to the Royal and the Rogano, to Guy's and Ferrari's and the One-O-One with its smart set. There were drives too to the smaller towns and villages dotted around Glasgow, to Eaglesham and Fintry and Drymen and others where there were splendid hotels with fine dining rooms. It was on one of those evenings that she had asked Rasool, calling him as did his other Scottish friends, Russell, about the woman who had been his wife.

'Were you very much in love?' she asked.

'Yes. Very much, I suppose you could say. But you mustn't equate the love that we have with a woman in Pakistan with the love that is expressed, or at least which I see expressed here.'

'I don't understand.'

'It's not easy . . . it often confuses me too. But there is a difference, a whole world of a difference, between the way of thinking about women in my country than there is here. So when you say, was I very much in love, I have to interpret that expression. For instance, right from the very beginning, from the way we meet women, everything is different. Our marriage, like most, was arranged. That is and always has been our custom.'

'But how can you marry and love someone when that someone is not your choice?'

'Well, it is easy if you don't ask questions like that. We accept

184

that the woman of our life will be chosen for us. If that is the way you are brought up to think, then why should you question it? And supposing you do question it? Is there not some logic in having your family, your very own family, choosing someone from a background which equates with your own background, someone they know is from an honourable family, someone they know will look after their son and make a good mother for his children? And let's face it, the alternative, the Western way, is so often one partner choosing another at a very young age as a result of some adolescent fascination. To be honest, isn't the very basis of choice of a woman here in how she looks? There is more to the human individual than appearance. But I do appreciate our ways are so strange and remote and are difficult to comprehend here. Can you imagine what would happen if the story got out that some Gorbals family were insisting that their daughter marry the son of a particular family because they were close friends of her parents! It would make front-page news in those sensational newspapers you have here.'

'Russell, now you're speaking like you are not one of us.'

'What do you mean?'

'When you said . . . *you* have here.'

'Ah, you caught me there. Yes, I suppose that despite all the years I have been here and the years before that when my masters at school were British and we were taught in the British fashion, there is a part of me which is not with you here. Some of me will be forever the outsider.'

'We seem to have strayed from what I really wanted to know . . . about your love . . . your love for the wife that you lost. Tell me about her.'

'Aneela was her name. She was my cousin. A first cousin. It is not all that unusual for us to marry first cousins, for who better, we consider, than a member of our own family circle? It's legal here too to marry your cousin, although I know it doesn't often happen.

'You'll remember me recounting the story of our flight from India and how Javaid helped save my life until we joined one of the long refugee columns where we met Maqbul. Javaid and Maqbul . . . Davie and Mac. I laugh every time I think of them as that. Anyway, when I eventually got back to Samanabad, a

very pretty place just outside Lahore where my uncle lives, I was in a shocking state, both physically and mentally. The work in helping the old and sick refugees had been more exhausting than I thought, plus the long trek itself. That had kept me busy without time to think about myself. But when I got to my uncle's it really hit me. There I was bereft of everything that had been near and dear to me in life . . . my father, my mother, my dear sister Nazia. Burned to death in the flames of hatred. I wanted to hate those Sikhs, the people that had done it to us. I wanted to hate the Hindus who had murdered and slaughtered so many more of us. I just wanted to hate everybody, I suppose. But my uncle was a great help to me. He is called Irshad. The name means Guidance and he was well named for he helped guide me in the way of love, in the way of our Koran, our bible. I know so many scoff at the varying religions and the peculiar ways, it seems, that some of them have. But how can one scoff at something which helps fill the heart with love instead of hatred? He helped me too in so many other ways. To readjust my life once more and to stand on my own two feet and face up to the world instead of thinking only of the loss of my family and all our possessions. Irshad took the role of my father and, as such, took it upon himself with my aunt to choose an appropriate wife for me. Aneela was the daughter of my father's other brother, Zaakir, a very wealthy merchant in stone and granite and onyx and things like that. She was one of the most beautiful girls . . .'
He paused and looked intently into Star's eyes and she returned the long, loving look.

'And it was love at first sight?'

'You mean like they say in the Hollywood movies? They just have to look at one another and it's love. But in fact it's . . . desire. The desire to share that person's body.'

'Was it desire, then, when your eyes first met Aneela's?'

'No . . . it was more than that. For I was being presented with a woman who was to share my life, not with someone who was merely to be a conquest. And she was being presented to the man who would be the father of her children and the provider for her future. So when we looked at each other it was like that feeling you get when you look for the first time into the eyes of the child that has come into your family as brother or sister. In the truest sense of the word love, you love them immediately you look at them because they are to be a lifelong friend and companion.'

'So you looked at her with the love of a brother for his new sister?'

'More than that, Star. You see, the Muslim views woman in a vastly different way from the Western mind. We are wary of this thing "love" that is so often spoken about here. Love, goes the Arabic saying, can either drive you crazy . . . or kill you. And there is another, perhaps more accurate, saying which is a prevalent attitude among Muslims and that is that whenever man looks at woman, *fitna* occurs. *Fitna* means chaos. And we see woman as the root of all chaos among men.'

'And was there this *fitna* when you looked at Aneela for the first time?'

'Of course there was *fitna* too. Remember, in Pakistan we do not go around looking into women's eyes. If a woman is not of your family, she wears the veil or hides her eyes in some way from you.'

'But why do you fear women so?'

'Again it is very difficult for one used to Western ways to quickly comprehend such things. But in Muslim thought it is perfectly reasonable to fear women. Being a Muslim, you know, is not exactly like being of a religion like you have here. Being a Muslim is a way of life. It is a much younger religion than Christianity and therefore we are as zealous as the Christian was seven or eight centuries ago when you warred for your religion, when you displaced kings and queens for your religion and when you conquered and subjugated other countries for your religion. In the conscience of the Muslim man is the fact that religious and social duties are first and foremost in life. Nothing, absolutely nothing, should come between him and that duty. Women are considered a distraction and therefore must be controlled.'

'And you saw and felt that too when you looked into Aneela's eyes?'

'Yes. I was looking into the eyes of one of God's most beautiful creatures.'

'And that she had to be controlled?'

'Yes . . . in our sense. Just as I see much the same when I look into your eyes.'

'And are they the eyes of someone that has to be controlled?'

'Yes. In the Western sense . . . not in our sense. Maybe you understand that.'

'Understand, yes. Appreciate . . . I'm not so sure. I would have to know an awful lot more about Eastern ways, I suppose, to appreciate. The veil, for instance. That is difficult to appreciate, let alone understand.'

'Again, it is getting back to that power which must be controlled. Our assumption is that women are powerful and dangerous things, therefore all our sexual institutions, such as polygamy, segregation, and so on, can be perceived as a strategy for containing that power. Hence the veil. They say, you know, that when a man and a woman are isolated in the presence of each other, their likeliest companion will be Satan.'

'Is he here with us just now?'

'He would be . . . if I was married to another and feeling about you like I do just now. That is why it is so confusing when we come to this country and we can look into the eyes of a strange woman. We know about that power all right when we come here at first.'

'So if I went to Pakistan I would have to wear the veil and cover my arms and legs?'

'When we go together, Star . . .'

'Is that an invitation?'

'Yes. I want to return to my homeland one day and establish myself there again. I have in mind to start factories of my own and make my own leather goods. That will create more jobs for my country's people. At the same time I will keep the agencies here and in Europe who will import the goods I make and I will retain and create even more jobs for the countrymen of my second homeland. And if all goes well, I will be able to spend half of the time in my homeland which I love so much and the other half in my adopted homeland which I have come to love so much. I have been planning it all for some time now and I know a beautiful spot to the north of Lahore in the foothills of Kashmir where, except when there's a heat haze, you have this wonderful backdrop of the beautiful mountains of the Karakorams and the Himalayas. I cannot think of a finer place to be. Your Highlands remind me so much . . .'

'*Our* Highlands.'

'I don't mean to forget. Our Highlands. You're right. Our Highlands remind me of the same beauty. The mountains of Pakistan and those that look down on us might be five times and more higher than the mountains here. But it is the proximity here that gives you that same feeling. Like that weekend we spent in Glencoe.'

'You mean at the hotel where they had the sign that said "No Campbells Allowed"?'

'Yes . . . that one. And I didn't know the story about the massacre and was foolish enough to joke that my name was Russell Campbell and they weren't going to let us in.'

'And I jokingly told the owner that you just said you were a Campbell as a jest and that you really were from a branch of the MacDonald family.'

'And he believed you . . .'

'So your place in Punjab is like up north?'

'In a way. At Glencoe you can reach out and touch the beauty . . . like that waterfall at Claddaig or at that place they called the Pass. I've never known such beauty, such savage beauty, so close, so overpowering. Whereas the beauty of the place where I will establish my home is distant . . . more mysterious . . . like you, Star. You will love being there.'

'Your plans then are for much more than yourself?'

'My plans, Star, are that you will be part of them . . . that you will be my wife . . . that you will be the mother of my children.'

'And what about the chaos, what is it . . . the *fitna*? . . . that I will cause?'

'You have already caused that, my dear.'

'But you cannot and will not contain me like you would a woman who has been raised the Muslim way.'

'Star, being what you are and as I know you, I could not imagine trying to contain you even in the Western way.'

'But you would have to compromise if we lived together in Pakistan.'

'That is so. And so would you. But is that not what harmony is about . . . compromise?'

'I'm glad you said that. I would have been so disappointed had you said otherwise. So many cannot compromise . . . I know lots of Catholics who can't. And I know lots of Protestants likewise. Their God gave them everything . . . except love and compassion for one another. Sadly, all God seems to have given so many is hatred.'

'Many of my people have that same failing. Their belief that there is only one God and that God is Allah often precludes them from trying to understand others and their ways. But any compromises I make will have to take the customs and lifestyle of my people into consideration.'

'You mean you will be Russell here and Rasool there and all that that means.'

'I think that sums it up. How do you feel about that?'

'Well . . . it looks like I'll have to do some shopping for an entirely new wardrobe if Star is to become Sitaara . . . Sitaara Jehan.'

They held hands once more and there was another long and loving look between them, interrupted by the subtle cough of the dining room's *maître* inquiring, 'And how was your meal, Mr Russell?'

It was nearly midnight when they arrived home and the lights were on in the big front lounge and the hall of Sammar. 'How unusual,' said Star. 'Sammy is usually in bed at this time and normally only leaves the small light on in the hall.'

They walked into the house together and Star stopped to listen as she heard voices, then turned to Rasool. 'Surprise, surprise . . . it *is* Sammy and he's got company. How unusual!'

'Well, well, well,' said Sammy jumping up from the couch in which he was sitting with an engaging brunette in her mid-forties. Another couple sat in the longer couch on the other side of the broad fireplace, the man a distinguished figure in smart flannels and blazer, the embroidered badge of which, with its Glasgow tree and bird and a beehive, Star recognised as being that of the Clydesdale Cricket Club. He stood up briskly as Star and Rasool approached, Sammy introducing them as Mr and Mrs Mackay, 'friends from the club', and then turning to the woman he had been sitting beside. 'And this is Emma . . . eh, Mrs Emma Hunter. She lives in Fotheringay. You know, in the big tenements?'

'The big what?' she chided in that cosy manner which younger couples often display in pretence that they've known each other all their lives but in fact are just recent acquaintances.

'Aye . . . I keep forgetting. I've not to call them tenements. They're houses or flats, as they say.'

She was looking up at him all the time as he spoke and when he had finished she turned to the others. 'You see, there's the snob in all of us. There I am living up a close and up a stair, yet because it's in Fotheringay Road, Pollokshields, you mustn't say it's a tenement. Come and sit beside me, Star, dear . . . I've heard so much about you.'

Rasool was immediately cornered by the man in the blazer who wanted to know all about the recent triumphs of the Pakistan cricket side and Sammy busied himself arranging drinks from his tall cocktail cabinet.

'So you're the brains behind the Sammar empire?' commented Emma, anxious to converse with Star.

'Empire hardly . . . as for the brains! Well, I prefer to say we've been very lucky. And there wouldn't be a Sammar in the first place had it not been for the enterprise of Uncle Sammy there in his younger days. It was quite an achievement what he did, starting from scratch and all that. Do you go to the Clydesdale Club too?'

'Oh yes. I even like cricket . . . and me a Gorbals girl as well.'

'You're from . . .?'

'That's right, Star. Rutherglen Road just near McNeil Street. Some folks used to say our house was on the other side of the Gorbals boundary. That was them being inverted snobs, I suppose. But we were all south side and south side is south side . . . is it not? And here in the 'Shields we're still technically in the south side.' At that point she elongated her words in an affected West End accent . . . 'And we never call our houses tenements . . . do we, darling?' Then she burst into a warm, infectious laugh. 'Aye, what was I saying there? Yes, cricket. I don't mind watching the game at all. Haven't a clue about all the rules. I thought it was sort of rounders for men, but there is a lot more to it. It was at Clydesdale I met Sammy. He's become one of the characters of the place even though he says he's terrified his friends in the Gorbals will find out he's a member of a cricket

club. He says that if the news got out it would make a front-page
story in the *Record*.'

'I didn't realise Sammy had been to the club that many
times.'

'You mean that many times to ask an old widow up to his
house?'

'Oh, Emma, I didn't . . .'

'I'm having you on, Star. I remember Sammy when I was a
youngster. Of course, as you can see,' she said jokingly, 'he's a
lot older than me. I knew him because of the Nelson family.
They were quite well-known . . . if you know what I mean. Then
I was at school with Peggy, your aunt. What a lovely girl. What a
terrible way to go, the poor dear. At least mine went quickly.
Myocardial infarction, as the death certificate said. As if they
couldn't just say a coronary.'

'And had you lived in the 'Shields long?'

'Since we married, although he originally came from here. Do
you know, he was the first boy with a pan-loaf accent that I had
ever met? He was a clerk of works at the time with the
Corporation Housing Department and I had a boyfriend who was
a wee joiner with them. He took me to their staff dance and I met
Charles . . . that was his name. He just swept me off my feet,
accent or not. Imagine never having met someone from here
before and us living virtually in the next district. Strange when
you think about it, the separate lives we lead. Flats and
tenements and all that sort of thing.'

It was two o'clock before they had all gone home, Emma
leaving with the Mackays, Rasool having left earlier.

'Right,' said Star, stopping her uncle as he hurried past her to
go upstairs to the bedrooms. 'Let's hear your story. You've been
a real quiet one about your lady friend . . . who I must say is a
lovely woman.'

'Oh, you know me, Star. Some things I like to keep to myself.'

'Like what?'

'Like having a girlfriend.'

'Oh, so she is your girlfriend?'

'You know what I mean.'

'Of course I do. But I would love to have heard about her and
to know that you were maybe thinking about . . . thinking about

having women friends again. It's a long time since Peggy, you know. A man needs a woman about the place. Especially you. Tell me, have you ever so much as boiled an egg or made yourself a cup of tea?'

'Of course I could . . . if I had to, that is.'

'Don't you kid me on. If it wasn't for our housekeeper and the odd thing I rustle up for supper, I think you'd starve, Sammy Nelson.'

'Och, I'm too busy for that kitchen carry-on. Anyways there's always been a woman about the house.'

'Yes, but there won't always be . . . will there?'

'What do you mean by that, Star?'

'Surely, Uncle Sammy, you must have thought, even just once, that one day I would get married and set up a home of my own?'

'What would you want to do that for? For God's sake. Look at the size of this place! Half of Florence Street could live here. Och, anyway, we're talking away about the future . . . look at the time. I'm away . . .'

'Uncle Sammy . . . Russell and I are getting married.'

'What?'

'That's right. Getting married.'

'To Russell. Russell the . . .'

'The what?'

'The Paki.'

'That's right. Russell Jehan, the very same Russell who was here tonight, the very same Russell you meet from time to time at the Clydesdale.'

'But . . .'

'But what? Shouldn't I be getting married . . . or shouldn't I be marrying someone from Pakistan?'

'Oh, c'mon, Star. You know I've nothing really against them. But marrying one?'

'What would you have said then had I announced I was going to marry someone called Joseph Murphy or Kelly and the wedding was to be in Holy Cross?'

'Well, you know I wouldn't like that . . . but these things happen. I know quite a few who've had that shock in their family. But things like that go on, don't they? I mean, mixed

193

marriages are getting quite common nowadays. But . . . I mean to say . . .'

He fumbled for a word; a right word, for he could see her anger rising and he knew she was waiting to pounce on whatever he said.

'You mean to say what, dear uncle?'

'I just meant to say . . . Star, I love you. Love you like you're my very own daughter and I just don't want you to be doing anything you might regret. And there's the weans to think about. That's when all the trouble starts when they marry Catholics. You might say that you're not going to be one of them, but as soon as the weans come, they're up at the door, the five-card-trick men, checking up on you to see that you bring them to chapel and send them to one of their schools. You take my word for it, Star. That's the truth, so it is. And it would be even worse if your weans were . . .'

'Slightly coloured . . . is that the words you were looking for?'

'You know what I mean.'

'Oh, I know all right. I love you too, uncle, but deep down you are like the others whether it's about religion or race. I don't know! It seems to be inbred in us, or something. People might say they have this or that view on the subject, but as soon as you say one is coming into the family then the shutters come down, the blinkers go on. It's like saying you're going to marry someone with a contagious disease.'

'Star . . . I'm saying nothing more. I just don't want you to get hurt, that's all. Losing you is more of a shock than anything. I cannae imagine this place without you.'

'Well, that's why I was delighted, absolutely thrilled, when I saw you with Emma tonight. She's a lovely person. It won't be nearly as bad as you think when I'm gone. And, one way or another, I'll still retain an interest in the business, especially when I'm back in Glasgow.'

'Back in Glasgow? Why . . . where are you going?'

'Pakistan, of course.'

Sammy looked at her in disbelief. The double shock of the night was almost too much for him. The very thought of his niece, his Star, going to Pakistan was just too much to bear.

'Pakistan!' he exclaimed loudly. 'What the bloody hell would you want to go there for?'

'Oh God, Sammy, you're off again. You haven't a clue what Pakistan is like, let alone what it's about, and you're wondering why I should be going there. I'm going there for the very simple reason I'm marrying a Pakistani. Tell me . . . what's wrong with my going there with Russell?'

'How would I know? I don't know a thing about the place except that it's full of . . .'

'What?'

'Star, don't do it. Don't go away there,' he said dolefully.

'Oh, poor Sammy, you really think I'm going off like some latter-day Mary Slessor to live among the poor tribes and to look after the lepers. Sammy, there are people in Pakistan with a lifestyle that very few of us have here. And from what I can see of the ones I've got to know here, I've a lot in common with their up-and-go attitude to life. You don't get them sitting back waiting on some bossman to give them a job. I wish more of us were like that.'

'Oh dear, Star. It's been too much for me. I'm away to my bed. Maybe you'll have changed your mind by the morning.'

'Why, you old incorrigible! Talk about sticking your head in the sand. You're like a wee boy at times . . . go to bed and everything will be better in the morning. I bet you're thinking that maybe when you come down in the morning I'll tell you I'm going to marry some nice Protestant boy.'

'Star . . . I'm away to my bed.'

It was to be more than a week before the subject was raised again, Sammy conversing about every subject he could think of, except marriage, Pakistanis, or anything about the future. And when the subject did come up, it was to be in a spectacular fashion. Star had become friendly with Meera, the wife of Maqbul, and she had asked her to help with the intricacies, such as there were, of Pakistani dress. Meera was well versed in the subject.

'There're no real complications,' she explained. 'Just a few rules. Unlike the Scottish girl who can dress any way she pleases and show off as much of her body as she wants, we are restricted by custom. Nothing to be seen from ankle to neck. We mustn't show the shape of our breasts or our hips or our waist. And we should have a scarf or the like available in order to avoid the gaze of the man, should one come into our presence. So we have our costume called the *shalwar qamiz*, which is really just a pyjama suit with a long tunic. It must not be tight or figure-fitting, although some girls I see are cheating a little bit on that. Basically they may all look the same, but the style of them does keep changing. Sometimes the trouser legs are tightly stitched at the ankles, other times they are without stitching. And the *doputta* is very important. It's just a long light scarf, really. They are mainly chiffon nowadays. And you use that to cover your head when need be, or across the front of your chest to hide the shape of your bust.'

'It's all so sexual,' laughed Star. 'I mean about the avoidance of the shape.'

'That's right,' said Meera. 'But then the Western woman's dress is all about your sexuality and the emphasis of it. Contrary to what you might think, our beliefs are based on the assumption that woman, as opposed to sexuality, is the powerful and dangerous force, which is why it is deemed we should be under the authority of our fathers, our brothers or our husbands. I found it all so strange when I came here, just as you will in Pakistan.

'I often speak about it with the other Pakistani women here. Some of us thought at first that there would be those who would want your ways and that they would be a great temptation to us. Then, when we got to know more about the customs here we discovered that as a group of people we were as happy as anyone. We don't really feel subjugated. All this freedom and equality which the women have here hasn't appeared to have made them any happier than us.'

'Yes, I've gathered that too, Meera. But then I've a lot to learn about your ways. Now help me choose the finest *shalwar qamiz* you can.'

She picked three outfits in varying colours from the shop in Bridge Street which specialised in the various women's clothing of the Sub-Continent. Rasool was calling for her that night and she rushed home in order to pick the best of the three costumes so that she could surprise him by wearing one when he came to the door. She had tried on the three of them, settling for a gentle pink colour in a silky material. In order to see herself more fully, she had come down from the bedroom upstairs to the huge mirror in the hall and she danced and twirled in front of it so that the light material of the tunic and the gossamer-like *doputta* floated out from her like a graceful filamental extension of her body. For a moment she was lost in herself, as though her body had taken another form, another exotic form, as she pirouetted once again in front of the ornately framed mirror. She hadn't known that dreamlike state since she was first put out to play on the pavements of the Gorbals and together with other little girls she would fantasise that they were nurses or mothers and their dollies, scratched and bashed, were patients or babies, real patients and real babies. And she twirled round once more and she was in a far-off land of the East. Then the doorbell rang and the dream was no more.

She ran to open the door, expecting Rasool. The man standing outside visibly gaped when the door opened.

'Jeeesus Caarrrist. Jeesus . . . bloody . . . Caarrrist!'

It was Sammy. The heavy front door gave a solid clunk as it slowly slid into its lock. He stepped into the house shaking his head. From time to time, if he was very angry, which was rare, or if he got highly excited about something, Sammy's speech and mannerisms would revert to that of the street Gorbals boy, like he was as a youth and when Jamesie, his brother, was king. The shock of seeing Star in her Eastern dress had the same effect.

'Have you gone aff yer heid? One minute you tell me you're marrying a Paki, the next minute you're floating about here like something out of Ali Baba. Jeesus Caarrrist, Star. You'll be wanting me to call you Salome next. Oh my God, what's happened to my poor lassie?' He shook his head again in disbelief. Then the mood of apparent anger suddenly lifted and he smiled. 'Know who you're like? That yin Yvonne de Carlo in the *Dance of the Seven Veils*.'

Star ran to him at that and threw her arms around him and hugged him tightly to her. 'You're a rogue, Sammy Nelson. A real rogue. I could never hate you, no matter what you say or think. I know you're all confused about what's happening to your dear niece.'

'You're more than a niece, Star. You're my lassie. That's the only way I can think of you. And I'll just have to get used to seeing you cutting about like this. You better no' let that John Hanson, the Red Shadow, see you or else you'll be off wi' him in his *Desert Song* show . . .' at which he burst into the first lines of that show's memorable tune: *Oh Song of Songs . . . Song of Memories . . . la da de da de da de da da da . . .*'

Star hugged him tightly once again. 'I can tell, Sammy Nelson. I can tell. You don't understand what is going on but inside you're pleased because I'm so happy.'

'Well, you always had the right words to say about everything. And you've got them once again. Of course I'm pleased for you, hen. I'm happy for both you and Russ. I really am. Got a date yet for the wedding? Where do they marry anyway : . . you know, the Pakis . . . the Pakistanis?'

'Usually in their mosque but we'll be calling the banns at Martha Street Registry Office within the next couple of months and we'll marry there. Then Russell has planned another ceremony over in Pakistan in the district where all his relatives live.'

'So you're going to live there right away?'

'Till Russell gets the first factory going and then we'll be back here again.'

'But no firm date yet for the wedding?'

'No.'

'Well . . . I have. We beat you to it. Emma and I had the banns posted today and we'll be there at Martha Street in a month's time.'

'Sammy, I'm thrilled . . . why, that's the best news I've heard. Oh I'm so happy. Wait till Russell hears.'

18

What is Freedom?

The acquittal of Sonny Riley and the tallymen gang was the
green light for the immediate expansion of their operations to
other centres throughout the Gorbals, but still mainly in public
houses, the occasional one in the proximity of an illegal betting
pitch. Prior to the trial, Riley controlled the tally operations in
ten public houses, from which he was netting about £200 a week,
all for the mere nod of the head from his seat by the door of the
gents' toilet in the Old Judge pub. The week after the trial, five
more pubs had come into his network. Two weeks after that
there were another ten. As the Gorbals declined, the tallymen
expanded like blowflies that laid eggs which survived on a rotting
corpse, and the more they consumed, the more the body rotted.
Riley had never known it so easy, never known it so good. The
vast increase in his wealth had given him a new dimension in the
holding of power. Before he could only command respect
because of the ruthless violence he exercised. Now he could see
that very same power also existed because of his wealth. That was
a revelation to him. Before terror had to be generated. People
had to be regularly challenged and injured and maimed and even
killed by him to demonstrate that he was power, the ultimate in
power in the Gorbals. Now there was no need to do that. The
money had that same grip over everyone. They would jump to
his command for money just like they used to for his superior
physical and fighting ability. Once there were loyalties to him for
the *camaraderie* of the battle, lieutenants and adjutants ready and
willing to obey for the fellowship of the fight. Now there were
mercenaries who would sell their souls to him for a share of his
silver. He had heard them say wealth was power. Now it was
being demonstrated to him.

But such was the quirk of his nature, the new-found authority
was also to be a source of frustration. There was a twisted sense
of achievement, a sort of joy, when he could cause pain or injury.

For others in combat, victory was the golden fruit. For Sonny Riley it was the way the fruit was achieved that was important. Victory in itself was merely the outcome, a sort of by-product, of what should and would happen to adversaries. The delights were in the slit and the slash and the plunge; the glory was the infliction of agony and the torture which a knife or a bayonet or a razor could impose on another. That was what pleasure and satisfaction were really about. And money couldn't replace that. Not even the sums that were effortlessly coming into his possession at that seat by the gents' in the Old Judge pub.

'Get the word out,' he said to one of his men. 'I want to see Freddie Holden . . . you know, the Da's brother, the wee modeller that comes to see me now and then.'

He was there the next day. As usual, they immediately armed him with the drink he knew would be there for him.

'We didn't get finishing that story the last time, Freddie . . . you know, about my Da and the Nelsons? What more do you know?'

'No' that much to tell, Sonny. Like I said, the story was that it was Nelson who did your Da, but nobody was arrested.'

'Must be more to it than that, Freddie. They don't talk for nothing.'

'Well, Nelson had this helper. Bloke by the name of Claney. He still works for him. Does his manager or something wi' they bars that he runs. Anyway, this Claney one was seen tailing your Da two or three times. It was chinas of your Da that saw him, like, but they didn't twig till after he was done.'

'So, what was the connection? What could Nelson or Claney want to do him for?'

'There were umpteen reasons. See's another pint, Sonny.' Another tumbler of whisky was also put down beside him. 'Aye, you're a great boy, so you are. What was I saying? Oh aye, the connection between them. Well, like I said, it goes right back to the old days. Your Da and the Jamesie one were in the same team thegether. Jamesie was the top man, then after doing a stretch up at the House, your Da did him.'

'A straight fight?'

'Dunno. Big gang fight somewhere in Crown Street. I was

respectable at the time. Worked as a joiner and never had time for a' that daft gang business.'

'But my Da did Jamesie?'

'Aye, that's right.'

He would dearly have loved to be told more of the details, for they were important. But he could visualise them. His Da, his father, had won; it had been in the street and it would be in the manner of the street; vicious and primeval, where you gave of everything and surrendered nothing, neither compassion nor chivalry; no going away when the other had had enough or when you had proved you were the better; for the only going away was when the other sank down on his knees and the life poured out of him before your very eyes. Yes, that's how it would have been, he thought, when the man who had fathered him had met the one they had called Jamesie; and the satisfaction welled inside him, almost as though he had been there himself and watched it.

'Then there was this connection wi' Nelson, Jamesie's brother Sammy, like, when your Da was living in the old houses in Cally Road. Nelson owned a lot of them and Steve was one of his tenants. That's where Nelson made his money. Anyway, the story goes that Steve got himself involved somehow wi' two of Nelson's men who were done in. Murdered, like. He wasn't charged or anything, but it was a' the talk round the pubs. And then, next thing we know your Da gets it. It must have been Nelson or Claney that did it in revenge. I mean you just don't get done for nothing . . . dae you? Nobody was arrested. They say they never even questioned Nelson or his china Claney. You know what the rozzers are like!'

'And you said there's a woman mixed up wi' them nowadays?'

'Aye, that's Nelson's niece. She runs a' his businesses now. Millionaires, they say. Shops, bars, everything. Rare pint that, son.'

'Big Frankie still doing his bag man for your Paki landlord?'

'Did you no' hear . . . oh, no . . . you'd be in the nick at the time on that charge you were up on. Big Frankie has moved in wi' a London mob. Does his shooter for them. So they say anyway. Still comes up here, mind you. But it's just to show aff his flash suits. Drives a motor and everything.'

'So what about the Paki?'

'He's got another Paki helping him. Sometimes there's two wi' him. Fly bastards, but. Come at different hours now since that time they got done. He's got even more houses now. Making a mint, so he is.'

Iftikhaar the landlord was also the subject of conversations once again at the Jamiat Ittihad. There had been yet another story about him and his activities in one of the Sunday newspapers which specialised in such scandal. He had evicted two of his tenants, one with a young family, and the paper heaped new scorn on the man they said was becoming one of the city's most infamous landlords.

The newspaper had put their top investigator on to him and he was the subject of their widely read feature which they called 'The Advocate', whose speciality was exposure of various sorts. The headline of the page read 'Money-Mad Ifty' and in smaller type beneath it 'The Advocate meets Glasgow's strangest bus conductor'. There was a series of pictures of him, one on the platform of a Corporation bus, another of him talking to a customer at his shop and a third of him coming out of one of the houses he owned. The story concluded: 'Scotland doesn't need you, Mr Ifty.'

Like the previous times they had discussed him, the men at the Jamiat meeting agreed that something would have to be done. Various solutions were suggested . . . another deputation, another appeal for him to attend one of their meetings.

'He won't listen to any of these,' said Maqbul.

'Maybe he will listen to me,' said the Imam, their spiritual leader. 'I am the voice of Islam. He must listen to me.'

They were sceptical about that, but nevertheless thought it an idea worth pursuing.

'I may go and visit him on my own,' said Rasool. 'Maybe I can plead with him on a man-to-man basis that he is disgracing his fellow nationals.'

'You know, I was thinking of doing that too,' said Maqbul. 'If you don't manage to see him, Rasool, I will go and talk to him.'

Javaid shook his head. 'What he needs are the *Goondas*.'

'*Goondas*?' queried Maqbul.

Javaid shook his head. 'You country boys . . . you have much to learn. You've heard of the *Goondas*, Rasool, . . . haven't you?'

'Yes, I heard about them when I was at university. Somebody pointed out one to me once. But I wasn't really all that interested at the time. I thought they were a bit of a myth, really.'

'They are no myth,' said Javaid. 'I knew some of them in the Old City where there are still a lot of them. And there're others you get at the Fort, where they mix with the Kabuli money-lenders and Pathan tobacco merchants. You have to be tough and sharp to mix with that lot.

'The one I knew best was called Amir. Like the other *Goondas* he liked to be seen by everyone and in the morning when his wife and children would be in the house having their breakfast, Amir would be in the market place at a particular foodstall having his breakfast out in the open where he could be seen . . . tall glasses of *lassi namkeen*, then a plate of *cholé* followed by lots of *halva*. Nothing but the best of food for Amir, just like an athlete would take, or the wrestlers that we had in the Old City. They were always drinking the glasses of salted yoghurt like Amir.'

'But what did they do, these *Goondas*?' queried Maqbul, impatient to learn.

'They had many strange ways and activities you did not know about. Some would maybe be burglars, but they would never steal from anyone in the community. A shopkeeper could lay out all his bank notes in front of him while he counted them and a *Goonda* would never even think of taking one.'

'Then they were crooked . . . just like Ifty is?'

'Yes, they did some illegal things but they would never act like Iftikhaar. And they would help the people of their district. Supposing you had a grievance, like someone was harassing you or you were being victimised by someone or some group and the authorities and the police were doing nothing because they are so slow, then you would ask a *Goonda* for his help. And when the *Goondas* helped you, there were never any further problems. They would punish people too who had thieved in the community. Or if there had been an Iftikhaar around our gate in the Old City, I would have asked Amir the *Goonda* for help and I can assure you, the landlord would have had his ways altered. That English one was like a *Goonda* . . . the one they still make stories about after hundreds of years. What's his name? Ah, yes . . .

Robin Hood. He was a sort of *Goonda*.'

'These *Goondas*,' said Maqbul, 'they are what Iftikhaar needs to teach him a lesson. Did any of them come here?'

'No,' assured Javaid. 'They would not leave Lahore. Trading is not their way, like you and I. Anyway, they would miss being the centre of attraction like they are in the Old City.'

'*Goondas* or not,' said Rasool, 'we must find a solution to our Iftikhaar problem. He is no good for us.'

Iftikhaar and the *Goondas* were being spoken about again the following evening when Rasool and Star had their usual Saturday together. Star was fascinated about life in Pakistan and after telling her about the continuing problem with the wayward Iftikhaar, Rasool had gone over Javaid's story of the Robin Hoods, as he had called them, of his area in the Old City of Lahore.

'So will you go and see him on your own?' Star had asked after being told about the various solutions they had considered.

'Yes . . . definitely. I was due to be in France this week on business, but it has been postponed for a week as the main French agent cannot be there, so I will go and see our problem friend on Thursday night . . . that's his rent night. After he was attacked that last time he had a strange Glasgow man going about with him. A sinister and unusually tall man. But he is away now and he has another Pakistani companion accompanying him. If my appeal doesn't work then I am going to consult our lawyers and see what they can do. But something . . . something must be done. He's not very pleasant news is our Iftikhaar . . . now let's forget him for the rest of the evening.'

The deeds of the Pakistani and the story of the Nelsons could not be so easily forgotten by Sonny Riley. His need for violence was like a sexual urge. Money power was a poor substitute for the power, the real power as he saw it, which he could exercise through violence.

It didn't matter either if that violence involved pain or injury to himself; the sadist was masochist. Even prison could be a satisfaction of sorts, for in his warped way prison was turmoil; there was an edge in that nether world which he appreciated, for violence could spring there in an instant and those who didn't manifest it had it manifested on them and Riley and his like could rule even more ruthlessly than they did when they were in the freedom of the outside.

Freedom! What is freedom when you have a mind that lusts for destruction, a mind that's in a concentration camp of hatred and hostility and can only find contentment when its narrow confines have been gratified? Sonny Riley couldn't reason why he was the way that he was. There was no need for him to do so. Anger and the short temper were a characteristic of so many about him. A wrong stare, an accidental bump, an inappropriate comment, or less, could spark the tight mouth and the need for challenge; it was like there was a longing to be provoked so that they could prove who they were; but who were they that needed such provoking? These were things that Sonny Riley never tried to fathom, nor could he, had he tried. His world was what he was about and he was about that strange complexity that seemed peculiar to the character of so many from that part of the world where he lived; where he ruled.

The Pakistani and the Nelsons had to be seen to; when, how and in what fashion would be appropriate to the occasion. There was no detailed pre-planning in such moves; only the ordaining was important. And Sonny Riley had decreed it must be thus.

'I want to see this Nelson bird,' he had told two of his men and that week they spent a lot of their time at the Star Lounge Bar in Ballater Street, the one that had once been Sammy's Bar and had been the Nelsons' first venture into lounges. With his enthusiasm and 'conversion' to being a company man, Bert Steed and the family, under the supervision of Claney, now General Manager of the company, had made the Star Lounge Bar one of the most popular in the south side. They had acquired premises next door and through Sammy's contacts at the City Chambers had quickly obtained the extra licence required for such an operation. But just like the Old Judge, a strange face was a strange face in their lounge and when Riley and his men appeared for a second time and then another time after that, Bert Steed took notice.

'It's Sonny Riley,' whispered one of the waitresses.

'Christ, so it is. His face was never out of the papers after that tallymen trial. It's one of these faces you don't forget as well.

Remember that cocky grin he had on that big front-page picture? Treated him like a bloody hero, so they did. What's he doing in here anyway? That's the second day running he's come in. Don't tell me the bastard is thinking about starting his rackets in here? Christ, that would ruin the lounge.'

'Take it easy, Bert,' said Betty, his wife, who was in charge of the waitress service. 'I've been watching him and so have the girls. They've been keeping to themselves. They might be up to something, but it's not moneylending. But we'll keep our eyes on them.'

They had to return for a third time on the Wednesday and yet again on the Thursday before they were to see the woman who had attracted them there.

Star and Claney always visited their lounge bars unannounced, a custom which, as Star put it, 'helped to maintain', or as Claney insisted, 'made bloody sure of' a good level of honesty in their premises. Because Rasool had said he was going to visit Iftikhaar on his own in order to prevail with him about his activities, Star had arranged with Claney to do their scheduled check at the Ballater Street lounge that evening. Riley and his men had been drinking there for about an hour before they had come in.

'That yer big bosses, hen?' Riley had asked one of the girls serving them.

'Aye,' she had replied. 'That's Miss Nelson, no less. You know, Star Nelson?'

'So it is her,' he said quietly. Then he said nothing more. He just stared at Star as she and Claney busied themselves behind the bar taking various measurements and counts between talking to the staff, then going to the cellar and returning again.

'That'll be Nelson that's with her,' he said. 'The Sammy one.'

'No, it's no',' said the man sitting next to him.

'How do you know?'

''Cos he comes into the Devon on a Friday night and meets a crowd there. They don't call him Sammy.'

'Claney then?'

'Aye, that's the name they give him. Claney.'

Riley took another long look at the man and an even longer look at Star.

'I think you fancy her, Sonny,' joked the one sitting across the table from him.

'You want your fuckin' face stitched?' The mood had suddenly changed and he was the unpredictable Sonny they knew and feared, the Sonny who could turn on them with the same viciousness he would a rival or an enemy in the street.

Then just as suddenly again, the evil look which had silenced his companions had gone and he laughed in the face of the one who had made the remark, ridiculing the fear he had so instantly instilled into him. 'You're right . . . I could fancy that yin. But no' the night. I've got other plans for her and her chinas. Tonight we've got another date . . . wi' the Paki. Remember? Thursday night's his rent night. Two more Specials and we're up the road. Freddie says he keeps changing his collecting hours. Must be frightened or something.'

At that he laughed again. And the others laughed loudly too.

One of them was ordered to fetch what Sonny called 'the tools' and to meet up with them in the vicinity of the Abbotsford Place and Cumberland Street junction, around where Iftikhaar had many of his houses.

A fine rain was in the air, so imperceptibly fine it could not be seen, only felt, and Riley cursed at his new Jackson getting soaked. They sheltered in a close-mouth to avoid a further soaking and he cursed again at the stench of the place.

They were to be there for over an hour before they saw two Pakistanis through the gloom of the night, one carrying a bag. Then another Pakistani joined them and the three of them walked together into the entranceway of one of the tenement houses.

'So he's two-handed the night,' said Riley before asking the details of 'the tools' the man had brought.

'Two hammers, a screwdriver and a rozzer's baton.'

'Christ . . . is that all?' Riley commented with an air of disgust. 'Just as well we're no' taking on the Cumbies the night . . . isn't it. Still it'll be enough for the Pakis.'

He then said he would take the two hammers and that the others would be better using their fists and feet.

'You were there the last time,' he said turning to the one called Harry. 'Which one's the landlord?'

'There was only two of them the last time, Sonny, and we went for the bag man.'

'But what one's Ifty?'

'I dunno. They a' fuckin' look alike.'

'Jesus Christ! He's probably the one that joined them there and the other two's the handlers. Right, youse go for them . . . I'll get him.'

Riley felt good at that point, just as he always did on such occasions: journeys into an unknown where they gave and sometimes received; where the kind of character which they revered could be bared in its truest form and where the hideous skills which they possessed could be displayed. And afterwards, as it always was when the excitement of it would be such that sleep would be a day away, they would carouse with each other and others too who had not been there and share with them their moments of squalid glory.

'Right, boys,' snapped Riley, a hammer tightly gripped in each hand. 'Let's get the bastards.'

19
Star Finds a Way

The voice seemed strangely quiet when Star answered the phone early that Friday morning.

'It's Javaid, Star. I'm sorry to call you so early. But I have to know . . . were you with Rasool last night?'

'No . . . he was going to see the one that's been giving you all the trouble. You know . . . Iftikhaar?'

'Yes, I know.'

Star waited for him to speak again but there was only a long pause.

'What is it, Javaid? Why did you want to know that? What is it? Is there something wrong?'

'Have you read the newspapers this morning, Star?'

'No. I'm just up. There'll be one at the door.'

'It's bad news, Star. Very bad news.'

'What is it, Javaid? Tell me. It's Russell . . . isn't it? He's had an accident. Tell me, Javaid. Tell me,' she pleaded.

'He's in hospital, Star. It's the story in the newspapers about the Pakistani men who were attacked last night. They have named Iftikhaar and his helper but the story said a third Pakistani, but not named, is in hospital. Rasool said he was going to see Iftikhaar last night. It must be him.'

'Which hospital?'

'The Victoria Infirmary . . . Intensive Care, it says, Star . . . Star! Star! Are you all right?' The line had gone suddenly dead.

'Are you a relative?' the ward sister asked.

'He's my fiancé.'

'Oh!' she replied, her mood going from concern to compassion. 'I am so sorry. The doctor has just left but will be back again soon.'

'Where is he? I must see him.'

'I'm afraid not. He's in an intensive care room with staff in

209

attendance. He's very heavily bandaged and still unconscious.'

'Just from the door then or the window. I must see him. Please.'

'Come with me.'

Between the activity round the bed, Star could see how heavily the face was bandaged. Then he was out of sight again as a nurse worked hastily at yet another appliance, one with dials and lights, which they were attaching to him.

The sister took Star gently by the arm. 'I really do think it better . . .'

'Yes, I understand. I just had to see him once more . . . even though . . .' The word didn't surface and Star turned quickly and left the hospital.

She tried to compose herself, but couldn't, and she walked from the big infirmary with unseeing eyes and into the outside world where there was noise and hustle and bustle, none of which she heard. Some basic instinct gave her the protection and the guidance to walk safely along the road that went by the side of the Queen's Park with its tall ashes and leafy sycamores, then down Victoria Road in the direction of Eglinton Toll and the road that took her from there to Pollokshields.

Only the thoughts of Rasool, her Russell, filled her mind on that journey she was never to remember back to the house in St Andrew's Drive. She had waited so long for the love that was to be the love of her life . . . and now! Her mind clouded, unable to foresee a future of which he was not a part. There was no tomorrow without her Russell. No one could ever replace that love which to them was unique, as all love affairs are unique; a bond the significance of which is only relevant between the partners who share it. The world could speak about love and love affairs; but love was just a word and no one could quantify its depth; it had a profundity that was beyond measurement, beyond compare. And none, she thought, was deeper, more intense, than the love that she had for him and he for her.

'It is the will of Allah,' he would have said had he been there to explain and to reason with her why the world didn't really have a logic as science knew the meaning of that word.

'The will of Allah,' she kept repeating to herself. 'The will of Allah.' Was this the God among whose people she was so soon to have lived . . . a God who willed that good people like Rasool Jehan could be taken from them and that other people, like those whoever they were who had injured him so, were not to be taken from life. What kind of Allah was this who ordained life so? And how could they hold their hands up to him and agree with his will and bless him and call him the Beneficent, the Merciful, the Lord of the Worlds and bear witness to him that there was no God apart from Allah; how could they say and do all these things to the one who could rob them of the most precious thing in all the world . . . their very own love?

If Allah was great then Allah was cruel and nothing was more cruel than what had happened to the man she had just left behind in that hospital; nothing was more cruel than the torture which she was now experiencing. Nothing.

She turned into the long driveway of their home, Sammar, not having remembered one moment of the long walk from the infirmary, her mind still benumbed and confused with the horror she had witnessed and with the prospect of a future that was beyond contemplation.

She was jolted into reality by a man hurrying towards her and taking her into his arms and telling her how horrible it must have been for her and slowly, like coming out of an ether cloud, the face that was speaking the gentle and reassuring words that everything would be all right came into focus. It was Sammy and he walked towards the main door with her, a comforting arm round her waist.

'Javaid is waiting for you, Star. He's just arrived. Like you, he's very upset, my dear . . . and he's also got something to tell you.'

He was standing at the foot of the wide staircase and the bright sunlight pouring through from the tall stained-glass window of the landing showed up the large tears running down his face. 'Did they tell you, Star . . . did they tell you?'

'Oh God . . . oh no. Dear God . . .'

'Star . . . it is not Rasool. It's Maqbul who is in the hospital. I don't know where Rasool is. I phoned the police this morning when I read the papers about the unnamed Pakistani man and told them it would be Rasool as I understood he had gone to see Iftikhaar. But he didn't. It was Maqbul. His wife phoned me later this morning to say he hadn't come home. And after that I went to the hospital and identified him. I also remembered him saying that if Rasool didn't go to see Iftikhaar, he would.'

Star turned round to her uncle. 'Oh, Sammy.' Then he helped her, weeping uncontrollably, into the lounge where he left her in one of the big armchairs before returning to speak with Javaid.

'I've never seen Star like this, Javaid. She's deeply shocked by it all. I may have to get the doctor. You are sure, aren't you, about who it is?'

'When Star recovers, tell her that nothing is more sure. I asked them at the hospital to let me look at his left hand. The little finger was missing. Maqbul lost it when he worked on the farm in the little town where he lived. It is him all right. Rasool must have gone on business somewhere.'

He then left saying that he had to go and comfort Meera, Maqbul's wife, and to get some other women to be with her before returning to the hospital.

After a half tumbler of cognac, Star said she felt more relaxed but still hadn't got over the shock of that morning. 'I can't really feel relieved or happy when I know that that man lying up there with all those bandages and machines and everything is Maqbul. Poor Maqbul . . . Russell admired him so much. He said he had learned so much from him during the long trek which they had together all those years ago when they were young men and their country was going through that terrible time. He had been so courageous and inspiring yet, here he was, the son of the poorest of peasants and destined to be one himself and showing Russell, the rich man's son, so much. And look at him now. Oh, the dear, poor soul. What happened anyway, Sammy? I haven't even given the actual event a thought.'

'A gang of neds went for them. It's the second time this bloke Ifty the landlord has been done. They got off with the money again but one of them with a couple of hammers, that's what they use, you know, bloody joiner's hammers, well he gave Mac a terrible going over. Battered him senseless. Front page in all the morning newspapers. I'll hear more about it when I get down to the Gorbals. How are you feeling now, Star?'

'I'll never forget this as long as I live. Nor will I forget whoever it was that did it. They'll have to be caught and punished . . .

one way or another, Sammy. One way or another.'

Her wide, soft eyes narrowed as she said that, looking straight at Sammy in that determined fashion which he had said so often to her reminded him of Jamesie.

'Aye, you're right, Star. These ones will need to be caught. But right now you take a rest, my dear. That's some morning you've had.'

She was still sound asleep when the call came through and after taking a look at her, Sammy told Rasool it was best not to disturb her.

'I'm in Paris and I tried to contact her last night but there was no reply. She would be working perhaps.'

'Yes, she was stocktaking with Claney.'

'Everything is all right then . . . I mean, she doesn't often have a sleep at this time of day?'

'Then you haven't heard, Russell?'

'Heard what?'

There was a long pause before Sammy spoke again.

'Russell . . . it's bad news. Your friend Mac. Well . . .'

Rasool didn't speak or ask any questions until Sammy had finished the story.

'Sammy . . . when Star wakens, tell her I'll be home tonight. There's only one direct flight but I'll make it back, perhaps through London. Whatever! I'll be home tonight.'

It was about an hour later when Javaid called with the news. Star was wakened and Sammy took the call. All she heard him say was how sorry he was, which he repeated three times.

'Maqbul?'

'Aye, Star. Poor Mac. He died just after you left the hospital. They tried everything. Javaid is leaving now to break the news to Mac's wife. It's really terrible, so it is.'

The news made the final editions of the evening papers with the headline: 'Murder Hunt'. It said that Superintendent Thomas Graham who had been in charge of the Talleymen Case had been called in to lead the detectives hunting the killer or killers. The story also said that the other two Pakistanis injured in the attack had been discharged from the hospital, one of them, Mr Iftikhaar Ghani, suffering from a broken arm.

'You know,' said Star after reading the story, 'it's like some weird dream to me. I still can't grasp so much has happened so quickly. Look at the time . . . just four o'clock; four o'clock on a Friday afternoon with everyone getting set for their weekend and life going on everywhere as normal and in this one day, which is just a little more than half over, I've suffered more mental anguish than in all my life, even worse than an experience I endured once in the country which also ended in the death of someone. Russell was lost to me this morning . . . then he was given back to me again. And all that suffering I have passed on now to poor Meera. Only she will have no reprieve. Promise me, Sammy – you *will* find out what really happened. You know the people in the Gorbals who know everything. You must find out for me, Sammy. I must know. I must.'

Star and Rasool were reunited that night when he arrived home from Paris and went straight from the airport to Sammar. It had been a mere five days since they had last seen each other. It was like five years, Star told him and they held each other again, closely and lovingly with eyes only for each other. And Sammy quietly left them together and alone in the big front lounge of the house.

Rasool and Javaid took charge of the funeral arrangements of Maqbul. As he would have wished, and just as so many of them wish, he was to be flown back to Pakistan for burial.

But first there were the Muslim rites before interment and which would be performed prior to Maqbul being placed in his coffin. As in their prayers, cleanliness is next to Godliness and it is the duty of the nearest relatives or friends to carry out the ritual cleansing of the body. First it is stripped of all clothing and bandages and then with tepid water washed three times with lightly soaped cloths and, just as they would a living person, they then thoroughly dry the body with towels. When this is completed they shroud the body with three sheets, each overlapping the other.

Maqbul was placed in his coffin and the Imam, who had come from the mosque in Oxford Street, then said the *Namaz Janaza*, the funeral prayer, in which he praised Allah who, he said, was 'free from all kinds of sins' and that all the holy names were for him, after which he praised their Prophet Mohammed, and each time he said the name, as each time they always said the name, he said Peace Be Upon Him, and then finally there were words of praise for Maqbul and for his own relatives who had died before him.

Star had visited Meera, Maqbul's wife, at their big stone villa in Langside Drive in Newlands, while the men had performed the first of the funeral rites. There were other women from their community there giving her comfort. They brought food with them for the house, as was the practice so that the widow of the deceased could concentrate on her grief in the immediate days following the death and thereafter they would also tend to her welfare during the four months and ten days in which the custom had it she would be confined to the house in mourning.

Three days later, the various documents completed, permits granted, Javaid left to accompany the coffin on its long journey back to their homeland for burial in the little cemetery just outside Gujrat, the town he had left to find his fortune, first of all in England, and then Scotland, fifteen years previously.

Rasool and Star went ahead with the plans for their wedding which was just three weeks away and for their honeymoon trip to Pakistan the day after they married, during which they would see work started on the house which they planned to build in the foothills near the Kashmir border. They would also go to Gujrat and pay their respects to Maqbul's remaining relatives and to Meera's parents as well as visit his grave.

Sammy was late home the day after Javaid had left for Pakistan with Maqbul's body and Star anxiously awaited him, hoping he might have some news about the murder.

'Well, what have you found out?' she asked as soon as he came into the big lounge and before he could answer she added . . . 'Was it Riley right enough?'

'Why did you say that name? What do you know about Riley?'

'Did you think I would be sitting still? I've got contacts too, you know. Well, was it him?'

'The talk says yes. He's got a thing about Pakis, they say.'

'That's not unusual . . . is it, Sammy?'

'I hope you're not implying I'm like that?'

'Of course I am. It's like I said before. Some might say they only mean it as a joke but still the feeling is there about them because they are different . . . and their colour is dark.'

'Well, I still think you're being a bit harsh lumping me in with the others that think like that.'

'I'm sorry . . . but it's the way I feel. I don't like being a nice girl at this moment. So it was Riley?'

'There's more.'

'What?'

'They say he's been bad-mouthing us.'

'Why?'

'This will shock you. His real name, or the name he was born with, isn't Riley. That's his stepfather's name. His real name is Holden. Steven Holden. Son of Snakey Holden. Another Steven Holden! You know . . . the one who did Jamesie? Like a bloody ghost from the past that's sent to haunt us. I thought that Holden affair was done and by with when . . .' Sammy hesitated slightly, making sure he would use the right word, but before he could proceed Star continued with the sentence.

' . . . when Claney bayoneted him. Is that what you meant to say? When Claney bayoneted him because he got to him first and if he hadn't you would have shot him.'

'Good Christ, Star. Who the bloody hell have you been talking to?'

'As I said, I wasn't sitting still. Don't worry, it's not a story that's around. That's obvious, isn't it? I had sort of figured it anyway and it doesn't make any difference to me. I wouldn't have worried had it been you that had got to him first. What happened to him was . . . appropriate, shall we say.'

'I'm really shocked, Star. Shocked, I am.'

'Tell me more . . . about Riley. He's after us because he too knows who did his father. Is that it?'

'Something like that. Apparently Riley only found out just recently about the connection through his old man, his real old man that is, and us. I don't know the boy but if he's anything like that old swine of a father that he had, his mind will have more twists than a piece of old rope. You know that saying the neds use about going "mental"? What it means is that they get so bad with hate and anger they go into a mental state about it. Well, old Snakey went about "mental" most of the time. And they're saying this one's the same. Full of nothing but hate and anger and viciousness. Right "mental", as they say.'

'What about the police?'

'They've questioned him but the landlord fellow couldn't identify them and there's no clues.'

'So he'll get off Scot free again?'

'It could be. But that's the way. Riley has been in jail for things they caught him at but you should hear the stories of the things he's done that they haven't done him for. Same as his old father. He did two murders I know about and they hadn't a single clue to connect him with them. And he lived the life of an old crook all of his days. Couldn't think straight if he tried and he got away with it most of the time.'

'By the way, Uncle Sammy, I would prefer if you didn't repeat any of this conversation to Russell. I don't want him to know about Riley and Holden and all that. But especially don't tell him anything about Riley. He might find out by himself, but we must keep it from him.'

'Why shouldn't he know?'

'Because he might want to take revenge of some sort on his own. The Muslims have the same eye-for-an-eye attitude as the Jews. It's in their Koran, you know . . . their bible? And if he tried anything against types like Riley . . . my God, I don't want to even think about it. They would massacre him. Russell is far too gentle a sort of person for that.'

'I wouldn't worry, Star. He's too clever to try anything like that. By the way, are you not going to tell me how you found out about Riley?'

'That's right . . . I'm not.'

'Oh well, no harm in asking, was there?'

'Don't think too hard of me, Sammy, for what I said earlier about you and the Pakistanis. But racism expresses itself in many forms and some of those more evil things that are going on can start off as little jokes, you know. It's just like we feel if the English or other foreigners make a joke about us being mean.'

'Aye, maybe you're right, Star.'

Star hadn't expected to discover the whole story about the Riley-Holden connection when she had a secret rendezvous the day before with Bert Steed, 'Big Bert', her manager at the Star Lounge Bar. But, as it was, things were to work out much more fruitfully than she had anticipated.

She had taken the stock books from Bert's bar away with her for closer study after the last visit, especially after Claney said he thought something was going wrong at the bar. 'There's some discrepancies I can see, but there's more to it than that,' he had said. 'You know, when you've been in the trade as long as I have you can smell what's happening in a bar. Well, something is happening in Big Bert's place and I just can't put my finger on it.' They had discovered more signs that night they did the stocktaking, which was the reason Star had taken the books away with her.

She was to discover a lot more, despite some fairly clever attempts to hide what was going on. But Star's eye had become as experienced as Claney's nose for such things and what she saw in the books she didn't like. She had called Bert to the bar on the Tuesday night and arranged to meet him for lunch the following day. 'I would like to go where we can talk privately . . . what about the Rogano? And . . . it's on me.'

Bert looked apprehensive when they met and ordered a large whisky to be brought to the table as an aperitif.

'I always find whisky overwhelms me and my tastebuds before lunch,' Star had smiled. She said nothing further till the waiter had taken their orders.

'Right,' she said, 'we won't wait till the dessert comes before we get down to business. How much have you been paying Riley?'

Bert's mouth visibly dropped in shock. 'How . . .? Who . . .?'

'Never mind, Bert, how I know, who told me, when I found out or why I found out. That's all irrelevant. How much have you been paying him? I estimate about £100 a week.'

'You're not far out. Some weeks it's £90. Other weeks £110.'

'And you thought you could hide it by using some of the old tricks from Sammy's Bar days?'

'It was against my better judgment, Star. But you're right. I thought I could hide it, but I knew I couldn't keep that up for long against the likes of Claney and yourself. At the same time I was hoping. You've got to have hope in this world. So now will you tell me who squealed on me?'

'You've just squealed on yourself, Bert. No one told me a

thing. I merely put the right two and two together. Your books were riddled with faults. I've trusted you and the family ever since the day I hired you for the lounge and I knew you wouldn't be back to your old ways again. I also knew that Riley has been in the bar and I know he's been taking protection money from two or three of the bars roundabout our place. So it didn't take too much figuring really . . . did it? So now you can tell me how it all happened.'

'It started a couple of months ago, maybe a wee bit longer. Two of his heavies came into the lounge one day and asked to see me. I knew what was coming when they started asking me about insurance. Christ, Star, their dialogue was straight out of an old George Raft picture. You know the kind of stuff . . . "The boys won't be very pleased if they know you're not insured. Look what's happening to some of the others who didn't take out a policy on their bars." You know. That kind of stuff. Then they mentioned the manager that had been nailed to his bar, the other one that got his throat cut and the ones that get their windows smashed every weekend. It was like a big joke at first and I found it hard to take them seriously. So I told them to . . . you know. Go away. In the language they understand. So they did, but they said they would be back. They were right. The very next day they were there, three of them this time, the new bloke with a face like a gorilla, and built like one as well. They said he was Sonny's special ambassador and that they would be back to see me that Friday for the insurance money. They said it would be £90 and it should be ready for them in an envelope.'

'Didn't you think of telling Claney or me . . . or the police?'

'Of course I did. But Star, these guys weren't messing this time. There was no funny dialogue stuff from them. Just the straight message. Scared me out of my wits, so they did. And before they left they mentioned that Sonny had taken a personal interest in you and that they knew where you and Sammy lived. They said a few more things. Not very nice things. I won't go into details. But, Star, they were not kidding, these guys. They were for real. So I started paying. They were nice as ninepence after that. Told me that everything would be all right in the bar and if I had any problems with troublemakers and the like, just to let them know. It was all part of their insurance service, they said. But they laughed when they said that. And once I was in their trap, that was it. So I had to get the money from somewhere. Well, you know the rest. I've had to use every trick in the book to try and squeeze it out of the lounge.'

'Coin in the measure?'

'Aye.'

'Slops back in the light beer barrel?'

'Aye.'

'Spirits in the black rum bottle?'

'Aye, Star. And bringing in cash 'n' carry whisky and soft drinks and under-ringing. The lot.'

'Does Riley know the connection between his father and Sammy and Claney?'

'I suppose he does. That's why he's talking so much about you and Sammy.'

'How did Holden die?'

'I thought you would have known that.'

'Well, I know he was murdered. Sammy told me that much. But how?'

'Well, I shouldn't be saying.'

'But you will . . . under the circumstances!'

'Claney told me one night he was drunk . . . that drunk he doesn't remember telling me. Anyway, Sammy and Claney were both out independent of each other to murder old Holden. He had done in two of their men, you see. Sammy had a gun and Claney had a bayonet . . . one he picked mines with during the war. And it was Claney who got there first with his bayonet. That's the gist of what he told me.'

'Well, that fills in a few of the gaps for me. So, was it Riley's gang who attacked the Pakistanis last Thursday night?'

'That's right. And Riley was there himself. His team had been after the landlord one for weeks, trying to get him to pay insurance money but he had refused. The two that have been coming about the bar told me the week before that Sonny would be doing something himself just as a warning to others who were refusing to pay. That was Riley who was in the bar on Thursday when you and Claney came to do the stocktaking.'

'I know. Betty pointed him out to me and said he was the one

220

who had been up on the tallyman charges. Therefore he must have left our bar to go and get Iftikhaar and murdered poor Maqbul instead.'

'Did you know the one who was murdered?'

'Yes. Very well. He was my fiancé's best friend.'

'Oh, I'm sorry.'

'So that's us then. We've got the finest legal system in the world, so they keep telling us. We've got a wonderful police force. We're supposed to have the best detectives. Yet we have this monster Sonny Riley who murders, terrorises, lends money with extortion, drives debtors into all sorts of crime and nothing can be done about him.'

'There's not even another ned in the Gorbals willing to take him on. Maybe just as well. If he did and won he would probably end up worse than Riley. That's the way they go.'

'But we mustn't just accept it, Bert. Something must be done.'

'Well, I'm telling you the cops are useless. They need evidence before the courts will convict, and plenty of it at that. Look at what happened at the tallymen trial. There were witnesses against them there but at the end of the day the judge thought there wasn't a case.'

'But there *is* a way, though.'

'Oh.'

'You know that I'm marrying a Pakistani and have learned a bit about life in their country? Well, one of the things I've learned about is the *Goondas*.'

'The what?'

'Yes, I know it's a funny name. Sounds like our Goons. But *Goondas* is what they are called.'

She then related the story Javaid had retold about the *Goondas* of the Old City district of Lahore.

'Aye, well, that may be so, Star, but we don't have any people handy like that in Glasgow who will up and do you a favour by sorting out Sonny Riley and his squad.'

'But you will admit if there was no Sonny Riley, most of the evil would disappear.'

'Of course it would.'

'I know we don't have any *Goondas*, Bert. But there are people who do certain things for money. Are there not?'

'Aye. So they say.'

'And don't they also say there's one from Glasgow . . . from the Calton to be precise. Quite well known apparently. Well enough known for the likes of you, Bert, to know him, particularly with you coming from nearby Bridgeton, and particularly with you being in the Scots Guards in Malaya, and particularly with your dad having something to do with stewards at the boxing.'

'What do you not know, Star?'

'I'm more interested in what you know . . . and who you know, Bert.'

'You know I know him . . . don't you?'

'Yes. And so now both of us know who we are talking about.'

At that, she reached for her handbag and from it took a notebook inside of which there was a slip of paper which she handed to him. 'That's a signed cheque and made out to you. Otherwise it's blank and undated. I trust you implicitly to fill in the appropriate amount for the sum he requires. Understand?'

'Totally.'

'I presume that he will do the job?'

'More than willingly, Star.'

'When?'

'He's back down in London again. But he's only a telephone call away. We keep in touch.'

'The reason why I met you here is that what has gone on between us today must never be known to anyone else. I haven't told and never will tell Rasool or Sammy and you mustn't even tell your wife Betty. You can make whatever arrangements there are as soon as you like, the sooner the better, perhaps. But whatever has to happen, I would prefer not to happen until Rasool and I have gone. Sammy gets married this Friday and is off to Majorca that night with Emma for their honeymoon. And my own wedding is a fortnight later.'

'That's no problem, Star. It usually takes him a couple of weeks anyway to . . .'

'Please, Bert. I don't want any details.'

'I know what you mean.'

Bert was at work that night in the bar and early in the evening went into the small office behind the main bar to make a call. It was to a London number and a woman with a broad Cockney accent answered.

'He's not here at the moment,' she said.

'Will he be home later?'

'Yes. He said he'd be home at ten o'clock.'

Bert said he would call back.

When Star arrived home, Rasool was waiting for her. She told him she had been lunching with Bert at the Rogano.

'Problems?' he asked.

'A few,' she smiled. 'But nothing a good working lunch couldn't sort out. How was your day, Russell?'

'Not so good. I felt a bit depressed actually. Delayed shock, I suppose.'

'Oh darling, I'm so sorry.'

'Who would have thought I would be feeling like this so soon before being married to the most wonderful woman in the world? I should be thinking more about that than anything else.'

'And you'll be back home again soon, Russell. Think about that too . . . just two days after we're married we'll be on the plane for Lahore. You've no idea how much I'm looking forward to the journey. That holiday we had on the Continent is the furthest I've ever been. You must be just longing to see your country and all your relatives and friends again.'

'I am, Star. I am . . . especially with you. I want to share so many places and things there with you. And I am longing to see Pakistan again. You know, I've never realised just how much I miss it. I miss it more now than ever I have. When I came to Scotland at first I was so overwhelmed by the friendliness of everyone. I used to think then what would it have been like had thousands of Scots emigrated to Pakistan? Would the Pakistanis have been so friendly to them? I'd better make no judgment on that. But really, the people here opened their hearts to me in those early years, especially at the beginning when I was going with the case. And it was the same for the others when they were working as bus drivers and conductors and ticket collectors on the Underground or going with the case. But now, sadly, I am seeing changes. More and more of our people are prospering and leaving these jobs to go into business for themselves. They want to have their own shops and after that they want to be even bigger traders with a cash and carry or a warehouse or a group of shops. Look at the way Javaid and poor Maqbul got on.

'Will the Scottish people think the same of us when they see so many Pakistanis driving about in their Mercedes and Jaguars and living in the big villas of Newlands and Pollokshields and sending their children to Kelvinside and Hutchesons' and other schools like that? Our people got on so well with them when they were like them and working in the same jobs as them. But I fear that may change, Star. And thinking ahead when the children take over from their fathers and prosper even more and when the community becomes even more successful . . . will we still be liked, Star? I'm already seeing some disturbing signs, hearing the occasional remark. And when they murdered poor Maqbul, were they so vicious because they connected him with the bad landlord . . . or were they that way because he was of another colour?

'Maybe I'm thinking too deeply about things, my dear. I hope I'm wrong.'

Star held his hand tightly and had it been at another time or occasion she would have agreed, for she knew what he said just might be true. 'I really hope you're wrong, my darling.'

Sharp on ten o'clock Bert, as he did every night, was calling 'Time please, ladies and gentlemen' in the Star Lounge and the staff stopped serving drink and began gathering in the glasses. He told Betty he had an urgent telephone call to make in the office and wasn't to be disturbed.

The operator put him through to the same London number and again it was the woman who answered. 'Hold on, luv,' she said, 'I'll go and get 'im.'

Bert smiled when he heard the voice. 'That you, Frankie?'

'Aye . . . Frankie Burns here.'